# INEXACT VENGEANCE

## D.S. LEONARD

Cover Design by Alex Ross
Formatting by Polgarus Studio

ISBN: 9780997474404 (ebook)
ISBN: 9780997474411 (hardcover)
ISBN: 9780997474428 (paperback)

# CHAPTER 1

The morning began in typical fashion. Each day at 5:00 A.M., the all too conditioned body rolls out of bed just a little less energetic than from years earlier. The buzzing from an alarm has yielded to an uncanny sense of time over the years. A quick stop in the bathroom to take care of some personal matters and off to a shortened run today, as a new work schedule places more restrictions on time and pleasure. As Nathan leaves the friendly confines of his newly decorated bedroom, he takes one last glance of his lifetime companion who still takes great comfort in sleeping unencumbered by the formalities of night time attire. A quick check on the kids, who won't wake for another two hours to begin their day of mandatory schooling, extra-curricular activities, and mindless computer games, and out the door.

The morning ritual has offered Nathan a place his very own for his mind to wander about. More and more, time like this has been stolen from him. What used to be a seven mile, fifty minute workout has been tapered to a quick three mile dash around the community. The morning was already a little balmy with temperatures predicted in the mid-eighties. As Nathan goes through his well-planned out run, the neighborhood is still very much quiet and has not yet awakened. Back in twenty minutes, Nathan picks up the papers from the driveway, the Herald and the other, the Times. For all the years that Nathan has been a rather permanent fixture in his community, he has never given up his early roots up North.

***

Nathan's home, still very much in the pre-dawn darkness, was slowly awakening. A dim light in the back of the house suggests some life. The sounds of a shower door closing and the steady force of water and a steamy mirror reassures Nathan that his wife, Joanne, had started her day. Usually, Nathan is back in time to shower off first but today Joanne was hoping to get an earlier start with the kids. Over the years, Nathan and Joanne parted from more economic use of shower time, with the kids somewhat encroaching on their private time. But this morning, Nathan decided to take advantage of the schedule change and join Joanne for a few minutes of very personal water play. After all these years of marriage, Nathan and Joanne, continued to have that magical feel and fit. Great lovers when the time was right which over the years, like Nathan's exercise time, was gradually reduced due to the pressures of life, time, and fatigue. Still, neither Joanne nor Nathan were complaining and certainly neither one found the need to look elsewhere or encourage their sexual appetites with performance enhancing drugs for the world's most commonly diagnosed "medical condition". Erectile dysfunction, "ED" has become such a household word that the kids have all but been banned from watching programming on T.V., as what parent wants to get into a discussion with prepubescent children on the merits of popping a Viagra or describing what it means for a guy to have the quality of performance he's looking for. The shower ended as it had begun, with eyes gazing into one another and of course more than a cursory look up and down each other's bodies. As Nathan was approaching the legendary mid-life point and Joanne was flirting with menopause, the couple was grateful to have one another in relatively good health.

\*\*\*

Nathan's drive time to work has been one of the fringe benefits of relocating from New York. A usual commute to and from work meant a three hour crusade either by car or railroad from the suburbs to the city. Now Nathan pulls out of his driveway and his perfectly calibrated five speed barely makes it out of third gear as he travels east on Royal Palm toward the intra-coastal. Oh, how he misses popping the stick into fifth but still Nathan wouldn't trade that for the long commute. The beautiful sunrises out over the Atlantic, reminds Nathan of how wonderful the vista is in this part of Florida. As he is constantly reminded, life is but a series of tradeoffs which we try our best to balance over the course of time. Nathan like so many are still trying to solve that equation. As he drives over to the office, a quick perfunctory check of overnight messages are retrieved. A computer generated voice greets Nathan. "Good morning, Dr. Stern. You have four new messages and eight saved messages." Nathan quickly scrolls through the eight to refresh his memory of any old business and then attends to the most recent ones. He's reminded of his luncheon meeting at the University where he will meet with faculty and students for the new academic year. It's going to be a busy day, busier than most. All four messages involved new patient referrals; one requesting a psychological evaluation, two requesting second opinion consultations, and one interested in setting up an appointment to begin a course of psychotherapy. The twenty minute commute ends as Nathan approaches the front of the office. Over the weekend, the property management finally reattached the signpost which identifies the office of Nathan Stern, Ph.D. and Joanne Stern, Ph.D.. The brutal hurricane season, still with two months to go, has left most everything tossed and damaged. It will be a while before everything gets back to normal around here.

By the time Nathan arrived to the office, Joanne was getting the kids ready for their new school week. Nathan and Joanne always felt that children go to school way too early and stay way too late. Such has been the life for the majority of families and parents who struggle finding the right balance of economics and childrearing. Joanne especially found it irresponsible to shelter kids away in either day care or aftercare and has devoted much of her professional career trying to right the wrong of modern day feminism. As a stay at home mom, with the privilege of education and the luxury of a limited fee-for service clinical practice, Joanne has written extensively on the perils and harm to the emotional wellness of the children who are signed up in droves to attend day care or carted off after school to extended day programs. Joanne too has been trying to find that special balance as she too has compromised economics and several prestigious opportunities in academia to provide for her children.

Joanne's cell jingled one of her favorite tunes to alert her that Nathan was calling in. Nathan in leaving early today broke one of his rules to not leave the home without saying goodbye to the kids. However, leaving earlier today, he didn't want to break the other time-honored rule, never wake a sleeping child or something like that; Nathan pondered if he made the wrong choice this morning. The phone was answered not by Joanne, but by the first child who was quick enough to grab the phone away from the other.

"Hi Dad, where are you and why didn't you wake me before you left…I had something really important to tell you." Well, the tone of Erik's voice and the sheer disappointment came across loud and clear, making Nathan know he clearly goofed this morning. Within a few seconds, Nathan smoothed over his son's disappointment and juvenile outrage, and went on to a more simple conversation.

"Oh Erik, you know I had to leave a little early today and I remembered how you like to sleep in. So what did you want to talk to me about?"

"Nothing really. I forget right now. Got to go Dad, we'll talk later." Like so many fathers in the professional and academic community, Nathan was constantly confronted with the invites and pressures of traveling away from home to attend conventions and conferences, conduct workshops, and teach across the country and abroad. Nathan seldom embraced the opportunities as he too felt the most important job he may ever have was joining with Joanne to raise their children.

The kids on their way to school, tossed the cell phone around like a football in the well-appointed comforts of Joanne's late model Honda Accord. Neither Nathan nor Joanne were impressed with vanity cars or high profile vehicles. Money they both felt was better off spent on something other than an object which takes you from one point to another point. As long as you arrive safe, what difference would it make if you arrive in a twenty thousand dollar vehicle or a sixty thousand dollar vehicle. Just prior to drop off at school, the other Stern prodigy wrestled for the phone and chimed in. Jack, two years younger than his pre-teen brother, was less interested and annoyed by his father's early departure. He was however, curious about his father's promise to score some tickets for this weekends' big series which may preview the playoffs later in the month.

"So Dad, did you get the tickets for the weekend series with the Giants yet? If the Marlins win two of three they are playoff bound," noted Jack.

Even at age nine, Jack had a very complex understanding of the game of baseball with all its intricacies and nuances. In many ways, Nathan was reminded of himself growing up in the shadows of Shea anticipating the next outing with his father to the stadium.

"The tickets are locked away safely," Nathan replied, knowing that he has not yet found the opportunity to purchase them. The conversation ended rather abruptly with the kids as both were jumping out of the car. In their place, Nathan heard the pleasant musings of Joanne who was on her way to the office for her first appointment of the day. Nathan anticipated her arrival as he was hoping to have a moment with his wife before the next part of the day began.

***

Nathan's schedule, which has become so compartmentalized recently with his hours being split between his practice and responsibilities at the University's clinical psychology training program, still allowed him the morning block of time to see a few patients early and then quickly make an exit. After years of being vetted by the school of psychology, Nathan finally acquiesced and embraced a contract which he personally took pride in negotiating on his own behalf. With all the years of independent practice and an outstanding reputation in the community, the University felt honored to have Nathan accept an appointment as the training director. Nathan would have full control and thereby direction of the program's clinical training of its doctoral candidates, interns and residents. While Nathan rarely needed his ego massaged, the type of influence and power he knew he could have in shaping the future of so many young psychologists did not go unnoticed.

***

Even though both Nathan and Joanne seemed reactionary in their attitudes about the technological applications to the field, they were at times sucked into the use of all the modern day high tech equipment. Both often chuckled about practicing in the wrong era. Nathan's one such compromise to technology rested in his daily review, usually between 7:30 A.M. and 8:30 A.M., of email correspondence. While not clearly understanding the inner workings of the computer or comprehending the depth and range of the internet, Nathan sat in front of his flat screen and pecked away on the keyboard as he instantly sent off professional and often personal communications. He limited his use of email to these types of correspondences as Nathan's ignorance of the technology did not preclude him from understanding the possible violations to patient care and privileged information.

An unopened email sent yesterday from an old friend and colleague again caught Nathan's eye. Nathan still was not sure as to why he couldn't find the time yesterday to open the email but today felt better prepared.

*"Nate, just wanted to again congratulate you on your appointment and wish you much success. Best to Joanne,"* the email read, and was signed *Ben*. Ben, Benjamin Solomon, M.D., and Nathan trained together at the Metro Psychiatric Pavilion. Ben, a board certified psychiatrist, took a very different path than Nathan and approached patient care through the pharmacological world of anti-psychotics, anti-depressants, and mood stabilizers. Both Nathan and Ben trained during the same time period at one of the most prestigious inpatient programs in the country, specializing in adolescent and adult services.

Ben's email provoked a number of overlapping feelings in Nathan. First, Nathan was notoriously delinquent in returning calls and messages, blaming it mostly on time but a leaning toward the more avoidant side typically left Nathan feeling first relieved but later guilty and internally anguished. Perhaps, the more overriding feeling had been deep sadness and void over seeing Ben's wife, Brittany, lose the fight to the full assault of the most invasive form of breast cancer which eventually spread to the brain. She was gone in just a few short months. The thoughts of what Ben must be confronting aggravated Nathan's own deepest fears of what life might be like without Joanne. As Nathan was just beginning to compose himself and write a response back to Ben, he heard the little chime from the front office door which either announced his first patient of the day or the arrival of Joanne. As he heard the secured-door of the waiting room open, he was glad to see that he had a few more minutes as Joanne greeted him for the second time today.

"Hi, how's the day starting off for you?"

"It's starting. Kids get off okay?"

"Yeah, it was a mad race to the door but we got out, breakfast in tow," relayed Joanne.

Nathan's momentary distraction, transfixed by Joanne's smile, was more than enough to detour him from completing his email. Already primed by images of Brittany's ordeal, Nathan took a few more moments to collect himself and chit chat with Joanne.

*** 

The practice, a partnership between husband and wife, was truly the envy around town. Guided by uncompromised values and a crystal clear understanding of traditional psychoanalytic psychotherapy principles, Nathan and Joanne developed a caring and safe environment for patients to bring their troubles to. While most, if not all, small and solo practices had been devoured by managed care and made financially insolvent by the insurance industry, Nathan and Joanne never wavered from a belief that their office would thrive without following the anxieties and fears of the majority of psychologists in the community. While most were being reimbursed at appallingly low rates, Nathan and Joanne remained disciplined and accepted very close to their full fees. Nathan, though would often get some backlash from Joanne, as he would often take on certain merited cases, usually of younger patients whose families did not have the ability to afford his fees. Although coming from a different social strata, Nathan's more middle class values often began to rub off on Joanne, whose family came from old money and thus placed her in at least a superior economic position.

The clientele for the practice came to understand the high professional level of the office and the ability to assure confidentiality and protect the sacred notion of privileged information. The office was quiet, not busy like so many of the practices. A back door to the office permitted patients most concerned of privacy an appropriate entrance and exit. As a result of the practice's reputation, mostly through word of mouth, the office attracted some of the more influential, successful and powerful in the community and outlying areas. It was not unusual for patients to travel from two or three counties away to take an hour in either Nathan's or Joanne's schedule. This was not a zip code type of service. It was that kind of reputation that continued to build a financially secure practice.

\*\*\*

Nathan invited his first patient of the day from the waiting room into his office.

"Hi, Dr. Stern, how was your weekend?" Julie quietly inquired of her therapist now for two years.

Nathan, who, after all these years, was still uncomfortable with patients asking about even such commonplace matters, hesitantly responded with the politeness and appropriateness he knew his patient was entitled to.

"Really nice, Julie. But like most it went way too quickly. Thanks for asking."

With Nathan's reply, the session almost automatically

transitioned to the work before Julie and Nathan. Julie who was one month shy of her twenty-fifth birthday, began working with Nathan following the death of her mother. Already predisposed from a family history of depression, the sudden loss tipped the psychological scales against Julie, resulting in her first major depressive episode. Nathan who has never been a big advocate for medication-based therapy, reluctantly offered the recommendation following the third month of treatment. Given the family history, it felt prudent to defer to genetics and bring in line a treatment plan to conform to a reasonable standard of care. While Julie was responding optimally to her low dose of Lexapro, she was making very nice strides in her therapy as she was sifting through the different levels of vulnerability left in the wake of her mother's death. Long after the Lexapro would be discontinued, Nathan knew that the gains made through treatment would remain with Julie a lifetime.

Between sessions, Nathan routinely accepted calls or returned calls. The fifty minute hour has held up even after all these years. *Still a little too early to place calls*, Nathan thought, as he took in his second patient of the day. Terry Jackson, a retired fire fighter, has been a patient of Nathan's on and off for three years. Mr. Jackson who lost most of his meaningful relationships during the 911 attack had very little to live for before identifying other significant relationships he felt close to. Unfortunately, his wife of twenty-five years had other thoughts and probably couldn't wait much longer for her husband Terry to get back on track. He returned to treatment upon learning of his wife's extramarital affair and her filing for divorce.

"Gee, Doc, I'm glad that I still have you," Terry commented in a clinging, dependent way.

Nathan who had a special admiration and respect for first responders felt especially close to Terry and knew he would always offer an empathic understanding for Terry and for the wounds brought on in such a horrific way.

"Take care today Terry, and I'll see you next week. We'll work on this together and find a way for you to feel better," commented Nathan as the session concluded.

By this time of day the phones usually get pretty busy. The muted ringing from another phone extension, reminded Nathan to return his calls now that his last hour is completed.

The office secretary who works half-time, typically from mid-morning to 4 P.M., was just arriving. Nathan and Joanne typically have their one big office dispute once a year as to the necessity of having Myra continue on answering phones, billing and such other administrative duties. Nathan who was constantly watching the bottom line felt for some time that the practices' very reliable answering service could function as the full time secretary. Joanne, who felt Myra was invaluable to the practice, goes through this dance with Nathan each time only to come out on top, assuring Myra another year of employment. Nathan had just a few minutes in between hours to return a few calls. He felt bad that he couldn't apportion some more time for each call, feeling more hurried today.

"Okay then. So, I will see your son in three weeks on the 20th of September at 3 P.M. If you have any questions or concerns before then, please call me."

Nathan also scheduled in a new patient for psych testing on that date which would take up much of the afternoon. The second call and third calls were managed fairly efficiently as both came in from colleagues who hoped Nathan would have an opportunity to see their patients and offer an opinion with regard to diagnosis. Both patients were in their mid-teens, and while Nathan continued to see adolescents, his own maturing over the years tended to raise the developmental mean of his caseload. Nathan was one of those rare psychologists who were twice board certified in both child clinical and adolescent psychology and clinical psychology allowing him greater comfort and scope in his level of expertise.

Myra, who now has settled in for the day, captures Nathan's attention with a nod to let him know his last morning patient has arrived. Nathan, checks off the phone messages now seeing he has one more left to return which will have to carry over to the afternoon.

Nathan's 10 A.M., Andrew Lawson, Ph.D., proved to be the more difficult patient in Nathan's work week. Dr. Lawson, a fellow psychologist, came referred through the State's Impaired Practitioners Program. The State of Florida, like so many states around the country has for some time now offered a diversionary program for professionals who have practiced in some compromised fashion and who are willing to undergo treatment and maintain a recovery program. The completion of such treatment would allow Dr. Lawson to return to practice under some restrictions of licensure, with limited patient populations and of course under continued supervision. Proving more problematic than most typical clinical cases, Nathan didn't know for how long he could contain his own disgust and thereby lose his professional stance. The key here, Nathan reflected, was to keep in mind that Dr. Lawson was operating from the inner workings of a confused, needy, and damaged self. Nathan's personal understanding of how a psychologist can step close or over the boundary line with a patient sent up a flare of recognition that even in the field there are less than healthy psychologists who are feeling just as vulnerable as the very patients they wish to help. The not so healthy Dr. Lawson was scheduled to be seen twice weekly over the next half-year. Although probably a pattern, Dr. Lawson admitted to on one occasion having an intimate sexual relationship with a patient's mother at the conclusion of the child's therapy hour. While the young teen awaited her mother, Dr. Lawson was having a very different type of parent-therapist conference in his office.

Claiming that this was a consensual relationship in no way impinging upon the therapy for the child did not hold well with the ethics board or predict a favorable outcome for Dr. Lawson.

After completing the session, Nathan quickly departed the office. A brief, non-verbal exchange shared with Joanne, as she was taking in her next patient, was all Nathan needed as he left for his mid-day lunch at the University to see what this years' trainees were like.

*\*\**

# CHAPTER 2

The letters, which included a compilation of lyrics and prose, started to come to the Stern residence about a year ago shortly after last Labor Day. It was the first Tuesday after the holiday. Thirteen in total. All delivered by mail with a local postmark. Typically six weeks would separate one from the other although there were some months where a flurry of letters would appear and other months without one. The envelopes addressed without variation to Dr. Nathan and Joanne Stern were all typed with Old English character set.

At first Nathan simply gave the first letter a quick glance and placed it aside. The boldfaced typed words appeared in red and black respectively. The words RUN RUN RUN **FEAR FEAR FEAR** which spanned the entire page from left to right and up and down didn't register much of a visceral response in Nathan. Even the image of a mushrooming cloud placed toward the bottom of the letter did not capture Nathan's concern. Joanne often accurately described Nathan as having zero awareness when it came to anything other than his professional work. Nathan often thought that he set his defenses much higher in his personal life, an area which he knew eventually he needed to address. Nathan was the quintessential non-alarmist.

With the arrival of the second and third letters, Nathan developed more than a passing concern. When shared with Joanne who instantly reacted with more appropriate caution, Nathan snapped out of his cool emotional exterior and joined in with Joanne's alarm.

"Call the police, Nathan," Joanne abruptly voiced. "This is no coincidence. You know my personal rule of three. Once an accident, twice a coincidence, the third time a troublesome pattern."

Nathan couldn't disagree with Joanne, but the investigative side of him wanted to explore this a little bit further before involving the police. Following several tedious hours, an internet search of common prose, lyrics and passages which Nathan thought may be identified in a published format, turned up empty with nothing discoverable by his effort. Vague references to childhood rhymes, religious references and mythical creatures punctuated many of the letters, which had both a rather fragmented, choppy style to the writing as well as carrying a foreboding type of message.

Nathan waited till the weekend to canvass his neighbors. A reasonable first step to see if others close in proximity to his home may have received a similar letter. Usually comfortable with his neighbors, Nathan began to feel a swell of hesitance as he realized he was widening the lens to his private world just a bit more. Before walking down the path to approach Mark and Donna Bishops' front door, Nathan found himself rehearsing what he was about to say. As Nathan began cordially speaking with Mark about neighborhood gossip, he realized that the question he was about to ask was already answered on some level. The probability that his immediate neighbors or for that matter others in the community might be receiving such letters was close to zero. An inner rumbling predisposed Nathan to intuitively know that the letters were very much personal. Yet, Nathan wanted to go through the more methodical approach to rule out the less likely explanations. A part of him of course wished to believe it was simply a principle of random reoccurrence which somehow would have reassured Nathan that others were in the same situation. Safety in numbers, Nathan was thinking.

"Mark, I have this kind of strange thing happening every few weeks," Nathan began as he took out the letters from his back pocket. Nathan continued as Mark looked on. "By any chance have you been receiving similar letters addressed to you and Donna. This started around last Labor Day and I'm not sure what to make of it yet." Mark, listening to the story with quiet interest, gestured to look over the letters.

"Let me see, Nathan. I'll take a look but nothing like this sounds familiar. I can get Donna. I usually don't take in the mail and junk mail we just toss."

By now, Nathan wished he too would have followed that same junk mail policy. As Mark was speaking, Nathan handed over the three letters. It was not until Mark looked over the second and third letter, that his facial expression began to change, noting a more serious concern. The second letter, with a fire breathing dragon logo, was composed in prose style:

The fire breathing dragon could not constrain its rage

Riveting first thru my brain, and then the eyes locked onto the benevolent Doctor

The heat pulsating through my head. Do the same to the benevolent Doctor's brain.

I could not fight the dragon alone. How about you?

For I will succumb. What about you?

I just want to make it stop. Don't you?

My head bled and bled and bled

The blood ran down my face

And dripped all over the place

I was frightened. Were you?

So I too ran and ran and ran

I had to hide or be tied

Prayer opens my eyes

For I am such a stupid fool

I only live to eventually die


The third letter, comprised of the typical borderline dilemma with the twin fears of abandonment and engulfment was articulated clearly, and included images of someone's hands tied and a 38 Special read as follows:


THE END IS COMING

WHO MAY LOVE ME, WHO MAY HATE ME
WHO MAY UNDERSTAND ME
WHO MAY INVALIDATE ME
WHO MAY ABANDONE ME
WHO MAY ENGULF ME

WHO MAY TEACH ME RIGHT FROM WRONG,
WHO MAY HEAL ME
WHO MAY BE CRUEL TO ME

WHO LOVES ME?
WHY NOT?

IN THE END
AS IN THE BEGINNING

FEEL THE RHYTHM OF THE EARTH?
WHAT IS LIFE? VALUE YOUR LIFE??????

Nathan knew simultaneously that Mark felt both relieved in not receiving such letters and concern for his neighbor and friend who was just at the beginning of his search. Strolling around the street and getting reacquainted with his neighbors was nice for Nathan but fell short in learning anything new other than proving that he and Joanne were probably being targeted for some reason.

*** 

With the weekend passing, Nathan had scheduled some time to speak with the local post office to see if the letters can be traced back in any way to the sender. Obviously, with no return address this did not seem a possibility. Nathan did wonder about the markings however on the envelope, what the Postal Service calls a postal bar code. Perhaps, Nathan queried, there might be a way to track down the sender or at least where the letter originated from. Nathan became a quick study of the postal service. Each "word" in the postal bar code has twelve digits, each digit being represented by short bars and longer bars. The first five digits is your zip code, the next digits are the extended zip code, the next two digits are the delivery point digits, and the last digit is a check digit. The unique language used by the postal system, Nathan unfortunately concluded, was to help only with the delivery of mail.

The postal service supervisor, Mr. Garrison, a heavy set, graying man with gold rimmed glasses did point Nathan in the direction of the U.S. Postal Inspection Service. "Dr. Stern, look, if you have some concerns here, and I'm not saying you don't, go pay a visit to the "postal police". Maybe, they can be of some help, but I seriously doubt it," Mr. Garrison concluded.

The postal police seemed less threatening in name than the U.S. Postal Inspection Service- Division of Forensic and Technical Services. Nathan thought he was not only getting way ahead of himself but felt he was blowing this whole thing way out of proportion and temporarily giving in to some irrational levels of anxiety and perhaps a little bit of paranoia. After all Nathan began to reason, to involve the postal inspectors; this isn't fraud, extortion, or blackmail. There's nothing criminal here and no one has been threatened or victimized. It's simply been a nuisance. After mulling it over, Nathan was determined to follow this up one more step.

That afternoon Nathan scheduled an appointment with the interim regional supervisor at the U.S. Postal Inspection Service in the southern part of the county. Nathan approached the one-story glass enclosed building which had security guards posted at the entrance of the parking facility. Nathan was greeted with the request of two forms of identification and asked to step out of the car to allow an inspection of the vehicle. Nathan followed the directions to visitor parking and entered the building where he was physically searched and cleared to proceed to his scheduled appointment. Nathan again wondered as to why he was here and thought for a few more moments about reversing his tracks.

"Mr. Stern please come in. I'm Anthony D'Amato. We spoke briefly this morning. How can I be of some help?"

For Nathan, this was oddly familiar as he usually had the same supportive words for new patients entering his office. Nathan immediately felt in a subordinate role and deferent to the figure before him who easily was twenty years junior in age. Nathan was initially apologetic for bringing such a minor concern to the postal service in light of all the demands and significantly higher profile cases requiring urgent attention.

"I don't mean to take up your time on irrelevant things and I know you have much more important business to take care of, but these letters are coming to my home and I'm not sure what to do about them."

"Let me explain how we work here," Mr. D'Amato started as he broke into a patented, well timed speech.

"We look at things on a case by case basis. Sometimes, we actually find some relationship between cases so we try to take things, even the smaller concerns just as seriously as the larger ones. And sometimes we just nip it in the bud. We take pretty seriously that you are entitled to quiet comfort and a peaceful surround which pertains just as much to your mail as it would to some loud persistent noise from a neighbor. No need to feel apologetic or like you are wasting my time. Honestly, I'm not sure what I can do here, but if I think we can be of some help you will have the full force of the Forensic and Technical Services Division."

With this in mind, Mr. D'Amato reviewed the infrastructure of the F&TSD which included over a hundred Postal Inspectors, highly trained forensic scientists, and technical specialists who perform all tasks from latent print analysis to handwriting and typewriting analysis.

"Mr. Stern, can I see the letters?" asked Mr. D'Amato.

Nathan volunteered the letters upon request and saw the glare of disappointment on Mr. D'Amato's face. "What's wrong?" Nathan inquired.

"No nothing, I was just hoping that you would have protected the integrity of the document. Should there be additional letters, and I think there may be, I'll have you place the unopened letter in a seal so that we can preserve the physical evidence," replied Mr. D'Amato.

"Well, what kind of work do you do Mr. Stern?"

"I've been in practice for some time, both my wife and myself are clinical..."

Before Nathan was able to complete the phrase clinical psychologists, he heard Mr. D'Amato chuckle inquisitively and add on, "Well Doctor, I think you might be having a problem with one of your patients. But before we jump to conclusions let me check our data base to see if there are other similar complaints in the county, state or nation that match up to the format of your letters. Excuse me for a few minutes."

The time alone permitted Nathan the moments of consolidation which he required to finally confront the last residual strands of denial. He was finally coming to see that the letters were anything but random and by no means a coincidence. It took a few minutes with a postal investigator to understand the complexities of this situation and the problems which may lay ahead.

Mr. D'Amato, returning with little new information, some advice and a warning, continued. "There were no matches and no additional complaints by anyone. Dr. Stern we simply know that the letters are being placed in one of eight-hundred fifty mailbox drops in the county and being processed in the main facility downtown. The postmark tells us that the letter is without exception being mailed on a Wednesday and you typically receive the letter the next day. Very local, very local indeed. Dr. Stern if you wish us to help further you will need to collect the document, seal it immediately in this envelope and forward it on to us. At that point, we may be able to harvest some prints, but it is unlikely. Our National Forensic Laboratory in Dulles, Virginia may be contacted for support. In the meantime, you may want to contact your local police department. You know your line of work better than I do. But I wouldn't want you to take too many chances." With those parting words, Nathan thanked Mr. D'Amato for the time spent and left the building contemplating his next several steps.

***

# CHAPTER 3

The beginning of a new year at a clinical psychology training program is always met with much excitement and anticipation. All involved, from the administrators to the supervisors to the trainees, are full of a strange combination of positive energy, impatience to begin, and the acute onset of being overwhelmed almost immediately. Nathan was no stranger to this array of emotions as he has taken on all these roles over the course of his career.

"Welcome aboard Nate," a strong voice came from across the conference room. Dean Gerald Zwick, tenured now for quite some time, approached Nathan with a jovial eagerness.

"It's really great having you join our staff at a such a pivotal time, how are you doing?" the Dean inquired.

"Just fine thanks. You know over the months as we were talking and going over ideas, I didn't think it could all come together like it did. But here I am and I am very happy to be here," replied Nathan with confidence.

"Okay then, let's start now," announced the Dean as he walked toward the center podium, clipped on the microphone to his lapel and without a word the group of a hundred or so quieted down and awaited the formal introduction. The audience, composed of faculty, staff, students, interns and trainees, were ready to hear about their new training director. Knowing that Nathan grew uncomfortable with long winded introductions and an exhausting recitation of accomplishments and credits, the Dean kept his opening comments brief.

"I have known this individual for over twenty years and simply know that Dr. Stern is the right person at the right time to be here with us as we again begin a new training year. Since training with him at New York University and at Metro Psychiatric Pavilion, and later at the Post-Graduate Center, and following his career path as a clinician and as distinguished faculty at Columbia University, I am very pleased that he decided to make his new professional home with us at the Institute of Clinical Psychology here at our prestigious university."

As the Dean concluded his remarks, he gestured over toward Nathan to take the microphone and say a few words about this year's training program. With Nathan's few steps toward the lectern he was able to really for the first time capture how large the group of trainees were. Although unique in their own way, everyone just blended in together. Recalling the size of his graduate school class, he was taken aback as to the sheer number of psychologists who will be flooding the market in a few short years. As he affixed the mike to the lapel of his tropical blend charcoal suit jacket, Nathan greeted the audience.

"Good morning, or no, good afternoon. I understand we all have a wonderful catered luncheon so I will keep my remarks brief. I am obviously very excited to be here as your new Training Director and I hope over the course of the next few weeks, I will get an opportunity to meet with all of you. As you heard, Dean Zwick and I go way back so now we have another chance to get reacquainted in working together. Some years back, he and I were in a very similar room, as you are today, wondering what the year has in store in terms of patients, treatment, assessment, therapy, supervision, all the things that go into a training year. Probably feeling all the things you're feeling right now. Like the Dean and myself, I know you too will have an extraordinary year of training filled with successes and yes some disappointments and even some failures. Hopefully and most important, a year of growth and maturing. So, that's all I have for now. No doubt you will be hearing from me again, but for now let's enjoy lunch."

The brief introductory comments apparently went over well. Nathan often had a way about him to relate well with his audience and to make them at ease by identifying with some dimension in common. As Nathan was guided toward the back of the conference room by a select group of faculty, partitioned walls folded in revealing a nicely arranged buffet luncheon of cold cut platters and desert trays.

"Dr. Stern, please sit with us," two or three faculty members gently pressured, "we'd like to hear your thoughts on developing, researching and utilizing evidenced-based treatment protocols here in the program."

"You know, today no shop talk. We'll have that discussion shortly. But for now, I think I'm going to sit with some of the students. You're welcome to join us."

And with that civil rebuff, Nathan very quickly sent the message that the program will be more about the students and their training, than the particular faculty sponsored academic interests and research. Carefully calculated, Nathan knew exactly what he wished to accomplish today.

\*\*\*

When placed back in the academic training community, it was not hard for Nathan to become nostalgic. Seeing a few trainees coupled off in an obvious romantic entanglement, Nathan began to reminisce about his training year when he and Joanne were together. Meeting actually the summer before their second post-doc year at the Post Graduate Center for Mental Health, Joanne and Nathan attended a summer symposia on Cape Cod. An annual conference, this was the second year in a row that both Nathan and Joanne were in attendance. Their relationship which seemed tepid at first began to heat up with some encouragement from both Ben Solomon and Gerald Zwick and their respective partners. A romance began and friendships blossomed amongst the three couples, who made yearly trips out to the Cape for a few weeks each summer. By the second summer, ferry rides out to Martha's Vineyard and Nantucket with antiquing and shopping along the cobblestone streets of the islands gradually replaced attendance at the conference. Nathan and Joanne often were missing in action as they would navigate the Cape from Woods Hole to Provincetown and all points in between. In more recent years, Nathan would be invited as a presenter at the symposium which filled his time up a little more but still Cape Cod became a beautiful retreat for Nathan and the family.

***

Nathan sat comfortably and made his rounds for the next hour with several trainees trying to make them feel reassured that this year's training program, unlike the year prior, will run smoothly and that the primary mission here at the Institute is training and education. As a result of internal and external audits combined with new regulatory measures, last year's funding dried up considerably which almost jeopardized a very healthy internship and post-doctoral program.

"Dr. Stern, I hope I'm going to make it through the year. I've been hearing all types of rumors about the program cutting back further and letting some slots go," boldly commented Jon

Michaelson, an intern who relocated from Kansas City to train under one of the senior psychologists who specializes in time-limited dynamic psychotherapy.

"Jon, I haven't heard anything like that, and now that I'm here, I will be working very hard to make sure that does not become a reality."

Nathan knew that his job here was going to be challenging and reparative. He didn't realize until now how much anxiety the students were experiencing. Others joined in and echoed Jon's concern for their future as well. Toward the end of the luncheon, Nathan felt a tap on his right shoulder and heard Dean Zwick ask for a moment of his time before he left.

"I'm sure you heard from Ben about his wife. Awful thing. Such a warm, loving person so full of life and a gift to give. Do you still stay in touch?" asked Gerald.

"We do but not nearly enough. He sent out an email this morning which I didn't get a chance yet to respond to."

"We made quite the trio back then at Metro. You and me, convincingly recommending and pushing the therapy and Ben pushing the drugs. You know… you think times have changed but when you think of it, it really hasn't. We're still fighting between ourselves… each camp thinking they know better."

Nathan sighed and replied, "You know we are better now in recommending an approach combining both psychotherapy and pharmacology but I still don't think we have come to the right balance to the equation. I think we are losing the fight. Look at all the major players in the pharmaceuticals, look how much money and power, look how many scripts are written for regulating psychological and psychiatric symptoms for adults and for the children. I'm waiting to see the backlash from all the irresponsible prescribing and to see what our role is in all of this."

"Yep, good points Nate. Another day, another discussion. How's Joanne and the kids?"

"Joanne's just fine. She seems to be approaching a comfortable place in time and the kids are great. One of our guys is preparing for a Bar Mitzvah and the other one is planning on a major league baseball career. Which reminds me, I need to step out of here and run an errand. We'll talk again, Gerald. Let me get my feet wet over the first week or two and then we should compare notes after that."

Nathan excused himself from the luncheon which was all but over. Nathan had some parting nods for a few students who smiled politely and some waves to faculty and staff as he left. He thought he had enough time before heading back to his office to take a side trip to Marlins Park, praised by the architectural community as a twenty-first century retractable roofed stadium contoured with elliptical concrete, steel and glass, to accept an invite for a stadium tour from a friend who works in the front office. Although prepared to purchase tickets to this weekend's series, Nathan had a feeling his friend would simply comp the tickets as a personal favor. He knew tickets would make Jack's day.

\*\*\*

"Myra, hi. It's Nathan. How's everything going?"

"Pretty good for a Monday, Dr. Stern."

"Can you do me a favor, I misplaced a phone number. Can you retrieve the number from voice mail and leave it on my desk. It was the call from a Ronnie who wanted to speak to me about setting up some time. I didn't get the last name so see what you can do. I'll be back by three."

"Okay. Will do. Anything else?" asked Myra.

"Is Joanne free?"

"Unfortunately not. She's still with her last appointment of the day. Any message?"

"No, I'll catch up with her later." Nathan ended the phone call and realized how lucky the office was to have such a dedicated and dependable secretary. Joanne was right all along about Myra.

\*\*\*

Nathan returned to the office in time to make some calls before he took in his afternoon appointments. Myra had already pulled the charts for Nathan's patients.

"Myra, thanks for taking care of all of that. Why don't you go home early. I don't think I'll need you."

"That's great. Thank you, Dr. Stern. Then I'll see you tomorrow."

Nathan's first call was placed to Ronnie. Apparently, a new patient requesting treatment. In dialing, Nathan realized he was calling a long distance number. Familiar with the New York area codes, he knew instantly he was calling the metropolitan area. A cell phone voice mail picked up.

"Hi, you reached Ronnie, leave a message and I'll get back to you. Later." The voice, female and young, had a rather spunky, raspy quality.

Nathan left a short professional message. "Hello, this is Dr. Stern. I'm returning your call. You can try to reach me again at my office number or I'll try back again tomorrow." Moments later, Nathan's phone rang and he picked up and heard on the other end that same youthful voice which he recognized as Ronnie's.

"Dr. Stern. Hi. Sorry I missed your call. This is Ronnie Fitz-Morris. Thanks for calling me back."

"I see you tried to reach me last night after office hours. What prompted your call?" asked Nathan.

"Oh, I don't know. I'm in the middle of moving down there and I know I need to find someone to talk to. It's been difficult to find someone with a good reputation and who is known up here."

"I see from your telephone number you live up in New York. When are you planning to be down here?"

"I'm back and forth right now. I still have a few things to settle up here."

"I see. Can you tell me how you got my name?" asked Nathan.

"Well…you know I started asking around and it seems a lot of people in New York seem to know you or have heard of you."

Feeling flattered, Nathan enjoyed the moment for a little longer but then tried to pin down a name. "That's always nice to hear, but who exactly suggested you come speak with me?" inquired Nathan a little firmer.

"Oh, my gynecologist . She's really great. She really didn't know anyone, but she connected me with some psychiatrist in the city…some guy that works with teens and adults… Dr. Solomon. I got your name from Dr. Solomon. His office said you're the best down here."

Glancing down at his watch, Nathan realized he had just a few more minutes before his next patient. Customarily, Nathan would spend some more time on the phone to gather additional information about a new patient such as a chief concern, relevant background information, psychiatric history, and medical history. Over the years, Nathan treated the first telephone contact as the beginning of treatment. However, today he was prepared to cut the interview short. This afternoon, feeling the pressure of time, Nathan was ready to discontinue the phone call with just a few more comments and the scheduling of a date and time for Ronnie's initial appointment.

"Ronnie, it was good that we found the time today to speak. Let's go ahead and set up a time for your initial consultation here in my office. I guess I need to know your schedule over the next few weeks."

"Okay. I'll be back in Florida the day after next and through the long Labor Day weekend. After that I'm not sure. It depends on a few things," replied Ronnie.

"Let me see. I can get you in my schedule Thursday afternoon at 5 P.M. if you can make it," Nathan suggested.

"That's great. See you then. Thanks Dr, Stern."

"Good-bye Ronnie. I look forward to meeting you on Thursday." As Nathan concluded the conversation, he realized his short-cut would place him at a slight disadvantage in preparing for Ronnie's appointment on Thursday.

\*\*\*

The afternoon of appointments proceeded unremarkably, at least from Nathan's perspective. Nathan's 5 o'clock, Marla Peters, a stable but demanding thirty year old, had been doing better of late. Violated as a child into her teen years, both physically and sexually, Marla presented with a history of self-mutilation. Up until recently, Marla left blood stained tissues in the office bathroom as yet another reminder to Nathan of how much more work was ahead of her. Marla also presented with the now classic borderline features, alternating between periods of idealizing and devaluing her therapist. Nathan, now much more comfortable than ever in handling these types of attitudes, would move through the destructive patterns and help Marla balance out her distorted perceptions of others' around her. Nathan, of course, was not exempt from the pattern and found himself frequently on one or the other side of Marla's vacillating mood.

"Why don't you go fuck yourself," screamed out a very disgruntled Marla. "I simply asked for your help with something and you blow it all out of proportion."

"I am here to help, but this is something you can do on your own. You're most upset because I'm suggesting that you take some responsibility here and be a little more independent," replied Nathan.

"You just don't understand," cried Marla.

"But I really do. My not helping you out here is not a signal of an uncaring attitude or some form of rejection as you are accustomed to. Perhaps it might be healthier for you to see it as a respect for your ability to deal with a very frustrating and uncomfortable feeling, and that I feel, Marla, that you are ready to do just that," echoed Nathan's warm, firm words..

"You're wrong today and you were wrong last time. I hate it when you say it in that way. This session is over." As Marla bellowed a few parting words, Nathan heard the waiting room door close with some force.

Nathan spent considerable time in conceptualizing Marla's dynamics and knew that the more histrionic she became the more accurate and meaningful his confrontations and interpretations were. Abandonment, at all different levels became a toxic emotional force for Marla. While at risk of cutting herself tonight, Nathan was more certain that he was getting closer to really helping Marla make some positive changes in her life. As Nathan was preparing to finish up his day, he made some routine entries in his patients' charts and completed some correspondences.

"Ben," the email started, "thanks for the well wishes and thanks for the referral. Someone called in today using your name as a referral source. How's everything up there. Bumped into an old friend today who said hi. Gerald and I were talking about our early days with you at Metro . Anyway, take care. We'll talk later." Nathan sent off the email, closed up the office and left today at a respectable time. Psychologists and mental health professionals in general tend to be known as P.M. workers, since a majority of their patient's request afternoon and evening hours. Nathan too got sucked up into that schedule early on in his practice, but now found himself respecting and defining time, commitments, and obligations differently.

\*\*\*

As Nathan headed home, he reflected on the day's events, feeling pretty good about his work and new found responsibilities at the University. Half-way home, Nathan realized he left the most important part of his day on his desk in his office. *Can't go home empty handed,* Nathan thought to himself, and abruptly made a U-turn and went back to the office. Re-entering from the back of the building, Nathan disarmed the security alarm and headed toward to his office which was still naturally lighted by the late summer sun. The floor to ceiling glass panels, tinted to allow more privacy, was a big selling point of the office. *Ah, there they are,* referring to the tickets. As Nathan placed the tickets in his jacket pocket, he noticed a new email from Ben and took a moment more to open it and read,

"*Hi Nate. Nice to hear from you. You know I think you're one of the good ones down there but I haven't given your name out in about six months. Be well.*" *That's strange,* Nathan thought, *I'll need to check that through on Thursday.*

As Nathan closed up the office and rearmed the security system, he made a mental note to remind Myra to call in to building maintenance to replace the door. Since the hurricane, the door wasn't quite right. Something was misaligned and Nathan wasn't comfortable just leaving it that way. Now ready to go home and prepared to make Jack's day, Nathan traveled home, his short commute, with the route he can do blindfolded.

\*\*\*

As Nathan approached his street, he was able to see the kids still playing basketball out on the driveway. Although several inches shorter, Nathan got a quick peak of how agile Jack was in dribbling and pulling up to shoot. Erik's expression on his face pretty much told it all. A quick beep of the horn and Nathan knew at least one of his boy's was ready to hang it up for the day. "You guys eat yet?" Nathan asked.

"No Dad," replied Erik.

"Not yet," added Jack.

Joanne usually held dinner until Nathan would arrive. A little later than most families, the Stern's made every attempt to have dinner as a family as often as possible.

"So then, let's get inside, cleaned up and ready for dinner. Hey, Jack. Got something you and your brother might be interested in." And with that comment, Nathan quickly flashed the set of tickets for the weekend.

"Excellent! Usual seats Dad?" inquired Jack as his eyes quickly scanned the tickets.

"Yes. Between home and first base. Bring your gloves."

As the boys raced into the house, Nathan was left to tidy up the outside and tuck away the two basketballs. As he entered the house, he was comforted both by the pleasant aroma of dinner and Joanne's voice heard in conversation on the phone.

"Hi Joanne. I'm home."

Joanne looked in Nathan's direction holding up one finger in a pausing gesture suggesting to give her one more moment on the phone. Joanne was finishing up a call with a patient. As was customary in the field, Nathan and Joanne returned after hour calls selectively and usually on basis of importance or urgency. As such, the home had two dedicated lines, both unpublished. One for home use. And the other for business. Incoming calls on the business line would automatically forward to the office line or to the answering service. Both Nathan and Joanne always practiced with much caution when it came to their privacy. As Joanne's call was coming to an end, Nathan flipped through the day's mail usually silently sighing with relief when not discovering another one of those creatively foreboding letters.

"Nothing important, already went through it," started Joanne.

"So, how were things today?"

"Well, I think things are going to be just fine at the University. Probably made some new friends today and pissed off some others. But I think I'm going to like it once I work out the schedule. How was your day?"

"Oh, it went alright. Terminated with a patient today after two years of therapy. You know, that's always difficult for me but it was the right time. The patient really has done well and was ready to move on." Joanne, referring to her own countertransference, became quite skilled over the years in using these feelings to move treatment ahead for her patients.

"Otherwise, the kids had a good day at school… Jack, Eric come for dinner now," Joanne blurted out so the kids could hear her in the back part of the house. Following dinner, Nathan and Joanne had a little more time with the boys and for themselves before calling it a night.

\*\*\*

# CHAPTER 4

As the months marched on, Nathan had collected more than a handful of letters. Each somewhat more intriguing than the next. Each suggestive of a strange dialogue the author of these letters believed he or she was having with Nathan. Upon receiving the fourth letter which had another image of a gun, Nathan contacted the local police department.

"Okay Dr. Stern. Come on in," directed Detective Bev Granger, "Let's take a look." The detective, young and dressed casually, was of slender build with cropped blonde hair.

"I know I probably did everything wrong here, but I'm now much more concerned about these than before," commented Nathan.

"Why is that Doctor?" asked Det. Granger.

"Well, I now know these aren't random…that it is personal, very personal… and the frequency is telling me that this person has become more frustrated. I don't know what to do here. I'm not sure who it is or what's this about," replied Nathan.

"Dr. Stern. I believe you're right on target here. Forgive the pun…and I'm going to prioritize the case and give it some more attention."

"What kind of attention?" asked Nathan.

"Okay. First, the next letter…I want you leave it unopened and preserve it in a plastic sealed envelope, like the one you told me the Postal Service gave you. Maybe, we can get lucky and get some prints off of it. If you need more, I'll supply you with some. Next, if you're feeling that shaky, we'll get you some support out there by sending patrol cars out several times a day around your office and house," responded Det. Granger.

"Do you think that's necessary?" inquired Nathan.

"I think I do. Also, let me know where your children go to school and I'll notify the school of what's happening. Who's allowed to pick up the kids?"

"Oh…no. You're really getting me worried here," commented Nathan.

"You know…I really don't think you should worry about the kids, but that's the general drill in situations like this," reassured Det. Granger.

"Still, that does seem unnecessary," added Nathan.

As Det. Granger skimmed over the letters, she made some notations on her legal pad. The most recent set of letters Det. Granger began to read with a curious, bewildering expression.


Here I am lost in the turbulence of the deep ocean
I have to get out or be sucked into the vortex

You are with me once again in the turbulence going
down. Can't you see clearly how I crave your care

The road is long and dark with curves as sharp as
razor blades - lead me out of this torment or get lost
with me and get buried under my decaying corpse

I don't want to be abandoned here—help me, please
help me
I don't believe I'll ever get out

I'll go down in the turbulence of the ocean—you are
my only out, come be with me
I'll take you down too.

Please find a way to set me straight
Don't give up on me again
Show me how to cope and survive without you

I have nothing more to say, but know that you are
listening to my desperation of prayers.

Only you have the answer to repair my despair.
Please rescue me before it's too late.

I hear no reply. Am I deaf to your call
I will wait… I will wait… I will wait…

What about you?


Detective Granger read on as she placed the letter neatly on her
desk next to the file.

Before the storm hits

I need to see some signal to let me know that you are
Still here to take care of me

All these emotions are crossing over the circuits
sending confusing messages,

I'm bleeding out …you're hurting me with your
countless rejections … I don't want to hurt back and
end your time

Shot an apple off my hand…ripe and rotten at the same
time
Make it stop and go away

The heaviness of my feelings will suck me down to the other
dark side, till my shadow is no longer seen to the naked eye
I'm getting into you cause you got to me and I need
you to survive. Don't die.

Just keep tearing at me, hurt me more…destroy
me…should I fight back.

The storm will come…
the life will be gone and I will be forgotten


The next letter Detective Granger held up to the light as to
compare the type and weight of the paper, now realizing that all the
letters to date were written on similar paper and probably written
with what appears to be the same computer and printer. "No, not a
computer," whispered Granger recognizing her error, "a typewriter".

Making some notes on her pad about the paper, typewriter and style of print she continued.


The sun is yellow

The sky is forever blue

I really need to talk to you.

But we all know

That it is true.

There is nothing that you can do.

I can't find you

And I can't say

Which means you'll just send me away.

The air is polluted

Thick and gray

Make it stop

Or I'll do it my way.

"Doc. Any ideas who may be sending you these…" as Detective Granger paused, noting the revolver printed toward the top center of the page, not really expecting a response from Nathan at this time. She read on:

Don't wait for me

I've crawled so long

I cannot get away

Make it stop today

Tears block my view

I look down the barrel do I aim at you

No not now I do not see you

I see little boy blue

What am I to do?

I know where it's coming from

You know too

It's time to be through

Kaboom!!! Goes the child's balloon

## And the cow jumps over the moon

"I think I'll need to speak to your wife too. We don't know, do we, if these letters are meant for you or your wife?" questioned Detective Granger.

"No, not really, but Joanne and I were just going on the assumption that my practice and caseload is a lot more complicated than hers."

"You mean sicker, more disturbed," Detective Granger concluded.

"No. Not necessarily. And certainly in more recent years our practices are much more similar with the type of patients we work with," stated Nathan.

"How long have you been practicing Dr. Stern?"

"Down here about fifteen years and before that up in New York for another ten or so."

"Anything like this ever happen before?" asked Det. Granger.

"No. Never."

"Anyone in the family capable of playing with you like this or any one friend capable of playing a practical joke or prank like this?"

"No, I couldn't imagine," Nathan said.

"Ever been sued or brought up on malpractice charges?"

"No."

"Do custody evaluations for divorcing people?"

"No, never got into that line of work. Too messy."

"Do any forensic work with jails, prisons, etc. Or perform competency evaluations?"

"No. I've been to court a few times, but nothing like that."

"Expert witness?"

"A few times."

"On what type of cases, if I may ask?"

"I've been called in more than a few times to render second opinions in cases where a patient was litigating against a current or former therapist usually claiming some form of clinical error," responded Nathan.

"Were you for the plaintiff or defendant in most cases?"

"No. That never entered into it. I am very impartial," Nathan commented.

"You know…I want to back up for a second," Nathan suggested. "Competency evals…I had to think for a second. Not recently, but in the early part of my career I did 2PC evaluations."

"What's that stand for?" asked Granger.

"It's like our Baker Act here in the State. Involuntary hospitalizations, commitment proceedings. Two physicians or one being a licensed mental health professional would be needed to involuntarily commit. Just wanted to mention it to be complete," Nathan replied.

"Okay. Very good. I'll need to go through the same line of questions with your wife so have her call me to set up a time. Dr. Stern, have any ideas about who might be doing this?" inquired Detective Granger, who now was anticipating a response from Nathan.

Nathan, who now was becoming fatigued by Detective Granger's line of questioning, pondered for a moment or two and began to recount his own analysis of his work, type of patients, dissatisfied patients, and any possible hints or signals in someone's treatment that may alert Nathan to the type of behavior expressed through the letters. A process completed numerous times by now by both Nathan and Joanne in their attempt to better understand and identify the individual responsible.

"I've been through this so many times and still nothing really jumps out at me. Sure, there are some patients I can think of but I would be hard pressed to be certain and even the most minimal confrontation of one of my patients may prove detrimental to treatment," Nathan explained. "Even if I was able to narrow it down…can you imagine how problematic in someone's therapy that might be." That's if the person sending you these letters is still under your care," said the Detective.

"Yes, but there is still the issue of privacy and privilege which exists for current patients as well as former patients. The privilege really is in place in perpetuity. It's a sacred confidential relationship between the psychologist and patient."

"Doctor, look I'm not telling you how to handle your business, but from my position there are times you can or have to step outside of that arrangement and take care of yourself, don't you think?" asked Det. Granger.

"Well, yes under certain situations of danger you are generally permitted to step outside the bounds of privilege. Actually, unlike in other States, say California, where there is a duty to warn, Florida operates with a looser interpretation, permitting psychologists to breach privilege under situations of imminent danger. And that's just it here, I have never felt in imminent danger or close to feeling threatened. I'm not about to go ahead and violate someone's privilege with nothing more than a few letters and some armchair hunches," professed Nathan.

Nathan, who by now had a few more contacts with the American Psychological Association's Practice Directorate and the Ethics Office was fairly clear with his ethical obligation in a situation like this. In fact, Nathan unfortunately was operating in somewhat of a gray area as the new Ethical Principles of Psychologists and Code of Conduct was in the final phase of approval by the APA Board of Trustees and was not anticipated to be released for several more months. At the current time, there were only the most general comments about disclosures in Section 5, Privacy and Confidentiality. In the revised edition, very specific language was being mapped out to protect the psychologist from harm. Moreover, if Nathan was convinced it was a current patient of his who was involved in the letter writing, the revised version clearly articulates that psychologists' may terminate therapy when threatened or otherwise endangered by the patient without being worried about being sued for abandonment of care. Still, Nathan was unable to equate his experience with being threatened or endangered. The letters were tantamount to some definition of harassment but for what purpose.

"Detective Granger," began Nathan, "this seems more like some type of harassment but I'm not sure what the legal definition of harassment is," queried Nathan.

Detective Granger reached for her code book and began flipping through pages until she came to the section on harassment. "Doctor Stern, I already know what it states in here but let me read out loud so we both can understand. There are different types of harassment so I'm going to read the general section which applies. Under the U.S. Code Title 18 Subsection 1514(c) and Florida 784.048 harassment is defined as "a course of conduct directed at a specific person that causes substantial emotional distress in such a person and serves no legitimate purpose". Well, that about sums it up. There is a further section that refers to the course of conduct in terms of a persistent action and to the perception of a credible threat. Let me also point out that harassment is punishable, depending on the form, course and type of credible threat from a misdemeanor 1$^{st}$ degree up to a felony of the 3$^{rd}$ degree. This comes under our stalking laws in the State." Nathan's conversation with Detective Granger was quite sobering which left Nathan feeling that much more unglued.

"Before you leave Dr. Stern, I just want to be complete in my work and take some extra footsteps. Won't take long. Have a seat. I need to put a call into the FBI to double check something," explained Det. Granger.

As Detective Granger stepped away from her desk, Nathan was trying to take in all the information from today's meeting and again began racking his brain for any clues about who may be behind the letters.

Detective Granger reappeared a few minutes later and explained her contact with the FBI. "Dr. Stern, I was interested in seeing when and if the FBI should play a role in a stalking or harassment case."

"Did you find out anything?" asked Nathan.

"With forms of this type of harassment, letters being sent to the target or victim, the FBI would intervene in alliance with the Postal Service if there is a suggestion that the letters would cease as a result of a financial payment or if their appears to be links to organized crime or a network of perpetrators operating across the country," Detective Granger clarified.

The words target and victim resonated in Nathan's mind for a few seconds. Stunned by the accuracy of the Detective Granger's terminology, Nathan forced himself to regroup from several physiological responses all akin to a developing panic attack. Feeling lightheaded and clammy, heart and pulse accelerating, and difficulty breathing, Nathan was a walking DSM-IV checklist of all the classic signs.

"Doctor Stern, are you alright?" asked Detective Granger.

Pausing for a few more moments, Nathan now appearing more flustered, was having trouble searching for the right words. "No. I don't know. It finally hit me," replied Nathan.

"Maybe we should call your wife to come down," Det. Granger asked with concern.

"No. That won't be necessary. I'm feeling better now. It's passed," said Nathan tentatively. "Is there anything else Detective Granger we need to do now?"

"No. I think we covered most everything today. Let's stay in touch over the weeks and if another letter is delivered or if anything unusual occurs which raises your suspicion, give me a call. I also put in that request for regular patrolling in your community and by the office which should begin tomorrow , so don't be alarmed when you see us."

Detective Granger handed Nathan her card on which she wrote out a case number and left a few telephone numbers. As she escorted Nathan out of her office, Detective Granger offered Nathan a few parting words of comfort and caution.

"Doctor Stern, you and your family are going to be just fine. It always pays to be cautious but don't stop living your life. These type of things usually go away as quickly as they started."

"Thanks Detective for your concern and attention to this matter. I'm feeling a lot better now," commented Nathan.

As Nathan walked toward the elevator to go down to the lobby he was wondering if he was able to convince Detective Granger that indeed he was feeling better. Nathan knew first hand that his appearance of a now calmer exterior was merely a product of some creative defenses erected to mask his internal unsettling emotions.

\*\*\*

# CHAPTER 5

Nathan's life and life style began to change accordingly. The twice daily checks by the police continued for about a month or so until more urgent commitments within the community needed to be addressed. Detective Granger had mentioned to be more careful and observant with respect to surroundings. Also, the detective suggested to change the schedule somewhat so that nothing appeared too predictable or routine. Detective Granger really didn't appreciate how much of Nathan's life and thereby his family's life had become so organized just to keep pace with a very busy schedule. The ambiguity of the letters combined with the initial attention given by the police, easily aroused an irrational paranoia in both Nathan and Joanne. Nathan who was very much a creature of habit, began feeling the tension upon forfeiting some of his most favored activities. Morning exercise, his pre-dawn run, gave way to a stationary bike and a treadmill located in the home. A security system, though casually and inconsistently used before, was now part of the daily regimen of security. And trips back and forth from the office and around town had both Nathan and Joanne glancing to their rearview mirror more than a few times during any given commute.

During certain weeks, Nathan's opinion vacillated in giving the letters any more importance than they should have had. At times, Nathan felt ridiculous in attributing significance to a letter and refused to allow himself to be ruled by such events. At other times, Nathan invested inordinate amounts of time and energy analyzing each letter and hypothesizing as to the sender's identity and motivation for such behavior. While falling just shy of a full blown obsession, Nathan did realize how preoccupied he had become with all of this and how much distraction he had succumbed to.

\*\*\*

"Joanne, come in here…unbelievable," an exasperated Nathan shouted. Nathan who was attempting to find out how someone can locate a name or address by accessing databases through a computer became adroit in surfing the internet. He located several sources which link to other domains which can easily retrieve specific personal information.

Joanne, leaning over her husband's shoulder, watched as Nathan keyed in an address to link to the county government web site and then to further scroll through the system and click on the window to access personal property and real estate taxes.

"Joanne, now look how easy it is for anyone to find an address. All you need is a name and a good educated guess if that party owns property in the county," Nathan explained.

"You mean there's no password, unique id, no secured link?" asked Joanne.

"None that I can see," replied Nathan.

"Now watch. Plug in our last name and there we are. Names, address, property location, lot number, and even what our annual tax is. Can you believe this. That's how easy it is for anyone wanting to locate an address. I bet that's how this person did it," concluded Nathan.

"I really can't believe it's that easy to get personal and private information. Anyone is so exposed out there and even though you and I go to some length to protect our privacy, the internet is available to tap into such sensitive data. All public records are available to anyone with a computer and internet service," an incredulous Joanne remarked.

"Enough time researching this tonight. I found out what I needed. Joanne, I think I'm going to talk this over with Simon to see what kind of perspective from a clinical stance he can offer. What do you think?" asked Nathan.

"You know, I think it's a good idea just to talk to someone to get an outside opinion who's in the field and can offer some objectivity," replied Joanne.

Simon Hirshfield, who was senior in both age and years in practice to Nathan, was called upon from time to time to discuss such clinical matters as diagnosis, transference and countertransference issues, and therapeutic impasses. Nathan's relationship with Simon began during graduate training and continued into Nathan's early career. A mentor, a sounding board and at times a personal therapist, Simon often brought an astute understanding to a clinical dilemma. Simon who was an old school psychoanalyst had for many decades now the prototypical graying, white beard. The European accent only further completed the traditional stereotype.

***

The drive to Simon took about forty-five minutes. Set off the intra-coastal waterway on Flagler, Simon's condo offered a magnificent view of the barrier islands. Simon, who was now approaching his mid-seventies, was enjoying the full amenities of retirement life. Retired from the field for about twelve years now, he still maintained an office where he would retreat to a few times a week to take care of professional correspondences. When hearing about Nathan's visit, Simon preferred to meet at the condo where lunch would be waiting.

Nathan was bringing to Simon a complete set of letters for his review. No longer in possession of the originals, Nathan kept copies of each letter which were forwarded to him by Detective Granger after the police processed the envelope and letter. To date, the police lab was unable to retrieve anything useful from the material.

The most recent letters followed a now predictable theme. The first letter of the New Year came a within the first week of January:

## New Year's Resolution

If I came to see you, would you be mad at me?

Would I be mad at you. Would you dismiss me or would I

destroy you.

I need some help.

Don't throw me aside again for I can't take much more.

I'm ready to act.

Six weeks later, around Valentine's Day, a letter arrived with the following prose:

If I sat in your office before you, what would you do?

Would you help me

or look down

and cast a sad eye upon me?

You're in a better emotional place. I'm but a small part of

your life which fills up a small space each time.

Can you see the emotional landscape? I had no choice as to

whether my mind was healthy or disturbed.

All was sadly predetermined.
The evolution of which in a split second was once quite
certain.

Now I question what could have been.

So if you tell me that I can be in a better place, don't look
so
convinced because I of all people know that this is quite
untrue.

When I look at you with your certain truths

I got a strange weird type of feeling....
that you too know of the falsehood of the confidence

that you have in yourself
This you would understand as your simple truth.

The next letter, even more engaging, came on April Fool's Day:

How I wish for a brighter day so that I may rejoice in the
brightness of my emotions. To feel alive and whole once
again

But we know the reality of my pain is never ending and

brightness is turned to darkness and the negative

overwhelms the positive.

There is no end, is there? Just a bunch of words to

momentarily release me of my suffering

That's all it is a temporary fix to a disabling permanent

condition

Make it stop! Can you make it stop!

Cut me free. Stop the pain. Or, should I inflict

the pain?

So how do I still wish for brighter days so that I may rejoice in the full range of my emotions. To feel alive and whole and

healed again. If you can take me there I will be forever in your debt.

But we both know that's something you can't do

\*\*\*

Whenever Nathan would meet with Simon, a feeling of security and a sense of reassurance would inevitably settle in. Simon, without attempting to, came across as a soothing paternalistic figure and probably represented something very endearing to Nathan. Simon always occupied a very special role in Nathan's adult life.

"Nathan, Happy Pesach. It's very nice to see you again. Come in," greeted Simon.

"Simon…Happy Passover. You're looking very well."

"Played a round of golf this morning, probably got too much sun. How's Joanne and the boys?" asked Simon.

"Everyone is just fine. Thank you for inviting me."

"No. No problem at all. You know how I like to help. Keeps me younger I think. Sit down… lets have some lunch and talk. I hope you don't mind I'm eating only matzah this week during the holiday."

"That's fine Simon, we're observing too," replied Nathan.

"So, Nathan what's this all about… you mentioned something about letters and a patient?" Simon inquired.

"I really don't know yet. I was hoping if you took a look at these letters I might be able to put some things together differently," explained Nathan.

"I imagine you invested some time into this already, so I'm not sure how helpful I will be but you never know…let me see."

Nathan handed over the letters and Simon put on a different pair of reading glasses and began to look through the small stack of letters.

"Well, I can see why you might be concerned but let's not overreact. No need to pack up and leave the state," Simon added sarcastically.

"And all of these letters come to your home, never to the office. It's as if the individual is making a special point to be certain you take this more seriously. It took an extra effort to obtain the home address and while this person easily could obtain your office address, the home is a clear violation of a boundary and I imagine this person understands and enjoys how much he or she stepped over that privacy boundary," suggested Simon.

"Nathan, tell me what your thoughts are about all this. What kind of individual are we looking for?" asked Simon.

For a moment, Nathan flashed back to his training years when a similar question of case conceptualization would have been asked by Simon. Nathan then went on to present to Simon a clinical profile of the type of person likely involved in compiling or creating, and then sending the letters:

*This is an adult, chronologically in the twenties or thirties, although developmentally arrested pre-oedipal. Suffered some form of psychic injury in the earliest years. Probably female with some rupture in the mother-child dyad. Unable to tolerate a whole lot of frustration, ambivalence, and disappointment, she is prone to various forms of acting out and impulse dyscontrol. When feeling invalidated, dismissed, rejected or misunderstood, she is very likely to become enraged and search for some way to neutralize the feeling. She can become needy, clingy and dependent and thus engulf some figure in her object world or become distant and disconnected and thus become estranged from her significant object choices. Either way this person is very likely operating from the vicissitudes of abandonment and will find some maladaptive way to quell the experience. She can pretend very well to be adult-like but regresses under the fears and stressors of separation, and would likely find methods to possess and control her figures of perceived attachment. Probably never psychotic, she may have moments or transient periods of psychotic-like experience. Most likely functioning with persistent thoughts of harming herself, she would be prone to forms of self-destructive behaviors like cutting herself and abusing alcohol and drugs. Potentially dangerous to others in cases where the transference mirrors a persistently devaluing, merging, and sadistic-like quality in her attitudes and behaviors. Looking for much attention, this person can be prone to histrionics and game playing. Major defense mechanisms would include projection, splitting, and projective identification. Diagnostic considerations lean toward higher level borderline personality organization or a type of narcissism, which has been termed malignant narcissistic personality organization; my best guess would be the former. Amenable to treatment of the longer term nature utilizing a more confrontational, psychodynamically-oriented form of therapy. Likely to be a protracted and at times feel like an intractable therapy with multiple ups and downs. For the therapist a constant barrage of vacillating transferences indicative of both idealization and devaluation. Generally not a great prognosis, but if both therapist and patient tolerate the therapeutic environment some dramatic gains can be seen. Most therapies for patients like this however would terminate prematurely, often with rage and abandonment reported by patients and frustration, anger, relief, and fear of legal retaliation reported by therapists.*

Nathan completed his conceptualization within two or three minutes without pausing in his well-thought out synopsis. For Nathan, he had already gone through this a few times. But now, he was interested in Simon's assessment.

"That's very good Nathan. I see you're just as sharp as ever. You still remember how to present a case after all this time," said Simon approvingly. "Your conceptualization, I think, is about right. I might have said it a little differently but the substance is accurate. The letters to me, at first, suggest a higher risk for self-destructive, suicidal tendencies. Yet, the letters shift somewhat and there becomes a blurring of boundaries and a sense of merger between the writer and the reader or at least a fantasized wish of there being a special relationship between the two. It's the joining of the two which reoccur in the later letters which concerns me. Okay then. Now let's see. Tell me about some of your patients, especially last year around this time extending through the summer, if you recall. I know it's been a while. Maybe you can remember anything unusual during that time, something that sticks out or was out of place in treatment, some of the central themes of some of those sessions, what your patients were talking about, what they weren't saying, any impasses or ruptures in treatment, any premature terminations, any patients referred out of the office, patients you chose not to treat or accept for treatment, any patients that left treatment angry or dissatisfied, any unusual transferences or any out of the ordinary countertransference feelings you may have been experiencing. This is where I would like to begin," recommended Simon

"Simon, it's reassuring to hear your thoughts on this. I went through a very similar line of inquiry a few weeks back. Both Joanne and I proceeded with the same line of reasoning but came up without anything really remarkable. I think it's helpful to do it one more time with an outsider looking in. Helps to narrow those blind spots."

Nathan then continued to review out loud an exhaustive list of active patients. In the end, Nathan zeroed in on the same four or five patients from his previous exercises in deductive and inferential reasoning. Even with the rigors of Simon's academic scrutiny, Nathan wasn't overwhelmed with optimism that they have come much further in what was beginning to look like a futile exercise.

"So, we have Janette B.... Marla P.... Patricia V.... Tamara L.... Natalie K... and I think we should add Leon J who I know doesn't quite fit your profile but I'm allowed a wild card, am I not," suggested Simon. "And you are telling me that only a few patients left your care in this time period and of those few all left apparently on good terms with you. And those you chose not to accept for treatment were referred accordingly and did not seem to be out of sorts with you over being denied care. And you had no patients complete an act of suicide where a family member blamed you and may come after you," summarized Simon.

Nathan had already sketched out each patient's history, treatment time line, and response to therapy. The list became a who's who in borderline pathology. Three of the five women, Marla Peters, Tamara Lockwood, and Natalie Klingel, were still under Nathan's care. Janette Bateman left the area and Patricia Vinton's care was discontinued after a few months due to financial hardship; a reduced fee was unable to be agreed upon and Patricia was referred on to some providers who participated in her insurance plans panel.

"Janette B's treatment ended early," inquired Simon

"Her husband was relocating to Washington D.C. to accept a high level position in the Justice Department. Her treatment was interrupted with less than a month of termination sessions after a year and a half of treatment. Although she was about a year away from completing therapy with me, we arranged treatment to continue in D.C. She felt mixed about ending and angry with her husband who she blamed for again dislocating her from therapy. Janette has been in touch since and apparently has made a nice adjustment to her new life in Washington and mentioned she continues working with her new psychologist," Nathan replied. "And Patricia V. How did she take it when you couldn't reduce your fees further to accommodate her financial situation?" asked Simon.

"Not too well. But I did most everything to work with her. An appropriate fee arrangement is an important aspect of someone's care and you know I'm well- schooled in this area," commented Nathan.

"She left your care in what kind of mood?" asked Simon.

"Not great. But I spent a significant amount of time with her in the termination phase of treatment just to take every precaution in helping her make the transition to a new therapist. She wasn't happy. But she wasn't threatening in any way and she wouldn't strike me as the type of person to pursue this behavior. Not organized enough and definitely wouldn't have the resources," Nathan explained.

"That leaves the three others," identified Simon.

"Marla P, Natalie K, and Tamara L," stated Nathan.

"All severely disturbed and all fit my clinical summary to a tee. All currently under my care. All making strong demands for my time and availability. All with major abandonment issues. All in treatment for some time now and all with a vacillating transference pattern, though typically the three are much more with the devaluation transference. Marla by far is the most enraged with me and the most vocal about her "hatred" toward me," clarified Nathan.

"You know, Nathan....I'm thinking that wouldn't be the person's style. I have a hunch that while this patient would be seething with anger toward you, that this emotion would be silenced in session. So let's not think of this patient in that way," commented Simon.

"Any of these patients violating any obvious boundaries with you? Telephone time, extending sessions, canceling sessions and then requesting more sessions which do not appear necessary, or, you failing to keep sessions?" asked Simon.

"Of this group of patients, only one. Tamara had a habit of abusing our telephone time and I placed stronger measures on her use of the telephone some time back," responded Nathan.

"And she complied?" Simon asked.

"She didn't like it much. But after a series of confrontations she respected that boundary as well as some others we were working on," replied Nathan.

"And…what about Natalie?" asked Simon.

"Natalie's treatment has been very problematic for me over the year. Just when I felt she was making some progress, she would retreat back into her most pathological ways and there we would begin again. She would be unavailable for hours, just sitting in my office looking away, looking angry, appearing sad but never expressing either feeling. I've thought of hospitalizing her a few times when she would mutilate herself and thought of referring her a few times, and then I reconsider. She's been a patient of mine for quite some time and I would like to see her through all of this," related Nathan.

"Your feelings toward her are different than the others?" asked Simon.

"No. Not really. It's just that she's somewhat more dependent and child-like than the others. She pulls for more nurturance and care. And that's just it. Just when you give it she snaps back and closes the door," replied Nathan.

"She's been very badly hurt by her caregivers and obviously you are part of this chaotic process now. But it's manageable. Just monitor your countertransference better. She certainly has the makeup to participate in the behavior…so let's just keep her in mind. "Well that brings me to Leon J," commented Simon. "I know we have been thinking in terms of a female patient, but there was something about this guy when we first spoke about him that left me feeling uneasy."

"What was that Simon?" asked Nathan.

"When you first described this patient…on first glance he seems to be a textbook narcissist with his sense of entitlement, his collection of such needs as power and status, and the way he manipulates and exploits relationships. But recall in your conceptualization, you made a comment about malignant narcissism which extends the narcissistic character to include both antisocial and sadistic qualities. This guy has some of that too. And the way he relates to you, like as if he's playing a game with you. I don't know. It goes against what we have been thinking of. But there's a strong possibility someone like Leon is very capable of carrying out such behavior and much more; a guy like Leon could be more volatile in an externalizing way than any one of your female patients we have discussed," explained Simon.

"That's an interesting take on things," replied Nathan. "I probably wouldn't have included Leon on my short list."

"Well, I think he belongs there until proven otherwise," responded Simon.

The two, working diligently as if still professor and student, all but lost track of time. The chimes from Simon's antique grandfathers' clock, faintly heard in the background, oriented Simon to the approaching time.

"Gee, look at the time. We've been doing this for two hours now," Simon commented. "I need to take care of something before 3 P.M."

"No. Don't let me stop you. Let's wrap up. You have been a great help Simon. I really do appreciate your time today," Nathan commented.

As the two friends parted and wished one another well, Nathan headed back to his office feeling his time here with Simon was well served. As he drove down the interstate, the few names identified resonated through his mind and he wondered how he could possibly confirm if one of these patients were responsible.

\*\*\*

Over the ensuing weeks, Nathan listened more carefully to his patients and paid attention to certain details differently in an attempt to draw some conclusions about the group of patients he suspected most. It probably was the least productive time in therapy for his patients as his distraction level was greatest. Instead of focusing in like a laser to his patient's therapeutic needs, Nathan found himself hopelessly entangled in his private preoccupations with certain phrases from the letters and several unproductive fantasies and countertransference reactions toward his patients. On a few occasions, Nathan found himself rescheduling appointments as even he knew he was less than there for his patients.

\*\*\*

The letters continued for another two months and just as Detective Granger predicted they suddenly stopped. No further action was ever taken by the police or the Postal Service. While Nathan kept in touch with Detective Granger, there was very little the police could do unless Nathan offered up the few names on his short list. While pressured by Detective Granger, this of course was ethically and legally impossible to accommodate to. Without any further evidence or concern of imminent danger, Nathan was left only with his clinical acumen to discover the individual responsible and to uncover the underlying motivation. The last three letters followed suit as the ten before:

I'm just waiting here for your call, a kind word,
a warm tone to your voice

I'm just waiting for our next time but perhaps
it will never arrive

Patiently waiting as your warmth melts within
me

It feels so good yet at once so confusing... so I

dismiss its intent and become enraged with dancing

flames which engulf you

I'm just waiting for the right time
How about you?
In the end, I know I will be all alone yet, I'm just
waiting to be proven right.


Dawn and Dusk


Each day the sun comes up with the pure

innocence of what lies ahead

By no surprise, very quickly the day turns to

torment and I want to reach out to you...

But you are not there for me

Distractions eventually give in to my urges
and I find myself at peril
But you are not there for me

Urges concede to actions

Do I dare commit to my familiar retreat

I call ... but you are not there

Dusk is upon us. I survived one more day

as darkness approaches

Still alone, very much on my own
I call, but you are not there

Life coming to a close, yet I live for another day
Hear me call out in pain.

The last of the three conveyed a more distinct depressive undertone with a sense of hopelessness and surrender:

Tried to reach you...but then you were Gone

What is wrong?

Everything is...Gone

Yesterday is...Gone

Tomorrow is...Gone

Today is...Gone
Life is decayed full of disease and irritation

I want to escape

I want to fly like Icarus

I want to stretch my arms up high

I want to glide beyond the sky

No more...just Gone

No touching...No more hurting...No more being

GONE...GONE...GONE.... BYE...JUST GONE

\*\*\*

# CHAPTER 6

The news of Ben Solomon's death trickled slowly through the professional community. Nathan however, probably received the notification earlier than most as he was named Dr. Solomon's responsible party to secure and manage clinical records in the event of a death. This was an agreement both Ben and Nathan ironed out over drinks several years ago and apparently, to Nathan's surprise, was never changed.

"Oh… no, I just can't believe it. I was just emailing with him a few days back. When did this happen?" asked a disbelieving Nathan. On the other end of the conversation was a sobbing, near hysterical Margaret who was Ben's colleague in his Manhattan practice.

"Tuesday, no Monday. We don't know yet. The police didn't say," a hyperventilating Margaret offered.

"Police, what happened?" asked Nathan.

"We're not sure. But they are saying…they are saying he killed himself. Left a note and did it in his home office."

Ben like most seasoned psychiatrists residing on Long Island had for the last two years established a part of his practice out of his home in Great Neck. Roughly an hour outside the city, this afforded Ben the flexibility of seeing patients at home while also spending more time with his wife. During the last few months of Brittany's life, Ben almost exclusively saw patients in his Great Neck office.

"Margaret, I'm so sorry. I know how rough this is for you," Nathan said thoughtfully. Margaret, a certified social worker, was an associate of Ben's who practiced with him for about three years.

"He left a letter?" asked Nathan.

"Yeah. That's what I heard. Something about not being able to go on after Brittany's death… and then he shot himself right in his office. They found him in his chair."

"He had a gun?" Nathan questioned with a puzzled tone.

"I guess. I know it doesn't sound like him, but maybe he kept a gun around that big old house for protection."

"Doctor Stern. I'm sorry to be the one to tell you. But Ben had a list of contacts…you know in case of emergencies, and there was your name," explained Margaret.

"Margaret, no I understand. It's just that we were in touch the other day, Monday I think, you know about general stuff…," Nathan rambled..

"Any arrangements yet?" asked Nathan.

"No, not yet. But my best guess is probably Sunday or Monday. Will you be coming up?"

"Definitely… yes. Just have to make some plans on this end," Nathan replied. "When I get up there I'll take care of some of the office matters. Margaret can you look after that until I get up there?"

"I will once the police let me and Ben's secretary back into the offices. I'm sorry again about the news. I know this is difficult for you too," a more coherent Margaret expressed.

The conversation concluded and Nathan was in shock, just sitting in his office and in his chair wondering what his friend was up against emotionally after his wife died. Nathan was planning to break the news to Joanne a little bit later. Joanne took the day off to attend to some school functions for one of the boys. Nathan knew better than to unload this right now.

"Myra, can you do me a favor. Start checking into flights up to New York for the weekend and see what my schedule looks like for the beginning of next week?"

At first, Nathan was contemplating on canceling all appointments unless there was something critical. But as the morning continued, he felt strong enough and alert enough to handle all his responsibilities. He took an early lunch, reshuffled a few things and felt prepared to finish out his afternoon appointments.

\*\*\*

The suicide death of Ben Solomon continued to pervade Nathan's consciousness throughout the day. Although Nathan had lost one maybe two patients to suicide over the tenure of his career, this was the first suicide to impact him in such a private and personal way. Nathan knew about the living legacy left behind to family and friends in the aftermath of a suicide. The range of emotions from sadness and anger to guilt were all quite common to experience, and Nathan was certain he too had begun to feel these emotions. By mid-afternoon, Nathan and Joanne consoled one another and were making arrangements to fly up for the funeral service. Joanne would travel back shortly after the funeral and Nathan planned to stay on for a few days into the business week to attend and secure Ben's clinical records.

\*\*\*

"Dr. Stern, your 5 o'clock is here a little early," Myra said as she poked her head into Nathan's office. "I'll have her complete the paper work and you can start a few minutes ahead of schedule if you would like," suggested Myra.

Myra, who stayed somewhat later because of the events of the day, would be leaving after taking care of the new patient file.

"You have a long day," commented Ronnie Fitz-Morris, as she took the folder from Myra.

"Oh me. I'm usually out of here by 3 or so, but Dr. Stern asked that I stay on today," replied Myra.

In a few minutes, Ms. Fitz-Morris handed back the folder with all the standard forms completed. Now a days, most records read like a legal doctrine with informed consents, HIPPA advisements, and contractual arrangements for fees.

"Ms. Fitz-Morris, how will you be paying today?" inquired Myra.

"I have insurance from my previous job up in New York, but I know Dr. Stern doesn't take insurance… I'll pay cash."

"That will be fine. Today's fee is $200," replied Myra.

Ronnie reached into her Louis Voitton handbag and removed two one hundred dollar bills and handed them to Myra.

"Let me get you a receipt and I will print out a statement if you would like to file it with your insurance company," Myra said.

While Myra prepared the statement, Ronnie sat herself down in a waiting room chair and flipped through some of the magazines, not really focusing on the material before her but wondering what she would be focusing on during her first session. A few minutes later, Nathan stepped into the waiting room and greeted his new patient. "Ronnie…I'm Dr. Stern. It's nice to meet you," Nathan said.

"Hi, Dr. Stern. Nice to meet you too. Thanks for getting me into your schedule," replied Ronnie.

As the two slowly walked back to Nathan's office, some small talk was made which often is the case as a prelude to a session. Nathan couldn't help but notice how attractive this twenty something year old woman was. Attired and accessorized with designer labels, Ronnie presented in a sophisticated way which set her apart from most of her peers. The session began in rather typical format for an initial visit with Nathan.

"Ronnie…we probably have a lot to cover today, but first perhaps you can tell me some of the reasons for coming to see me today?" inquired Nathan.

"Ronnie, that's short for Veronica, if you're wondering. Most everyone calls me Ronnie. So why am I here? You know, I've been curious about it and people tell me I should talk to someone."

"People…who for example?" asked Nathan.

"Well friends mostly."

"And why do you think your friends suggest that you speak to a therapist?" Nathan asked gently.

"My friends who really, really know me, know I have issues and that I haven't come from the best of family situations," replied Ronnie.

Nathan pondered for a moment on whether to explore the issues side of the equation or delve right into the family system, although intuitively he knew they were inextricably linked.

"Well, why don't you tell me about your family first?" suggested Nathan.

"Oh, not much to tell," Ronnie said.

Nathan who was accustomed to hearing that phrase, knew instinctively that a comment of this type was almost without exception the furthest from the truth.

"I was given up by my mother pretty early in life, never really knew her. I was told she had some serious problems. Probably could have used someone like you. I lived through a string of foster care placements arranged through the Division of Youth and Family Services in New York and eventually adopted at age ten by a childless couple who really had no business adopting in the first place…clueless about kids. Basically, raised by the nanny."

"That's quite a story of your early life. Did you ever have the opportunity to meet your birth mother?" Nathan asked.

"No. Never did. I later learned that somewhere between the ninth and tenth foster placement she killed herself."

"How old were you when you found out?"

"I was around fifteen or sixteen."

"That must have been difficult to hear?" inquired Nathan.

"No, not really. It's not like I was looking for her. There was nothing there at the time. Anyway, you go through the system and you feel less and less as time passes," explained Ronnie.

"And now. Do you feel different?"

"That's just it. I'm going through stuff now and I think my past is catching up with me," replied Ronnie.

"How do you mean that?" Nathan asked.

"Well…a couple of years back, I was getting real serious with this guy and we were planning to get married and you know he was asking questions about my family and although I told him about my adoption and all that, his questions started to make me think again about my real mother and father as well. That's when I started to search around for information on my mother. I just wanted a more complete picture of who I was and you know if we were planning on kids I wanted to know more about the family genetics. The adoption agency was useless, closed or private records or something like that, and the Division of Youth and Family was difficult to navigate around…records discarded, lost or destroyed. So I was at a loss. I later hired a private eye to look into it and he found some things out which started to complete the picture."

"Are you still in the process of learning more about your mother?" asked Nathan.

"I think so, it seems like it is never ending. But you know it has really opened up a lot of wounds."

"Maybe now would be a good time to tell me about some of those wounds," suggested Nathan softly.

"How much time do we have left?" Ronnie asked.

"We have a few more minutes, but since you're asking… perhaps it would be better if we wait to your next visit to talk more about this, if that's okay with you," recommended Nathan.

"That sounds right," Ronnie replied.

"Well, we will remember to bring that up next time, but for the moment we can shift gears. Tell me about your move down to Florida?" Nathan asked.

"You know it has a lot to do with my break up from George," Ronnie started to say.

"This is the guy you were going to marry?"

"Oh no, that was Jared. We went our separate ways about a year and a half ago. I started going with George about ten months later," Ronnie replied in a correcting fashion.

"So how serious was it with George?" asked Nathan.

"Not so serious from my side, but George that's another story. He got like all over me and made plans. It started to really suffocate me. You never see it coming. He got like real controlling…into a power trip. I couldn't take it. And when I told him about ending, he really freaked. I got a restraining order and everything."

"Did that help?" asked Nathan.

"Not really. George became like enraged and that's when I knew I had to leave the city. Moved out to a friend on the Island, quit my job and made some plans to really move out of the area."

"And how did you decide on coming here?"

"This area was like a second home for me. My parents, you know my adoptive parents had a winter home down here, so I'm real comfortable here."

"Did you find a place to live already?"

"Oh that. No that's taken care of. My parents left me the home," said Ronnie.

"Left you? Something happened to your parents?" inquired Nathan.

"I thought I mentioned it. They died in 911. Went down in Tower #1."

"Ronnie, I'm very sorry," Nathan responded compassionately.

"Thanks. I try not to dwell on it."

"Do you want to talk some more about this now?" Nathan asked.

"I don't think so. We must be out of time by now?" Ronnie inquired abruptly.

"I know how difficult this all must be for you. We've talked about a few things which I know are all interrelated. We can stop here if you want and we'll find a way to pick up somewhere next time. How would that be?" asked Nathan.

"That will be great. Can I see you in a few days?"

"Well… actually I'll be away probably through Wednesday. Let's schedule for next Thursday at the same time. How's that?" Nathan suggested.

"That sounds like a long time away," Ronnie replied.

"Are you anticipating some problems over the week?"

"No. I can't think of any. I just thought I'd see you sooner."

"Well, when I return we can talk about the frequency of your sessions with me. But in the meantime, if you need to speak to someone, here is a name of a doctor who covers emergency calls for me when I'm away."

Nathan turned over his business card and wrote out the name and telephone number of Dr. Martin Glazer. Dr. Glazer, a few doors down from the office, was the on-call psychologist for both Joanne and Nathan when they took vacation or went out of town.

"Ronnie, I'll see you in one week," said Nathan as he handed Ronnie the card.

"Okay then. Have a good trip. Where are you going anyway?" a curious Ronnie asked.

Nathan would typically field this question differently for new patients than from existing patients in which a strong therapeutic relationship was clearly established. However, this afternoon, perhaps getting caught up in the events of his friend and his new patient's New York background, Nathan commented loosely about his departure to New York.

"Actually, I'm heading up to New York."

"That's weird isn't it. I'm coming down here and you'll be up there. Well. Have a good time," commented Ronnie without knowing how very far from a good time Nathan was about to have.

As Ronnie left the office, Nathan began to dictate the information gathered from this session and tentatively formulated a diagnosis and treatment plan. Myra would transcribe his dictation sometime early next week. Nathan's 6 P.M. session was cancelled earlier which gave Nathan a chance to close up the office knowing that he would not be back until next Wednesday the earliest. He left some notes for Myra to attend to and some scheduling concerns for next week after the holiday and for the week after. Nathan also sent out a few emails advising of his absence from the university.

\*\*\*

By late afternoon, Joanne had already finalized plane and hotel reservations for tomorrow which would have them arrive at JFK by 3 P.M. Arrangements were also made for the kids to stay with a friends' family until Joanne arrived back home late Sunday evening. Erik and Jack would be staying with the Bishops' next door who often shuttle their own kids over to Joanne and Nathan's when in need of a night out. The kids who go to the same school and play nicely together would enjoy their time together. Nathan planned to sweeten the arrangement by giving the weekend tickets for the games to Mark and Donna. Hopefully, they would democratically determine the best way to accommodate all the kids interested in going with the number of tickets available.

Margaret had called Joanne about Ben's funeral which was scheduled for early Sunday morning, many days beyond the customary Jewish tradition of interring the body as soon as possible after a death. Apparently, the police were just completing their investigation and were planning to release Ben's body to family sometime late Friday afternoon. As it wasn't possible to bury Ben on the Sabbath, Sunday was the earliest date possible. The long summer ending Labor Day weekend now had a different meaning for the Sterns'. Instead of a family weekend of Labor Day celebrations including an annual block party and tickets to the hottest match-up in the National League, Joanne and Nathan and the children will co-exist separately over the next few days, focusing on very different events.

\*\*\*

# CHAPTER 7

Traveling by plane for most is usually met with a special type of anticipation. Perhaps one is at the beginning or ending of a vacation or a business trip and thereby one's thoughts and feelings are necessarily colored by those very experiences. Stepping aboard an airplane to attend a somber event as in the case of a funeral leaves the traveler in a very different space. For Nathan and Joanne the trip up to New York was subdued. Nathan, who has made a number of these bereavement trips up north primarily for family members was often struck by the same degree of isolation and loss. Left alone with his thoughts, Nathan was growing uncomfortable with how familiar these feelings have unfortunately become. Even though Joanne was sitting next to him it was a painfully long and lonely plane ride to New York.

As the plane was descending into JFK, Nathan's conversation briefly continued with Joanne. "Joanne, let's make a promise that next time we take a trip to New York it's for a happy event."

"I know. What was it. A little less than six months ago we were up here for Brittany's service and now Ben. He must have really been tortured without her," replied Joanne.

"What did Margaret say about the police report?" asked Joanne.

"That they ruled it a suicide. They were trying though to reconstruct his last day including appointments which he had at the house."

"What about the note?"

"A few sentences. That was all. Written on his PC. Words about understanding what his life was like and asking for forgiveness."

As the plane made its final approach to JFK, the conversation quieted down again.

\*\*\*

The seventy-five minute cab ride from JFK into the city was just as quiet. Rush hour traffic already had begun to build and the bumper-to-bumper crawl north on the Van Wyck and then west on the Long Island Expressway through the tunnel made the trip to mid-town that much longer. Nathan and Joanne decided to stay in Manhattan as Nathan would eventually need to have access to Ben's Park Row office. Even though the service was out in Great Neck and the funeral further out on Long Island, Nathan always preferred staying in the city.

Check in at the Hilton went remarkably smooth and while Joanne and Nathan's luggage was taken up to their room, Nathan wanted to walk up Fifth Avenue toward the Park. Still warm from the 6 o'clock summer sun, they walked for some time up through the Eighties and then found a bench to rest a bit.

"Do you miss it?" asked Nathan.

"The city. Yes I do. But I like our life back home," replied Joanne.

"That's our old street down there. And not too far away the old office right on Analyst's Alley. Seems like just yesterday, don't you think?"

"I don't know, seems like a long time ago for me," said Joanne.

"For a short period of time, Ben and I shared that office and then went our separate ways. You know, we seldom saw one another after that but still over the years we stayed in touch. I'm going to miss him," commented Nathan.

"Oh I know. We're all going to miss him in different ways," replied Joanne.

"Are you ready for that brisk walk back to the hotel?" asked Nathan.

"Nate, what about dinner first? What was that French restaurant we liked? Do you remember that cute, little Bistro around mid-town?"

"Yeah. That's not too far away. We'll get a cab and hop over to Madison," replied Nathan.

In a few minutes, Joanne and Nathan revisited an old romantic meeting place and for the next hour or so transported themselves away from the purpose of their visit and got lost within themselves.

***

Both decided to walk off some of the calories from dinner and strolled the evening streets back to the hotel. Holding hands and having some quickened pace to their steps, Joanne and Nathan looked very much like a New York couple. By the time Joanne and Nathan returned to their hotel it was close to 10 P.M. Whether it was the moment, the events of the day or the need to connect during this period of grief, Joanne and Nathan felt the energy between them and did not plan to detour their passion. Their embrace was strong and tight. The connection, at this moment, so much in contrast to the distance Nathan was feeling on the trip up. Both took turns hurriedly unbuttoning shirts and slipping off each other's pants. The anticipation of their bodies entwined and nurturing one another with the pleasures they both knew how to so skillfully locate and amplify commanded all of their attention. Nothing else now seemed so important. And for the next several minutes, Joanne and Nathan entered a very special world reserved only for the two them. As Joanne's relaxed, slender physique draped across Nathan's now depleted body, Nathan found himself in a twilight mumbling to Joanne, "I think we should come to New York more often."

\*\*\*

The Sunday morning service left Nathan with Saturday to meet with Margaret and the secretary at Ben's Manhattan office. The notion of walking into his friend's office as well as a psychiatrist's office felt uncomfortable to Nathan as he realized he would be entering the very private sanctuary where Ben spent much of his life helping others. Margaret, who shared in the overhead of this office, planned to keep the office and eventually would be transferring the lease to her name. The secretary, Ruth, was planning to retire by the end of the year. Nathan, Margaret, and Ruth planned to meet in the lobby around noon.

"Dr. Stern. Over here," an older woman's scratchy voice called out. "Hello, I'm Ruth Lowell. We spoke the other day."

"Hello, Ruth. Sorry we're meeting under these circumstances. Thank you for meeting with me and Margaret on a Saturday. I hope it wasn't too much trouble for you."

As Nathan and Ruth were getting acquainted, Margaret entered the building and approached.

"Hi, Dr. Stern. I'm Margaret. Thank you so much for coming up and being here. Ben constantly talked about you around the office." Margaret's voice hesitated a bit as she was ending her greeting to Nathan.

"Margaret, nice to meet you. Ben too spoke about you. He was very comfortable with you and your work," Nathan replied. "If you both think we should do this another time, just let me know and I'll make other arrangements."

"No this seems to be the best time," Margaret responded.

"Shall we go up," suggested Ruth.

The three walked down the lobby corridor to the elevator which took them to the office on the seventh floor. Ruth, who lead the way, opened the door to the office. something she had done a few thousand times for Ben and Margaret. As Ruth flipped on the light switch, Nathan entered his friend's office for the very first time noting how beautifully appointed the waiting room was. The room decorated in antique Victorian era furniture had all the markings of Brittany's interior decorating taste. Ben, who wasn't much for such details left Brittany in total control of the office design. As Ruth and Margaret gave Nathan a brief tour of the suite, Nathan was able to appreciate how much of Ben's life was here in the office.

For the next few hours, Nathan settled into Ben's office and with Ruth and Margaret's help, attended to the job before them. Nathan, who had closed down a practice before for an ailing colleague, was able to streamline his effort. Knowing that Margaret had decided to continue her work out of this office, helped make life a little easier. Also, that Ruth would be around for the next few months to manage the office was reassuring to Nathan that business would go on as usual to the best of their ability despite Ben's death.

"Ruth, some things like Ben's license to practice medicine and his malpractice insurance I'll leave to you to contact the appropriate agencies to notify of his death and reconcile any payments due or refunds back. Taxes and things of that nature we'll leave for the attorney and accountant who will be addressing those issues. We should place a notice in a few professional association publications and a professional obituary in the local paper reporting Ben's death. Margaret, I know you and Ben were sharing office expenses, so I will leave you to take control over the bills and obligations you had together and to alter the lease for this office to reflect your name as the principal party leasing the space. As far as the records go, Ben primarily had a medication practice out of this office, so we need to notify all current patients of his death and make appropriate referrals for continued care. For inactive patients, Ruth if you can compile a list and then send a letter to each former patient notifying them of Ben's death and where records will be stored and how to obtain records if needed. Current patients too will need to know the same mechanism for obtaining records."

"How far back should I go?" inquired Ruth.

"Well, that's a good question. Go ahead and check with the New York State Medical Association. The time frame may vary from state to state and between disciplines. What's required of me in the State of Florida as a psychologist and Ben as a psychiatrist or Margaret as a social worker will be different. It's probably somewhere between seven and twelve years," replied Nathan.

"That's a lot of patients," Margaret chimed in.

"I'm sure it is. The alternative is to notify all previous patients from day one of Ben's practice since some believe records should be stored in perpetuity. We'll give ourselves permission to take a short-cut and follow the State guidelines," Nathan concluded.

"Next, if it hasn't been done already, Ruth, you need to go through Ben's appointment book for the last week and weeks as far ahead as Ben scheduled and cancel all appointments and make sure each patient has a referral. Maybe, Margaret can help you out with that. Also, I need to locate one of Ben's psychiatrist peers, perhaps someone he used as coverage when he was away on vacation and have this person review with me current cases and make a final entry in the record. Obviously, this is something I can't do coming from a different discipline but I will prepare a brief termination summary based on my review of the record for that psychiatrist to sign. As you can see, there's much to do. We'll get started today and see how much of a dent we can make. I'll be around, I think through Wednesday, and after that let's see where we are. Also, I'll need to go out to Ben's Great Neck office to do pretty much the same thing although I imagine the caseload out there is significantly less."

With Nathan's last set of instructions the three worked well into the afternoon and finally left the office around seven. Knowing that they would be seeing one another in the morning at the funeral service, they exchanged brief greetings good night and went their separate ways.

The next morning Joanne and Nathan dressed in the customary dark colors reserved for funerals and left the hotel en route to Great Neck via a car service limo. Typically, the trip to Great Neck would take approximately forty minutes from the city on a Sunday morning. However, this being the middle of the Labor Day weekend, there would still be some late travelers escaping Manhattan this morning hoping to make their beach dates out on the Island by mid-day. The driver left sufficient time to arrive at the funeral home by the ten o'clock service time.

Ben's service was arranged at Riverside Chapel just off of North Station Plaza in the heart of downtown Great Neck. By ten o'clock, the small sitting room only had family remaining which included Ben's children, Jason, 15, and Kimberly, 17, Ben's brother and sister-in-law and their three children. Just prior to stepping out of the vestibule room, Nathan was able to spend a few minutes with the family and shared in his expression of sympathy and related some personable stories and memories about their friendship, training and work history together. Nathan was particularly concerned about the children but later understood that Ben's brother would be taking care of Jason and Kimberly for the years which remained prior to going off to college.

The parlor room where Rabbi Lefcourt would preside over the

short ceremony sat approximately seventy-five but it would appear only half of the seating would be required as only immediate family and several long-time friends and colleagues were invited to attend. Apparently, after Brittany's death, Ben left specific instructions as to how his own funeral was to be handled. And so, the Rabbi said a few prayers in both English and Hebrew, and then proceeded to say a few words about Ben's family and professional life. Not a word of suicide was expressed other than how Ben's untimely death now offers him the opportunity to once again be with his partner, Brittany.

Following the service, the limousines and cars lined up in the procession which would make its way out on the Island to Farmingdale where Ben would be interred at New Montefiore Cemetery. There, Rabbi Lefcourt continued the graveside service with the traditional Mourners' Prayer and concluded the service with mourners asked to lay some soil onto the casket which would shortly be lowered into the ground. Always moving at the moment, the historical religious gesture symbolizes how the mourners participate in the burial of their own. A dipping bowl rested to the side of the gravesite to not only help those congregated to wash off the dirt, but to more importantly cleanse themselves symbolically from the grief. Before leaving the gravesite, Nathan and Joanne stood over both Ben and Brittany's grave, said a silent prayer and walked away embracing one another.

\*\*\*

The ride from the cemetery to Great Neck seemed to take less time. Those in attendance were welcomed back to the home for a traditional buffet lunch of assorted deli and fish platters. The family would be sitting shiva for just the day as any more probably would have been hypocritical for the family who were less observant practicing Jews. Ben's office which was built as an extension to the house was closed off from the inside today. In attendance was Ben's attorney, Brian Michaels, who approached Nathan as the two met up in the living room.

"Hi. I'm Brian Michaels. I know you will be looking after some of Ben's records. You may want to arrange that through me."

"Okay, that sounds right…we'll talk later," replied Nathan.

Nathan, who was just about finished with his meal, had not planned on having a discussion today about his administrative function as custodian to Ben's patient files.

"Well, thanks for being here. Such a tragic thing," commented the attorney.

"It really is. How long have you known Ben?" asked Nathan.

"Oh, not very long. I met him while his wife was sick. Had handled some matters related to their estate back then. How about you?"

"For some time," replied Nathan.

"That must sting," said the attorney in a rather disinterested way. "I'm going to get some coffee and dessert. Can I get you something?"

"No. No thanks. I'm fine. Brian, do me a favor and leave your number with me and I'll contact you later tonight about scheduling a time to come out to the house and to look over things in the office," Nathan suggested. Mr. Michaels jotted down a number on his business card and handed it to Nathan and then parted in the direction of the dining room.

By mid-afternoon, Joanne and Nathan decided to leave the Solomon home. The somber, respectful day of saying good-bye to Ben was coming to an end. Joanne, who had a flight to catch, planned on being home by evening to kiss her boys good-night.

\*\*\*

Joanne's separation from her children was never very comfortable. Probably a little more difficult for Joanne than most mothers. Having lost her own mother at a very young age left its emotional mark which colored most every relationship in a very special way. Having checked in with the Bishops', Jack, and Erik several times each day since she left, this last call was comforting to Joanne as she knew she would be home in a few hours.

"So, how's everything today?" asked Joanne.

"Really good mom," Erik reported from the cell phone, which Joanne insisted on him having while she was away. "We're out here in the middle of our block party."

"Yeah, I hear… pretty noisy in the background," replied Joanne. "Alright then, I'll be home probably close to eight. Is your brother around?"

Jack who was down the street a bit speaking to someone heard his brother yell out that mom was on the phone. Running quickly to get to the phone, Jack was somewhat out of breath by the time he said hello. "Hi mom. You'll be home tonight?" asked Jack.

"Yes, I will be," replied Joanne. "So what are you up to?"

"Just stuff. Skate boarding and shooting baskets. We'll be eating soon. I'll save you a hamburger. Bye mom."

"Bye honey, see you soon."

"Kids doing okay?" Nathan asked.

"Sounds like it. Donna's kept them busy. It will be nice to be back home with them tonight," Joanne replied.

*** 

Joanne's return flight was scheduled to depart at five. On the way back to the city, their driver was going to swing by Kennedy and then proceed into Manhattan to return Nathan to his hotel. As they approached the airport terminal, Nathan made sure that Joanne had all the telephone numbers where he could be reached over the next few days. With tighter airport security it was impossible to escort passengers beyond a certain point in the terminal and so the driver was asked to pull up in front of Delta departures, where Joanne would say her good-byes.

"Okay, Joanne. Have a good flight. I'll most likely be back by Wednesday night the latest. We'll talk later."

"Nate, take good care of yourself and try to get through Ben's office stuff quickly. I need you back home. I'll miss you."

With a quick kiss on the lips, Joanne left the car, gathered up her overnight bag and disappeared into the terminal amongst the other travelers. By now the car was being directed to exit the drop-off lane by a New York City police officer who was trying to keep cars stationary for only a minute or two. The trip into the city took only twenty minutes this time as the driver was eager to complete his day and apparently Sunday afternoon traffic was cooperating.

***

Joanne's uneventful flight had her arriving ahead of schedule. The captain mentioned something about a tail wind which Joanne was grateful for. As the cab dropped her off in front of the house, she saw Erik and Jack playing outside by the Bishops' driveway. When they finally saw the cab, the two ran over to greet their mother. In unison, both eagerly welcomed Joanne home with hugs and kisses.

"I missed you guys. How's everything?" asked Joanne.

"We're good," said Erik who appointed himself as the spokesperson for he and his brother.

"So….how was everything?"

Jack who replied first focused mainly on the ball games. "You and Dad missed some great games Friday and Saturday. Can you go to tomorrow's game Mom?" asked Jack.

"You know I think we'll all go. We'll have an extra ticket, so think about inviting one of your friends."

"Everything okay Erik?" asked Joanne.

"Yeah, Mom. When's Dad coming back?" inquired Erik.

"Wednesday, for sure. Let's give him a call…so he knows I'm back," suggested Joanne who picked up on Erik's need for connection with his father.

"Let's go inside, let me settle in and we'll reach your Dad."

As the three walked into the home, Joanne collected the mail for the last two days and got comfortable. Joanne poured a glass of wine and from the kitchen phone she dialed his cell phone number and Nathan picked up on the third ring.

"Hi, Nate. Just got in," said Joanne.

"How was the flight back?"

"Weird flying alone without you, but otherwise alright. Hold on for a second, Erik wants to say hi."

"Hi Dad. What are you doing?"

"Oh, just hanging out in the hotel tonight, had some dinner, going to watch some T.V."

"What about you?"

"Yeah, I'm hanging out too," replied Erik.

"How was the weekend?"

"It was good."

"Must be nice to have Mom back tonight?"

"It is. When will you be home? I know it has been just a night or two but it seems like a lot longer."

"Erik, I'm planning to be home late Wednesday. It will be Wednesday before you know it. Hey, is your brother around?"

"Let me see, hold on." A few seconds later Erik returned to the phone and continued.

"He's in the shower. Do you want him to call back?" asked Erik.

"Sure he can if he wants to. Otherwise, let him know I'll speak to him tomorrow."

"Okay Dad. Do you want to speak to Mom?"

"Sure put her back on. Take care."

"Hi. I'm back. So how's everything in our hotel room?" asked Joanne.

"Pretty empty without you. What are you up to?"

"You know. I think I'll catch up on some laundry and then go to bed early."

"Sounds exciting as my night. I'll let you go. Speak to you tomorrow."

"Okay Nate. Have a good night."

\*\*\*

As the kids were settling in for the night, Joanne was getting serious with some laundry accumulating from the boys over the weekend and some of her clothes from the trip. By now she was used to going through her children's pockets for the various and sundry stuff that only boys would come to collect. Countless loads of wash had been ruined over the years due to laziness and indifference.

"Jack, get over here," shouted Joanne from the laundry area. "Where did this come from?" referring to a folded up small envelope containing a sympathy card in which the envelope had typed Dr. Nathan and Joanne Stern.

"Oh that. I don't know…some guy came up to me during the block party and handed it to me saying it was for your parents when they got back from New York," explained Jack.

"Was it one of our neighbors?" asked Joanne.

"No Mom. I said it was some guy."

"What did he look like?"

"I don't know. Why?"

"Can you remember anything about him?" a more anxious Joanne asked.

"He was wearing a baseball cap, shorts and one of those cut-off shirts. Looked like he was part of the block party…just hanging out."

"How long did he talk with you?"

"Maybe a few seconds and then he walked off somewhere."

"Did he say anything else or talk to anyone else?"

"No. I don't think so. Why all the questions?" Jack inquired.

"Oh. It has something to do with our office, honey. That's why I'm asking all these questions."

The envelope, which by now was opened by Joanne, held a simple, plain sympathy card on which was typewritten *Sorry for your loss*. As Joanne was looking over the card, she dialed Nathan's cell number again. This time Joanne's voice alerted Nathan that something was not quite right.

"I didn't expect to hear from you again tonight. You don't sound so well. What's up?"

"Nate, we got a problem down here. Some guy during the block party approached Jack and gave him a sympathy card to give to us and its addressed like all those letters. I need you to get back down here."

"Calm down for a second. It's going to be awhile before I can get back home. Do you want to call the police? Contact Detective Granger?"

"Tomorrow. Right now I just want you home," replied Joanne.

"I wish I could be there right now. We'll talk for awhile…close up the house, put the alarm on…. let's get you to feel safe. Everything is going to be alright."

"No. You don't understand. This guy talked to Jack and reached out to him. He was within a few inches of him."

"To give him this card, that's all. It's another message," explained Nathan who was failing in his reassurance by minimizing the situation.

"Well, this one is just too damn close. I'm going to call for Detective Granger and explain what happened. Maybe she can get a car out here over night," indicated Joanne.

"I'll call too from here, Joanne. Calm down, take a few breaths. Let me put a call in to Detective Granger first and I will call you right back. Okay. I'll call right back," Nathan said.

***

Nathan, feeling somewhat at a loss due to the distance which separated he and his family, placed a call to Detective Granger's cell phone which transferred to voice mail. Nathan left a brief, precise description of what transpired.

"Detective Granger. Hi. This is Nathan Stern. There's been a new development. I'm out of town through Wednesday. My wife, Joanne, is home tonight with the children and she's very upset after one of our boys was given a sympathy card this afternoon by a male stranger during our block party. The envelope was addressed just like the letters we have received. When you receive this call please contact my wife Joanne on her cell and you can reach me either on my cell phone or at the Hilton room 945."

A few minutes later, Joanne's phone rang with Detective Granger returning the call.

"Hello, Dr. Stern. This is Det. Granger," the voice said. "Your husband just tried to reach me. Is he in New York today?"

"Yes. We were up there for a funeral. I just got back tonight," shared Joanne.

"He mentioned something about a sympathy card?" inquired the Det. Granger.

"That's right. Some guy walked up to my son Jack and told him to give it to his parents," explained Joanne.

"Is he alright?" asked Granger.

"Yeah. He's fine but I'm a mess. Can you please send a car out tonight?" Joanne pleaded.

"It's done already. There should be a patrol car by your corner in a few minutes."

"Thank you," Joanne acknowledged with appreciation.

"Dr. Stern...I'm driving back from across the state tonight. I won't be back until much later. I would like to meet with you sometime tomorrow. When is a good time?"

"How about morning, around ten?" suggested Joanne.

"I'll see you then. Do you see the police car yet?" asked Det. Granger.

As Joanne walked to the front of the house, she leaned over the sofa and peered through the front window. "Yes. I see it. Thank you so much," a grateful Joanne replied.

"Okay. Dr. Stern. Feeling better?"

"I am."

"You'll be fine now. Try to get a good night sleep and we'll talk tomorrow."

"Okay, Detective Granger. See you tomorrow."

A moment later after Joanne said good bye to Detective Granger, the phone rang again.

"Joanne, hi it's me. How are you doing?" asked Nathan.

"Calmer now. I just got off the phone with Detective Granger. She arranged a patrol car which is out in front for now. We're going to meet tomorrow. I'm going to have Jack talk with her."

"That sounds good. Did she say anything about it?" inquired Nathan.

"No. Not really. Just wanted to make sure we were okay," replied Joanne.

"That person...knew about this...Ben's death. I wonder how?" queried Nathan.

"I don't know. But whoever it is knows things about us. Somehow knew about Ben, knew we were away attending a funeral, and knew to approach one of our kids. Nathan, I'm really scared. Try to get back here sooner than Wednesday. Please try."

"I'll do what I can here tomorrow. I'm going out to Ben's home office and then I think I'll push up my flight to Tuesday morning. How does that sound?"

"Not as good as having you back tonight. But I know that's not possible," stated Joanne.

"Are you okay?" Nathan asked again.

"I'll be alright. You know I'm going to speak to Erik and Jack tonight about all of this. I think they need to know some of what's going on, so that I can talk to them about being alert and safe."

"That's a good idea. Did Jack say anything about this?"

"No. You know. He was pretty nonchalant about the whole thing," replied Joanne.

"When you speak with the kids, just be careful to use the right amount of concern. Take a few more minutes for yourself before you speak with the boys," Nathan suggested.

"Don't worry. I'm not going to blow this out of proportion. I just want them to know what's been going on and to use the appropriate level of caution."

"That sounds right Joanne. I'll let you go. Call me again if you need me."

With their last exchange, Joanne and Nathan hesitantly said good night.

\*\*\*

The discussion with Erik and Jack moved along very smoothly with Joanne covering some of the history of the letters and the concerns related to the privacy and security of the Stern family. Joanne spoke about the police investigation and the likelihood that Detective Granger will want to speak with both Erik and Jack tomorrow and perhaps get a better description from Jack of the man who gave him the card.

After their discussion, Joanne poured another glass from her favorite stock of a German Riesling which eased her into a more relaxed, inebriated mood. Not accustomed to bringing drinks back to the bedroom, Joanne placed both the bottle and wine glass down on the edge of the Roman tub, undressed and stepped into the bath. The warm, honey beaded water along with the pulsating jets placed Joanne in the zone she was aiming for. Thirty minutes later, Joanne was sufficiently tendered to and ready for bed.

***

# CHAPTER 8

As the next day began, Nathan imagined he had slept more restfully than Joanne. Nathan, who was heading out to Great Neck via the Long Island Railroad allowed a few more minutes to elapse before calling home. Alone with his thoughts, Nathan was trying to piece together the recent events in the context of the several month history of receiving the letters. It was about a year now since having received the first of many letters. And, it had been a few months since receiving the last letter. Now, after all this time, this person was determined to be bolder in his strategy to make his presence known. The opportunity to impress upon Nathan and Joanne knowledge of time sensitive information about their life was quite alarming. Nathan's furrowed brow and distant expression accurately captured the realistic concern he had for his situation. The ringing of the phone served as a distraction which re-focused Nathan. On the other end was Joanne.

"Hi. Good morning. I was just about to call. How are you doing?" asked Nathan.

"Not so well. Got a few hours of sleep. But in between kept on thinking about this guy and Jack. It's creeping me out," Joanne replied.

"I know Joanne, me too. Let's hope Detective Granger can do more this time with our case. You think Jack can give a better description?"

"I don't know. He only got a brief look at this guy. We'll see what more he can tell Det. Granger."

"I'm taking an 8:15 train to Great Neck to take care of some things at Ben's office. I'll call you from there around noon. If something comes up....call me on my cell number."

"Okay. That sounds good. We'll speak later," replied Joanne.

*** 

Nathan's train arrived at the Great Neck station a few minutes before 9:00 A.M. where he was met by Ben's attorney, Brian Michaels. Nathan, who was not so impressed with their first exchange at the funeral, decided to hold off on any further judgments until after this second meeting. Mr. Michaels insisted rather strongly that he accompany Nathan to the home office. Nathan was unclear as to the reasons for this escort and Mr. Michaels did very little to clarify his role.

"How was your ride out of the city?" inquired the attorney.

"Probably a lot different than the commuters riding in," replied Nathan.

"You have commuted from the Island to the city and back before, haven't you?" asked Mr. Michaels.

"Oh, just a few times, I guess," quipped Nathan.

"Do you mind...I thought we would get something to eat and then I have some errands to run around town before we go to the house," suggested Mr. Michaels.

Nathan, who found the request imposing, paused for a moment and then unequivocally expressed to Mr. Michaels the need to go straight to Ben's home. "You know Brian, I'm on a very tight schedule. I have to push everything up and get home sometime later today. Take me to the house first and then if you need to run some errands you can do that on your own."

"Okay. Doc. I got it. Just business."

Within a few minutes, Brian's car pulled up to Ben's home and parked alongside the swale. The two walked up the slate walkway and approached the front door.

"I'll let you in and show you to Ben's office where you can work for a few hours. When you're done, you can call me on my cell and I'll come back and pick you up. The kids are with their Uncle so you should have the house to yourself," Brian abruptly commented.

"That will be fine," replied Nathan.

As the two walked into the foyer, the emptiness of the house felt powerful to Nathan. Brian on the other hand, only felt the emptiness of his stomach. "I wonder if there's any leftovers from yesterday. I'm going to check in the kitchen."

Nathan's picture of Brian Michaels was now pretty complete but he knew he had to tolerate him for just a few more hours. "Brian, I'm going to get to work. I remember where the office is. So we'll meet up later," suggested Nathan. Nathan made his way to Ben's office admiring some of the smartly framed photographs of family pictures. Amongst the many on the wall leading up to the office, were snapshots over time of Ben and Brittany's life together. Nathan eventually located one of he and Joanne and Ben and Brittany some years back walking down the cobblestone streets of Martha's Vineyard.

Upon entering the office, Nathan's eyes quickly focused to the chair where Ben's body was found. When the Crime Scene Investigative team completed their inquiry into Ben's death, apparently there was not sufficient time to adequately clean up the area. Residual blood stained areas were still quite visible on the desk, chair, carpet and walls. Nathan could not help but react with a gagging reflex which had him searching for the nearest waste paper basket in the office. He quickly found one and vomited up his very light breakfast. Adjoining Ben's office was a bathroom which Nathan stepped into to wash and refresh himself.

As Nathan reentered the office, he made a path to Ben's desk and sat just looking around the office. Several file cabinets were off to the right of the desk and Ben's computer station was off to the left. Mr. Michaels, in one of his more helpful moments mentioned that the key to the file cabinets would be tucked away in the lower left hand corner of the desk blotter. Scattered on top of the desk were some professional journals, reports and correspondences, an appointment book, and some personal papers and bills. Although appearing disorganized to Nathan, he knew Ben well enough to know that there was some order to the arrangement. Ben's practice out of the home was very limited and only one drawer of the file cabinets were identified for active patients. A second drawer was identified for inactive patients. All in all, Nathan totaled up thirty-two cases which required his attention; fourteen of which were current patients requiring some follow-up. Nathan was relieved to know that his work here would be completed within a couple of hours. The same set of instructions given to Ruth Lowell the other day would be followed for these cases as well. Nathan made a list of the patients to be contacted for follow up and referral and boxed up the records in one storage carton to be brought back to the city and left with both Ruth and Margaret. Nathan tossed in the appointment book as an afterthought and sealed and labeled the box.

Nathan's work in his friend's office was now drawing to a close. As he was finishing up he locked the cabinets even though they were now emptied and returned the key to the same place on the desk. Tucked under the other side of the blotter, folded over in thirds, a letter clipped to an envelope entered Nathan's line of vision. It was first the lettering which caught his eye. As he reached for the letter and slipped it out from the grasp of the blotter, Nathan began to identify a strangely familiar writing style. Removing the clip from the letter revealed an envelope which was addressed to Dr. and Mrs. Benjamin Solomon. Feverishly unfolding the letter, Nathan looked on with disbelief and then a sunken, hollow feeling struck him somewhere in the pit of his stomach. Reflexively, he purged for the second time this morning. Nathan began to read the letter which he held before him:

### Before the storm hits

I need to see some signal to let me know that you are still here to take care of me

All these emotions are crossing over the circuits sending confusing messages,

I'm bleeding out... you're hurting me with your countless rejections...I don't want to hurt back and end your time

Shot an apple off my hand...ripe and rotten at the same time
Make it stop and go away

The heaviness of my feelings will suck me down to the other dark side, till my shadow is no longer seen to the naked eye

I'm getting into you cause you got to me and I need

you to survive...Don't die.

Just keep tearing at me, hurt me more...destroy
Me...should I fight back.

The storm will come...

the life will be gone and I will be forgotten

Nathan took a minute or two to collect his thoughts and catch his breath which was only now showing some signs of regulating. *This was impossible. How could this be?* Nathan pondered softly to himself. His thoughts raced to some possible explanations which all converged on the notion of a relationship, a likely triangulation between Ben, the letter writer, and himself. Nathan safely assumed, that if this was the case, then there must be a commonality across patient care which existed some time ago. As Nathan continued his aggressive inquiry, he realized the subgroup of patients would therefore date back to their period of training or during the brief time he shared an office with Ben. *Was there a connection here which resulted in Ben's suicide or were the police mistaken in that Ben's death was not an act of suicide but made to appear like a suicide? If all of this is related and Ben's death was not by his own hands, then there is a clear danger posed to us as well.* Before Nathan heard a knock on the door he concluded, *and that guy who hand delivered the card to Jack is quite possibly a very dangerous character.*

***

The door to Ben's office opened with an irritated Brian Michaels peering in from the threshold. "Dr. Stern...you get carried away or something. It's sometime after you said you would call. I got to get going and you said something about a plane." Nathan looked down to his watch and saw that the time really got away from him. "Oh my gosh. It's a few minutes after noon," Nathan noted.

"Are you okay. Doc. You look out of sorts, discombobulated I guess," observed Michaels.

"Brian, how long have you been Ben's attorney?" asked Nathan.

"Not very long. Maybe a few months before his wife died, so maybe a year or so. I was called in for estate planning and related issues. Why?" inquired Michaels.

"Oh. I was just wondering…no he probably wouldn't have… it's probably something Ben would have kept to himself."

"No, what is it? You would be surprised what people tell their estate planners."

"No it's really unrelated to the estate and your role with him. More related to his work," shared Nathan.

"Did he ever talk to you about work?" asked Nathan.

"No, he never did. He was pretty private about that. I'm sure just like yourself," Michaels commented.

"Did he seem worried about anything or preoccupied with anything?" asked Nathan.

"No not that I could tell, but you know I'm not the most observant kind of guy."

"When did you see him last?" the next question was fired from Nathan.

"Gee, I can't really recall. It was a while back. At least some months," replied Michaels. Michaels paused for a moment and then asked firmly, "You want to tell me what's going on with all these questions?"

"I really can't say. I don't know myself. I have to do a little more research about something," replied Nathan very hesitantly and cautiously. Nathan knew Brian Michaels had little to offer and his interest would be strictly self-serving. Nathan however, underestimated what Michaels' response would be to his dismissive demeanor.

"You know what Doc. I got the message. Why don't you close up the house. Keep the key. I got a copy. I'm out of here. You can cab back to the city, the airport or any fucking place you want to go to. I'm done with you," a disgruntled Michaels stated angrily. Nathan was taken aback by the coarse language but realized in part he created Michaels' level of frustration with his own evasiveness and aloofness. The door slammed behind him and Nathan was again left in the home alone.

Nathan needed to make a few more calls as well as search one more time in Ben's office for anything that resembled a file or folder of additional letters. Like himself, Ben was a hoarder and if there were other letters, which Nathan was certain of, then his friend would have them tucked away for safe keeping. But where?

Another thorough check of the office came up empty handed. His flight was scheduled to depart in three hours which really didn't give Nathan much time. Nathan's first call went to a local cab company in Great Neck which would be at the house in ten minutes. His second call was placed to Margaret who mentioned she would be available most of Monday if Nathan needed her. Nathan left a brief message on her answering machine, leaving his cell number. He was curious if Margaret knew anything about this. The third call went through to Joanne who was wrapping up with Detective Granger.

\*\*\*

"Nate, hold on… back up, I didn't get all that," voiced Joanne with concern. "Start over, the call was breaking up a bit. What's all connected? What did you find in Ben's office?"

As Nathan described his discovery to Joanne, he was just barely cognizant of the pressure to his speech and the rapidity of his thoughts. Attempts to calm himself down seemed to only work momentarily before another round of accelerated energy took on a life of its own.

"Nate, honey, take a few deep breaths, try to regulate your breathing," Joanne suggested calmly. "I'm right here with Detective Granger. I'm going to put her on speaker phone with us."

"Hello Dr. Stern, Bev Granger here. What's going on up there?"

Over the next few minutes, Nathan more calmly shared with both Joanne and Detective Granger his hypothesis and his troubled concern that Ben's death was in some way related to all this.

"Nathan, did you speak with the police up there?" asked Det. Granger.

"No. Haven't had a chance and the way it looks, I'm leaving for the airport in a few minutes and won't have an opportunity," replied Nathan.

"Okay then. I'll pursue it from this end today. Also, I'll need to see the letter," commented Det. Granger.

By now, most if not all of Nathan's emotional grounding took hold. And with it, came renewed reasoning and analytic ability which was no longer usurped by his emotions. Joanne and Det. Granger could hear in Nathan's voice a sense of control and resolve.

"If I'm right about this, there is a common denominator between myself, Ben and some former patient with an ax to grind. And if I'm right about Ben's death, one way or another this person is responsible. Detective Granger, I want to make sure you take all the necessary steps to keep us safe. Did anything come out of this morning's meeting with my wife and son?"

"Well, we got a better description. Your son Jack is going to work with an artist to draw up a composite and I'm going to talk to some of your neighbors to see if they remember this guy yesterday. And, I'll run the card for fingerprints. Dr. Stern, trust me, we'll get to the bottom of this. You and your family will be safe," Det. Granger voiced reassuringly.

Maybe Detective Granger's words would have carried more weight if Nathan received them in a different environment. But somehow, sitting in Ben's office in the aftermath of his death and with a new and alarming development, Nathan's sense of security and safety for his family was unlikely to be buttressed by Det. Granger's perfunctory statements of reassurance.

"Oh, here's my cab. We'll cut this short for now. Joanne. I'm heading to the airport and I should be home in the early evening. Detective Granger, we'll talk tomorrow. Thanks for your help today." With that comment, Nathan packed up the box of records, closed up the house and walked quickly to the cab. On his way to the airport, he placed another call to Margaret. This time Margaret picked up on the third ring. In the manner that she answered, Margaret was obviously waiting on a call from a friend and was surprised to hear Nathan's voice on the other end.

"I just stepped out of the shower. You want to come up or wait a few minutes and I'll be right down, don't leave without me," Nathan heard Margaret blurt out.

"Hello Margaret. No, this is Nathan Stern, I'm sorry, you were obviously expecting someone else. Sorry for the inconvenience. Do you have a moment?"

"Not really. But what's up?" replied Margaret.

"There's something you and Ruth will need to do for me over the next few days. But first, did Ben ever mention to you being harassed by a former patient?"

"No. He never mentioned anything like that," commented Margaret.

"Why?" asked Margaret.

"It's a long story…. and I'm not certain, but I think Ben and I were being targeted by the same person for some reason and it has to be a former patient. I can't see it happening any other way. So, what I need are old case records which date back to Ben's first years of practice, especially the years in which Ben and I shared an office together," Nathan explained.

"Wow, that's a tall order. What makes you think he kept those records?" inquired Margaret.

"You know what. Ben was a hoarder, a pack-rat, and I bet he kept every chart for every patient he ever treated. Check and double check. They must be archived somewhere. Ruth may know," suggested Nathan.

"So what years would we be looking for?" an intrigued Margaret asked.

"Let me think for a moment or two," Nathan replied. "I would think you want to go back to the mid- 1980's and pull all charts from say 1984 through 1986…no through 1988 to be safe. Also, and I don't think it would be possible, but if Ben retained any records, notes, evaluations, reports, and the like during his year of residency at Metro, I want those too. After everything is all boxed up, I want the records sent to my office. List me as the agent or representative to secure the data. While I'm entrusted to do so, I never thought I would actually take physical custody of the records."

"That's a lot of charts," Margaret stated.

"I know it is. But I want everything. I'll go through them when I get them. I'm not sure what I will be looking for yet, but I guess I'll know when I find it," replied Nathan.

"Okay, Dr. Stern. Is there anything else we should do?" asked Margaret.

"Margaret, not right now. That's going to keep you busy for a while. Thank you for all your help. I'll be in touch in a few days to see how you are doing with all this."

As Nathan looked around, he noticed he was still probably a good forty minutes away from the airport. He leaned back, closed his eyes, and made every effort to relax for the duration of the ride. That in itself was a challenging undertaking for Nathan right at this time.

*** 

By 3 P.M., Nathan was boarding his flight back home with Ben's records tucked away in three sections of his carry-on luggage. Not the ideal way to travel with confidential files, but Nathan knew there was really no other way to safeguard the material. His original plan to drop them off with Ruth and Margaret in the city was no longer possible due to time constraints. The luggage, which was routinely checked at the security point, barely raised any suspicion and when Nathan was asked about the files, he commented about research and reading material for the trip home. Nathan did indeed reflect briefly as to how many ethical principles he may have just violated.

An hour or so into the flight, as the plane was passing over Washington, Nathan became somewhat more disinterested with an in-flight neighbor's personal struggles with his family. Nathan had made the mistake of informing Barry, who was sitting one seat over, of his line of work. Typically, this is a bonus for a passenger who may think nothing of encroaching on a psychologist for some free advice. After a few more comments of interest and some traditionally comforting words, Nathan excused himself, stepped up to reach for the overhead compartment and took down some of Ben's files to leaf through hoping that Barry would take the hint and find some other activity to occupy his time for the duration of the flight.

As Nathan briefly scanned over the files, he was reminded of how thorough Ben was in treating his patients and how well organized each chart was. Each chart had a comprehensive evaluation including developmental, family, medical, psychological, social, psychiatric, occupational, and educational history. He also reserved a section to conceptualize his findings of a patient along psychoanalytic nomenclature. This type of formulation, Nathan knew, became less and less acceptable as a standard of psychiatric care as the years progressed. Psychiatrists by and large were devoting most of their time to prescribing with little interest or time in examining the patients' psychological makeup. Ben took the extra time and therefore became known in the field as a psychologists' psychiatrist for his willingness to work collaboratively with a therapist for the benefit of the patient. Nathan also saw to what length Ben would document his rationale of choosing one type of medication over another. The chart also provided a running record of medication trials and responses as well as how the regimens were titrated. It was clear that at least with this group of patients, Ben utilized medication conservatively and had backed off from an earlier, more aggressive stance in the use of agents to control for certain conditions. Each evaluation stressed the significance of combining medication trials with psychotherapy and a few recommended only psychotherapy as the treatment of choice.

Nathan spent the remaining time of the flight glancing over charts and Ben's appointment book. He looked through the schedule of appointments up through the day of Ben's suicide and compared the schedule to the entries in the record. Most everything was accounted for including brief progress notes from Ben's last two scheduled visits on the day of his death.

As the plane began to make its descent, the overhead light to fasten seat belts signaled passengers to prepare for landing. Nathan found himself hovering over his seat as he was trying to return the charts to his baggage. The flight attendant gently encouraged Nathan to take his seat as she offered some assistance in closing the overhead compartment. It was getting close to 5:30 P.M. Nathan was looking forward to being home once again.

\*\*\*

Nathan arrived home drained both physically and emotionally. It was not until Nathan passed through the front door to an unusually quiet home that he recalled Joanne's plan to get things back on track for the family. Joanne and the kids were taking in a late afternoon game at the stadium. Joanne had mentioned earlier in the day about keeping her promise to Erik and Jack. Nathan collapsed on the sofa, opened his second Heineken, and tuned in to the game to get a score. Nathan was pretty certain that Joanne was heading home as the game was in the eighth inning with our team up by five. She more than likely would take a persuasive tone with the kids in an effort to beat most of the traffic exiting the stadium. Joanne was good for a few innings of baseball taken in small doses. The only protest would come from Jack who more than likely would insist on waiting till the field is covered with the tarp and the lights turned down. To put it to the test, Nathan called Joanne to learn that she was already en route home, probably half an hour away.

"Hi. I'm home. Forgot for a moment about the game. How's everyone?" asked Nathan.

"We're good. The boys really needed this time out. We'll be home soon. Sorry we weren't home when you got there. How are you doing?" Joanne asked.

"Pretty tired from everything. A lot of things racing through my head," said Nathan.

"I can imagine. We'll talk when I get home. See you in a few minutes."

"Okay. Drive safely. See you in a few."

\*\*\*

Nathan was in a twilight sleep when he faintly heard the alarm chime from the back door go off. By the time he was more alert, Nathan first saw Jack and then Erik swing around the kitchen wall followed by Joanne.

"Nate, we're home," announced Joanne.

"Hi guys. Nice to see you. How was the game?" asked Nathan.

"We won 6-1. Outplayed them in every way," Jack was quick to point out.

"Yeah, Dad. You missed a good game," Erik commented.

"Yeah Dad, a really great game," Joanne playfully yet sarcastically added as she went over toward Nathan to give him a hug and kiss.

"I know guys. But you know with everything that's come up, I actually cut my trip short to be home today for everyone," replied Nathan.

"That's good. You know it's not like every day we have a detective in our house talking to us," shared Jack.

"So Dad, which one of your patients is coming after you?" Erik asked.

"Oh Erik...I don't know if it's like that. We're not really sure, but mom and I and the detective will figure this out. It's a little like a puzzle and all we have to do is put the pieces correctly together. That's all. In the meantime, we'll be a little more careful and watchful for things around us," replied a reassuringly confident Nathan.

"Okay guys. Let Dad and I have some time together. You both have to get ready for school tomorrow. Back to our normal crazy schedule," voiced Joanne. On that cue, both Erik and Jack gathered up their stuff and headed back to their bedrooms.

"See you guys later," Nathan said.

"A little puzzle...put the pieces together...you sound pretty confident or was that for the kids' benefit?" asked Joanne

"Mostly all show for the kids. I don't wish to unnecessarily alarm them further until we think this through some more. Best to keep an attitude of calm and reassurance and let Erik and Jack see that we are taking some active steps to solve this."

"And what about me? How alarmed should I be?" asked Joanne.

"Well, for us, right now with so little answered… and you know I can't speak for you… but I'm feeling extremely concerned. It looks like we are facing some danger and not knowing why or from whom is the very alarming thing about this."

For the next hour or so, Nathan and Joanne sat and reviewed together almost all of the new information to surface over the last week. They had some very similar views as to how to proceed and agreed upon a plan of action. The plan, at least in theory, would bind most of their anxious and vulnerable feelings, permitting both to move ahead with a somewhat normal schedule. The two fell asleep side by side, nestled together on the couch, until a sharp spasm in Nathan's calf rudely awakened him first. By then, Joanne too woke up with sleepy eyes to see that it was already a few minutes past midnight. They closed up the house, put the alarm on, checked on the kids, and got ready for bed. The new day was quickly advancing upon Nathan and Joanne.

***

# CHAPTER 9

The recent week of events now can be seen clearly to have weathered Nathan's unusually well put together appearance and dress. His cleanly shaven more youthful and tanned face has now given way to a long, drawn, ruddy-like complexion with two day old stubble, redden- swollen eyes with darkened rings, and attire resembling someone who just as easily might have slept in his clothes. Nathan, who typically would be able to separate his personal from his professional life, now found it increasingly difficult to hide behind the fortress of defenses that he had erected over the years.

As he walked through the double doors of the graduate psychology building, the handful of administrative staffers and students did not seem to take notice of anything out of sorts. Several casual and informal greetings on the way to the elevator ended in a solo trip up to the third floor where Nathan rather briskly walked to his office. The box he was carrying could have easily been construed as another series of move-in storage boxes containing various office mementos, as Nathan did not yet have a good opportunity to settle into his new office suite. The reinforced storage box with the label Iron Clad however also contained the thirty or so files of Ben's patients which now rested to the left of Nathan on his wrap- around walnut veneered desk. Although the box proved to be a distraction for Nathan, several roundtable meetings with faculty and staff were already placed as a priority on his agenda for the morning.

"Good morning Nate," as his somber and soft toned friend greeted Nathan. Dean Zwick continued, "it looks like you had a very rough couple of days," commented Gerald. "I haven't been in touch with Ben for some time, but you guys I think were closer," added Gerald.

"Morning, Gerry," replied Nathan. "It's been tough for both myself and Joanne, having been through his wife's death and now his. On top of everything else, I must have gotten some bug up there which has knocked me out," commented Nathan, in an attempt to camouflage the real explanation.

"Well Nate, our first discussion group centers around a possible curriculum change as a small group of newly appointed faculty within the past two years are aggressively lobbying for a more strict allegiance to the cognitive behavioral model emphasizing evidenced based treatment protocols," noted Gerald. "And our second meeting", continued Gerald, "addresses student enrollment and retention as well as reduction in size of our internship and residency programs."

\*\*\*

It was clear from the outset that the Dean had recruited Nathan in great part due to his strong leaning toward more traditional psychodynamic psychotherapy and a particular disgust for the rapidly developing agenda for evidenced based or manualized therapies. Gerald knew that Nathan, by training and professional practice, was classified by his peers as a pure psychotherapist informed by the volumes of literature steeped in psychoanalytic and psychodynamic thought , and would be up for the fight against any progressive movement which incorporates EBT's.

While Nathan and Gerald shared similar theoretical models, during the early part of their training and professional lives both often found themselves in vigorous debate over the use of psychological testing to better understand the human condition. Both were somewhat inflexible in their positions which attempted to best one modality over the other.

"Do you remember the battles and endless discussions Nate, as you argued that ten hours of psychotherapy can trump the same time allotment for testing in learning and knowing your patient," stated Gerald.

"I do remember how pig headed you were in sticking to that point," Nathan jabbed back. "All you wanted to do was specialize in psychometrics and assessment as applied to the forensic arena," noted Nathan.

"And all you wanted was to see your therapy patients," replied Gerald.

"We did make a great team however, which I think in the end was mutually beneficial for both of us and in some way I think enriched our practices, don't you think Gerry," commented Nathan.

"We got to work on some pretty interesting cases over the post-doc years, you, me and Ben," noted Gerald. "Let's not forget how forceful Ben was in his pharmaceutical approach at that point," continued Gerald.

"Ben really found the pharmacology to be quite compelling in his treatment approach to a wide range of psychiatric conditions. He was one of those psychiatrists initially trained in both the medical model utilizing medication management as well as the art of psychiatric interviewing and psychotherapy," noted Nathan.

"Psychiatrists, very much like Ben, however, sadly caved to Big-Pharma and found themselves becoming primary prescribers and pill pushers. Ben got caught up in that firestorm during his training years to only revert back to a more pragmatic approach in treating patients with one hand on the pen and the other orchestrating a psychotherapy intervention," added Nathan.

Nathan's first discussion group consisted of seven faculty members comprised of three professors, fully tenured with traditional psychoanalytic principles in place, one associate professor who espoused an integrated psychotherapy model, and three cognitive-behavioral psychologists, all at the assistant professor level. The Dean and Nathan completed the roundtable of nine. The debate that ensued placed the more progressive CBT faculty, Drs. Stevenson, Newberry and Thomas, against the more established and entrenched senior staff, Drs. Tisdale, Isaacs, and Josephson.

"The tenets and values of this training program," Nathan began hesitantly, "certainly has been challenged over time to succumb to the ever changing pressures from our accreditors and national organization to replace our time honored philosophy of therapeutic principles with treatment interventions consisting of short term, briefer, and increasingly superficial models of addressing the human condition. What seems to ostensibly work just fine in a controlled, research setting, hardly ever follows through with application to the realities of treatment. I for one did not assume this position to begin to deconstruct our curriculum and training program."

"However," Nathan continued, "at the same time I do recognize the need to develop and stay current with various treatment modalities to make certain that our students are at least exposed to the more contemporary interventions and remain license eligible and marketable in the very near future."

"So, what are you recommending, Dr. Stern," announced Dr. Newberry, who was nominated by Drs. Stevenson and Thomas to take the lead. Dr. Newberry, Liz, to many of her peers and friends, appeared somewhat perplexed in Nathan's two somewhat opposing viewpoints. "If you are suggesting an expansive curriculum to now include required course work in cognitive behavioral psychology and research in the development of evidenced-based interventions, then that sounds appropriate," Newberry voiced. "However, if we only get apportioned a class here and there on an elective basis, to meet the standard of your "exposed to" statement, then this approach would be wholly unacceptable," concluded Liz.

"Well what else do you think Dr. Stern was recommending," commented Dr. Tisdale. "Any other solution would be quite unsatisfactory," added Tisdale

"I think Dr. Newberry," Nathan began to affirm, "that my solution is the only compromise that will be placed on the table at this meeting. Please appreciate that I am recognizing the need to explore the introduction of some limited course work of the cognitive nature into our current curriculum, but indeed our students would be afforded the opportunity to take these classes only on an elective basis. We will revisit the issue in about a year to determine the need and interest level of our faculty and our students," concluded Nathan. With that statement, Dean Zwick adjourned the meeting.

As the next meeting was to start in twenty minutes, Nathan found some welcomed time to try to reach Joanne but had only reached her voicemail. Nathan left a very brief message, "sorry I missed you, hope your day is starting out okay, we'll talk later." Nathan's next call was placed to Myra at the office to check messages and to see how his schedule looked for the afternoon. Myra noted Nathan's standing appointments between 3 P.M and 6 P.M.. "See you later Nathan," commented Myra. "Okay, Myra, see you later too and let Joanne know that I will be home by 7:30."

Nathan's third call was placed to Det. Granger at which time the call went directly to Granger's voicemail. "Hi there Det. Granger, this is Nathan, Dr. Stern. Sorry I missed you but wanted to let you know that I am back in town . We should try to speak later," suggested Nathan.

The second meeting was comprised by a different set of players as the focus centered upon the interim fiscal integrity of the program. Although Nathan was on the standing committee, his role was more peripheral to Dean Zwick's role along with the Chief Financial Officer and the Center Administrator. Nathan's disinterest during the meeting was apparent although he quietly recognized how significant the economics were for the survival of the program.

"I know the faculty has been quite troubled by the size of our program," began the Dean, "but unfortunately we see no alternative but to boost the number of seats in next year's class again to level out our deficit. This combined with a very strong retention rate, should help us in staying afloat in the near term. On the other hand, we find it fiscally imprudent to maintain the current level of funding for all our intern and post –doc positions and recommend a fifty percent reduction in the number of slots by next year."

Nathan's attention was quickly peaked and accompanied by a puzzled, surprised look upon hearing the Dean's last comment. "Gerald, you know as well as I know that the backbone of a training program is the financial and administrative commitment to an internship program and residency program for our post-docs," began Nathan. "A fifty percent reduction in funding and in positions, can render any program as irrelevant. I don't think I would have considered the position if I knew this was in the offering."

"It's one of a few possible recommendations to mull over," commented Gerald, "and I hope we do not need to go there." Gerald directed the conversation to the CFO, James Reston, who along with his team of accounting assistants began a PowerPoint presentation on the past fiscal year and the current fiscal year with the full accompaniment of charts, graphs and tables depicting the programs' revenue streams and offsetting expenses and liabilities. By the end of the presentation, it was clear that the program was indeed running a substantial deficit. Reston's recommendation included projections over the next three years with both maintaining the current level of funding for intern and post doc positions as well as a reduction of up to fifty percent. At this point, even Nathan's untrained mind from an accounting standpoint, was able to see the fragile financial state of the program should the status quo remain in place.

The Center Administrator, Priscilla Hickman, in concluding the meeting noted "this is a very difficult road ahead but we need to act with caution and conservatism to reach a fiscally sound decision."

*\*\**

As Nathan's schedule on campus lightened up after the second meeting his attention now could be more carefully drawn again to some of Ben's clinical records. Nathan wasn't due back to his office until 3 P.M. which gave him a sizeable block of time to continue the process which started on his flight home. Nathan knew that his preliminary review of the records were scanned with tired eyes and an overwhelming feeling of exhaustion. As such, he readily recognized that his somewhat obsessive personality trait would preclude any other behavior which was less than comprehensive and complete. Without a closer scrutiny of the records, Nathan would later ruminate and question that he may have missed something important during his first review.

Ben's appointment book didn't reflect anything out of the ordinary for a psychiatrist's practice. Blocked in were mostly initials of patient's names which appeared to correspond to reoccurring time slots over a several month period. Most patients appeared to be seeing Ben for some time for either medication monitoring or ongoing psychotherapy or both. As Nathan flipped through the appointment book, he was able to locate and pair up the patients' initials to the name on each chart. Of the fourteen active patients, all had visited with Ben within the past few weeks leading up to his death. Six were seen on a monthly basis and appeared to be stable. None of these six, BC- Beryl Cohen, NF- Nilda Fuchs, AV- Arnold Vineland, PW- Patty White, DB- David Bolston, and TE- Tyler Edwards, raised any particular concern or interest in terms of the profile Nathan had reviewed with Simon a few months earlier. Four of Ben's patients were relatively new to his practice, one a recently divorced guy, CS- Charles Stevens, was noted to be fairly depressed over court proceedings and alimony; VT- Vickie Thomas, and EZ- Elizabeth Zeller, were both dealing with chronic medical issues; and LP- Louis Peters was addressing a relapse of alcohol. Two of Ben's longer term, active patients, JQ- Jason Quick, and TM- Toni Morris, according to the chart, were seen over several years for ongoing medication supervision for a diagnosis of schizoaffective disorder, bipolar type and borderline personality disorder, respectively. Both patients appeared to be in and out of private psychiatric facilities on the Island and in the City. Neither patient seemed to respond well to mood stabilizing medication and one was clearly non-compliant to Ben's treatment recommendations. With the exception of the latter two, none of these patients appeared to raise any concern for acting out potential as there was no history of violence to others.

On the morning of Ben's death two clients were scheduled, one at 10 and the other at noon. Nathan initially was only able to refer to the patients' initials inscribed both in the appointment book and on the progress note. One other client appeared to be scheduled on that day at 2 P.M. It was this client, Ann Marie Templeton, who found Ben slumped over his desk and called the police. The earlier appointment, MT, and the later appointment, GA, appeared to be new patients seen for their initial appointment. There did not appear to be any formal records created as Ben would have completed that task later in the day. Ben simply documented MT's presenting complaint as mixed anxiety and depression and GA's presenting problem noted as interpersonal issues/relationship concerns. Clipped to the back of MT's progress note was an envelope with $275. And fastened to GA's progress note was three rather crisp one hundred dollar bills. Both progress notes also had a very fine, almost symmetrical pattern of blood which was splattered on the upper left corner of each page

Nathan methodically searched Ben's appointment book for any entries which may have corresponded to the patient's initials to match to their names. Nathan figured that Ben probably would have noted the date of the first telephone contact , name and referral source as this also was Nathan's practice and would be common practice in the field. Nathan's logical thought process was confirmed as a few weeks earlier MT's and GA's information appeared with some notations scribbled to the side of each client's name with their respective telephone numbers; MT was Michelle Tate, and GA was Giorgio Armis.

Nathan reflected for a few minutes mulling over his next several steps:

*As the police have ruled Ben's death as a suicide, the Great Neck police department gave every indication that the case would be closed... they were not at all interested in Ben's patient load to question nor would that be ethically proper to provide patient names... Ruth Lowell, I asked to contact clients and advise as to the Ben's sudden death and then to make some disposition to the cases... she would be contacting most of Ben's clients... also, both Ruth and Margaret were asked to locate Ben's records during the mid- 80's and forward them to me...Granger would be following up with the Great Neck police, and seems most concerned about our safety...I need to look over Ben's closed charts shortly but it makes the most sense to contact Ben's last several patient hours including contacting his last two patient hours first.*

Upon reaching Michelle Tate and after introducing himself and referring to the nature of the call, Nathan heard in her voice how emotionally shaken she was. Michelle noted that it took her a very long time to commit to seeing a psychiatrist and thought she may have found someone who would understand and help her. Although clearly having no basis for any therapeutic attachment, Michelle was simply attached to the notion of getting assistance. Having lost a child recently as a result of an auto accident involving alcohol, made it all that more difficult when she heard the news about her new doctor's untimely and sudden death. All Nathan could do was provide a limited supportive stance and suggest that someone from the office would be calling with referrals. The call concluded with Nathan hearing Michelle's sobbing in the background.

Nathan's next call was placed to Giorgio Armis. There was however no answer and no voice mail to leave a message. Nathan jotted down Giorgio's name and number, circled, and noted to call later.

One by one Nathan went down the short list of active patients and repeated again and again words that in no way could console some of Ben's patients. When reaching Toni Morris, Nathan however was greeted with several uncomplimentary phrases about her psychiatrist's treatment. "I told Solomon to fuck off and drop dead more times than I care to mention, but he was always there for me when I needed him. Tell me Dr. Stern what am I going to do now," stated Toni in a pathetic, clinging tone. Nathan could not respond soon enough and heard Toni comment "That's what I thought, fuck you too," as Toni concluded the conversation abruptly. Nathan's clinical experience with patients like Toni confirmed for him that

Toni's enraged expressed emotions were mostly internalized machinations which would be self-directed to herself and less probably directed to others. No doubt her transference toward Ben was all consuming but it was clear that Toni would have difficulty in the coming weeks without Ben's clinical stewardship.

Nathan glanced down to his modestly priced Seiko watch and noted that he had about thirty-five minutes before leaving campus to commute to his office. The remaining charts to be reviewed amounted to eighteen which were all patients discharged from Ben's Great Neck office over the past two years. A few of Ben's Manhattan patients apparently decided to see him on the Island when he began spending more time at home caring for his wife. The mutually convenient arrangement seemed to be a plus for both Ben and some of his patients who lived within the greater Nassau county vicinity. Several others decided to take the hour long drive out of the City or hop on the Long Island Railroad to keep their appointment with Ben if he did not have scheduled hours in Manhattan to accommodate their requests. By and large, the group of patients were seen for medication management, and by all clinical standards, appeared to be stable and would be best classified as the "worried well." Ben appeared to be treating simple anxiety cases and low grade depressives with rather straight forward medication regimens, with his patients being seen on a one time monthly basis or on a quarterly basis. Nothing alarming or troublesome to consider with these patients in terms of risk or potential threat. All seem to have reported getting better, all were in some form of psychotherapy with either a clinical social worker or psychologist, and all apparently had their medications discontinued or followed by their primary care physician in advance of their discharge from Ben's care. No apparent disgruntled patients, none threatening litigation or threatening to report some issue to the licensing board. Nathan was very certain that there would be no risk management concerns from this group of patients.

***

Arriving to his practice a few minutes early, after nearly a week being away, gave Nathan a chance to catch up on some incomplete work from previous sessions. Myra, who left a note about leaving a little early, had arranged a few charts on Nathan's desk to complete some remaining documentation as well as having set aside the afternoon's charts. The office seemed more quiet today with only the ever present humming sound coming from the fluorescent lights and the slight vibration coming from the air conditioning unit to break the still silence.

Nathan's 3 P.M. hour was a high achieving seventeen year old high school football star who found himself conflicted over figuring out how to maintain his first string quarterback status while at the same time sharing with his parents, coach and players that he is gay. Justin's work with Nathan began during spring practice in May when his grades seemed to slip, which according to Justin's parents would have eroded their child's possibilities for both an academic and athletic scholarship. During the past several months, Nathan and Justin have been focusing on strengthening his support network, both straight and gay , as he was taking steps closer to bring his parents up to speed on his sexual orientation. Justin's mom was not anticipated to be a major concern, but his father, a police officer and ex-marine, was seen as a formidable obstacle in educating both as to their son's orientation. "I'm not sure how much longer I can wait without telling my parents," expressed Justin. "I think they need to know. I want to be honest with them and true to me, otherwise I'm living a lie and remain feeling ashamed as to who I am."

"You know, I think we have worked well together over the past months and that you are better prepared to talk with your parents and find a direct way to tell them. It takes some guts and courage to come out," commented Nathan. "With the season already underway, you may want to pick the right time and place to tell them, either here during a session, if you would prefer , or at home… your words, thoughts and feelings. Justin, either way you let me know when you are ready and we will go from there. On the field, you've been pretty good in reading the defense, calling an audible, and making your adjustments. I think you can do the very same off the field with your parents and team," noted Nathan. The session continued a little longer with both Justin and Nathan engaged in a conversation to finalize a strategy.

"See you next time, Doc," said Justin.

"Okay , we'll continue to work on this," commented Nathan.

Before taking Mr. Jackson in for his 4 P.M. appointment, Nathan was able to speak for a few minutes with Det. Granger whose preliminary investigation of the person of interest, who left the mysterious sympathy card with Jack, was not turning up anything new.

"Nothing from the fingerprints but here's something interesting. The set type from the card and the card's envelope as well as from those letters and envelopes appears to be from the same style of typewriter, either an IBM Selectric or IBM Wheelwriter Series mostly manufactured and used as personal or business typewriters during the 70's and 80's." Granger also updated Nathan on her brief conversation with the Great Neck lead detective, Munson, who mostly regurgitated old information packaged with new language.

"The upshot Dr. Stern is that the police up there are done with the case and not interested in pursuing any new information about Dr. Solomon's patients or anything that may be going on down here. Closed case… their coroner ruled the death as a suicide with the forensics investigation finding no other plausible explanation. Solomon's fingerprints on the firearm, a suicide note and family circumstances suggesting a despondent widower who chose not to go on," summarized Granger.

"I see," commented Nathan. "Doesn't look like Great Neck believes there is any compelling information for them to reconsider or to take a second look. Okay. Let's stay in touch. I'm looking over Ben's records and contacting a few of his patients," added Nathan.

"Perhaps I should be doing that?" replied Granger, with a questionable tone.

"I don't think I can do that Detective, given some of the privacy issues involved, but I will let you know if anything comes up; however I have nothing so far," noted Nathan.

Mr. Jackson's session went by rather uneventful as he had reviewed the week's mundane activities and his ruminations over his wife's affair. Nathan's patient, who is typically focused only upon himself, did take note of Nathan's near nodding off during the middle part of the hour.

"Am I boring you Dr. Stern?", Jackson quietly asked.

"No sorry," Nathan alertly responded almost reflexively. "That's on me, it seems I need a little more sleep. Why don't you go on and tell me more about your plans to get an attorney to represent you in the upcoming divorce."

Mr. Jackson's session came to an end without much of anything being accomplished and with that in mind Nathan felt that his client should probably get a refund or credit. Nathan's next session called to let him know that she was running a few minutes late, which gave Nathan a moment to rest his eyes and grab a cup of coffee and a granola bar. In the minutes prior to Ronnie Fitz-Morris' session, Nathan reviewed some of his notes from the initial visit. Upon entering his office, Nathan observed that Ronnie's dress and appearance was more in line with her age, attired in distressed blue jeans, a NY Yankee's T, and a pair of powder blue Nike running shoes. As Ronnie got comfortable on the leather upholstered couch she began commenting about how much more settled in she now feels. "I've done some rearranging in my condo, started looking for a job and met some new people," related Ronnie.

"That's good, glad to hear you're making a nice adjustment," commented Nathan. "What kind of work are you looking for?"

"Well my degree is in computer science so I'm trying to find something in IT. I've actually set up an interview at the University sometime over next week. We just may be working together," laughed Ronnie. "There seems to be tech openings in the Law School, Business School and in Psychology." Nathan did not seem so thrilled yet he wished his patient good luck in her job pursuit and for next week's interview. "So Ronnie, I wanted to go back to how you were referred to me," stated Nathan. "I remember you saying something along the lines of getting my name from your gynecologist or from a psychiatrist, Dr Solomon."

"That's right, actually both," expressed Ronnie. My gynecologist, Dr. Fleisher, I think has referred to that psychiatrist and she had a card for me. They are in the same building. And when I called Dr. Solomon, the receptionist told me that Dr. Solomon was not taking on any new patients in the city and Great Neck was too far for me to travel for an hour or so appointment. When I mentioned that I'm leaving the city to move down to Florida, the receptionist got your name I think from the Rolodex directory. I thought that was nice of her. I guess if I was going to stay up there I might have considered seeing Dr. Solomon on the Island."

"But didn't you say last time that you moved out of the city to the Island to get away from that ex. I guess I'm more than a little confused here. Why didn't you see Dr. Solomon when you moved, certainly you would have been closer at that point."

"That's true but I knew I was coming down here and I didn't want to start therapy only to end so quickly," described Ronnie.

"So you and Dr. Solomon never spoke?" queried Nathan in a somewhat awkward cadence.

"No, never," replied Ronnie, thinking that was phrased strangely. "Can we move onto something else," commented Ronnie in an abrupt way.

"Sure, that would be fine," an acquiescing Nathan replied. "Let's pick up from last time."

"Yeah, okay, you wanted to hear more about my childhood," commented Ronnie.

"That would be a good place to start," affirmed Nathan.

Over the next twenty minutes Nathan listened attentively to Ronnie's depiction of her stormy childhood complete with multiple adverse events. Nathan was certainly familiar with the literature that studied the link between adverse childhood experiences and trauma, especially complex trauma, as well as the research on resiliency which allowed so many to adapt and survive where others may not have. Nathan was not yet clear into which camp Ronnie fell into, yet he was beginning to sense it was the former group.

"What a joke Protective Services is," related Ronnie. "What's that called…an oxymoron; nothing protective about it. Not one of my foster homes was truly safe and free of some type of neglect or abuse. I was told I was placed outside of the home as an infant under a year. Who knows what kind of care I got when I was real young but from the time that I could remember I got really bad care. I'm not saying I was abused or beaten, but my foster parents just saw me as a dollar sign. None of them seemed to really care about me and I guess I just kind of existed as I was sent from home to home. By the time I was ten, I had been to six different schools," asserted Ronnie.

"I see, incredibly difficult and unstable, invalidating environments for you," noted Nathan as he continued, "Ronnie, how do you think you survived these earlier events?"

"I wonder that myself," replied Ronnie.

"These kinds of events, with all the unpredictability, leaves wounds which often never heal, but if you are fortunate somewhere along the line things turnaround and you have an opportunity for the course to change. It sound like you had that chance when you were adopted," commented Nathan.

"I thought so too", stated Ronnie. "First I thought just another set of foster parents. I did a lot of testing, feeling uncertain and unsafe, but then gradually got the big picture that things were going to be different. When I realized this was the real thing, I remember thinking it was the best day of my life." Ronnie continued, "though I will never know, maybe it took those ten years to get to my adoptive parents."

"And how were things in your new home?" questioned Nathan.

"First pretty good. Things with my parents, Beth and James Fitz-Morris, started out real positive, spending a lot of time with me, it felt like a family. However, that seemed to last for just over a year. Both Beth and James got back to their busy lives on Wall Street and like overnight I became invisible, being mostly cared for by my nanny. Some weekends they went away without me and a few consecutive summers, they sent me off to camp, and they went off traveling abroad somewhere," an angered Ronnie commented.

"What was that like for you?" asked Nathan.

"What do you think, like I was being left all over again. I was pretty angry and started to find distractions," noted Ronnie. "And the distractions got more elaborate as I got a little older. First some drinking, then some weed, later pain killers and eventually all of that plus boys and sex by the time I was fifteen. Then 911 and poof both parents gone. I was sixteen by then and inherited the estate which remained under trust and then I legally emancipated myself. After they were gone, I really became much more unglued and ramped up the drugs."

"Did you get some help during that time?" inquired Nathan.

"Oh yeah, several rehabs both before my parents died and many after. It was during one of my stays shortly after my parents died that one of my therapists suggested that I look for my real mom and I thought why not, who else do I have. I did some basic database checks, and found some information out there identifying my mother but the pathetic part of all of that was that she died around the time when my adoption was finalized . Cause of death ruled heart failure but I'm fairly certain it was suicide," related Ronnie.

"How can you be so certain that it was a suicide?" asked Nathan.

"A few years later I had hired a private eye who also did some digging and located the toxicology report from the coroners which noted the cause of death as myocardial infarction secondary to unusually high levels of amphetamine, cocaine, oxycodone and alcohol," commented Ronnie.

"That's quite a range of events in your life which I'm sure has left you feeling empty, at times enraged and at other times simply depressed. Losing your birth mother once, then your adoptive parents through first disinterest and lack of availability and then through the tragedy of 911, and kind of losing your mother a second time after searching for her, is much more that any one person should endure but here you are," Nathan summarized. "Are you drug free now?" asked Nathan.

"I am now two years," noted Ronnie.

"Okay that's really good," Nathan commented supportively. "Takes a lot of work and day to day monitoring. I think we got through much today, so let's end and meet next week," Nathan suggested.

As Nathan walked Ronnie out toward the waiting room, his next and final appointment for the day, David Lugar, was sitting comfortably reading a magazine.

"See you next week," Ronnie said, as she swung the office door open.

Nathan's busy day was quickly winding down with Mr. Lugar's hour. David, an eighty-two year old widow diagnosed with an inoperable Stage 4 brain tumor was being seen for end of life counseling. David's oncologist apparently gave him maybe three months at this point as both chemotherapy and radiation treatments have not really slowed the advancement of his cancer. With no hope for any cure and only palliative medications to relieve pain, David was beginning to process his acceptance of his imminent demise. Nathan was mostly approaching therapy with a retrospective and existential analysis of life as well as an acceptance of his mortality. David and his deceased spouse, Anne, of fifty- one years were childless throughout their marriage. Both had seen brothers and sisters pass on decades earlier and David's more painful experience is one of being alone and dying alone.

"I know the philosophers say we come into this world alone and die alone," commented David, "and I guess that's right, but I'm really scared about the end… so, it's been helpful to have this time together with you and talk about it. At some point, I know I will no longer have some of my mental abilities to intelligently deal with things but for the moment talking to you has helped."

"I'm glad I can be here for you David, and hear whatever thoughts and feelings you're having," shared Nathan. You've been so strong through all of this and putting up the good fight… use this time in any way you see fit." The session continued for a little longer but Nathan could see David's fatigue, part emotional and part medication related. "I think we should end David and have Rosie, your aid, take you home.

We'll see one another next week," suggested Nathan.

"Okay. I think that's a good idea, you take care Doc," David softly replied.

"You too," Nathan replied, never quiet knowing if he would see David again.

Nathan had a few psychotherapy progress notes to write up which would briefly summarize each patient contact and content of session before he would close up the office. On his way out he left a few things at Myra's desk to take care of the next day and had called Joanne to let her know that he was on his way home. As he checked his next day schedule he had seen the circled name of Giorgio Armis to contact later in the day, a chore Nathan was too exhausted to accomplish at the current moment.

*** 

Joanne had prepared a nice dinner of roasted rosemary chicken, smashed potatoes and broccoli au gratin for Nathan, Erik, Jack, and herself to enjoy as the family sat together around their kitchen table for the first time in about a week. Although difficult to do, Joanne and Nathan tried their best to have as many sit down dinners with everyone as possible during the week. For most weeks that translated to about four out of seven days, which was a pretty good percentage for a busy professional couple with kids in school.

"How was everyone's day?" began Nathan.

"Alright," Erik replied and continued, "slammed with homework and a project for next week."

"Not great," blurted out Jack, "Miss Rosenberg wasn't in today and we got this sub who just had us do our long division and word problems all day."

"Well on the bright side, if Miss Rosenberg is out one more day, you and your class will be experts on long division and be ready for that quiz next week," playfully noted Joanne.

"Yeah, right," Jack replied without much enthusiasm. "Did they find that guy from the other day?" added Jack.

"No, I'm afraid not. The police officer is still investigating. Chances are they won't be able to find him," replied Nathan.

"That's not good," Erik chimed in. "Is that guy like dangerous or something?"

"We just don't know what that was about. While a sympathy card would be normal, the way it was given to your brother, so anonymously, makes us concerned," commented Joanne, "but we're looking into it to be safe. Let's just all be careful and more mindful of our surroundings in the meantime, but definitely go on with our regular activities and routines...okay guys," Joanne confidently expressed.

As their dinner came to an end, Joanne and Nathan cleared the table with only a modicum of help from Erik and Jack, who were ready to bail out and return to the back of the house to entertain themselves.

"Let them go, gives us a few minutes. What's going on with you?" asked Nathan.

"Oh, not a whole lot. Probably too much time on my hands this week... not really focusing on my work, distracted by that card and all that has happened surrounding Ben's death and these letters," Joanne commented.

"I know there's a lot to take in, and so much unsettled," replied Nathan.

"Look, Ben's records came by FedEx late today, four boxes, catalogued by year for the time period you requested," noted Joanne. "But do me a favor, if you would like I'll help, but leave that till tomorrow," firmly suggested Joanne.

"Sure, it can wait another day," agreed Nathan.

\*\*\*

# CHAPTER 10

Nathan appeared determined to read through Ben's records before the approaching weekend and decided to take the day to focus exclusively on the charts. Work at home was not Nathan's preference, but the number of boxes and charts to get through convinced him quickly to work from his home office. Nathan could see that Ruth and Margaret did a really good job organizing Ben's records, forwarding exactly what he requested including Ben's personal notes during his residency years. Should his hypothesis be correct, Nathan would begin to search records of patients he and Ben co-treated during the overlapping years of residency training and during the first year after post-doc when Nathan and Ben shared office space. This group of patients Nathan speculated should therefore be a rather finite group of patients given the specific time parameters.

Nathan noted that Ben apparently retained all treatment records and notes in perpetuity. Nathan realized that if Ben had followed more closely the New York State regulations of record retention, then his role and labor at this point although being simplified would nonetheless have been futile and unnecessary. In contrast to Ben's record keeping, Nathan followed the more expedient regulations defined by the state statutes which allowed psychologists to first condense in summary fashion after three years and then purge records after seven. Nathan's only exception and consistent with state law were retention of records for minors which he nevertheless held for several years after the age of majority. Given that Nathan did not have any of his own Metro records at his disposal he knew that his only recourse was relying upon his own sketchy memory of patients' he had consulted with or treated along with Ben, which were now in some cases twenty five years plus in the past.

Clinical rotations at Metro were comprised of two inpatient psych units, an involuntary commitment ward and a voluntary status ward, and one comprehensive outpatient mental health center. Nathan, in thinking back, had figured that he and Ben only overlapped time in their rotation on the involuntary unit for a period of four months sometime between September 1985 and August 1986. Otherwise, Nathan spent most of his time with the outpatient center. The two were supervised by their respective department heads, a chief psychologist and attending psychiatrist, for most of the twelve months. Nathan in reviewing Ben's residency notes figured that Ben had treated roughly seventy-two patients and from Ben's private entries, which were only identified by initials, none upon first exam seemed all that familiar to Nathan. Nathan could see that Ben had made multiple referrals for most of his patients including medical, neurology, and psychology. The psychology referrals were further broken down to referrals for either psychotherapy or psychological testing but in most cases for both. Nathan considered that he would have been one of four post docs in the rotation to have received Ben's psychotherapy referrals. Upon parceling out what he could from Ben's notes, Nathan still could not readily recognize any of the patients' histories primarily due to Ben's short hand and rather cryptic way of phrasing things to obviously protect confidentiality. It was clear however to Nathan that all the cases had troublesome backgrounds, extensive psychiatric treatment and severe and often multiple diagnoses. While the two did co-treat a number of patients at Metro, if there were to be some common denominator during the treatment process, Nathan was thinking it may be clearer from the formal records from Ben's practice after he left Metro.

As Nathan began examining Ben's files for the period following his residency, Nathan noted the high frequency of patients that continued with Ben in one way or another following discharge, a practice not all that uncommon where patients particularly attached to one psychiatrist or another would wish to continue outpatient care after a hospitalization. It would seem that Ben had a rather large following of these patients which apparently comprised a significant portion of his growing Manhattan practice. In contrast, Nathan upon leaving his post doc was not afforded the same privilege to take some of his clients with him into practice. Nathan often wondered about the difference between the two disciplines and approaches but was convinced by his mentors, all psychoanalysts, that termination of psychotherapy during an inpatient phase of treatment should be considered essential without any further blurring of boundaries during the outpatient phase. Over the years, Nathan challenged this approach through lecture and through his writings to suggest that continuity of care should be sacrosanct. Nathan endorsed a more humanistic approach, which suggested to follow a patient through the difficult ordeal of a psychiatric hospitalization and then transition with the patient to an outpatient level of care. Nathan firmly believed that this should be the standard of care and not discouraged or considered to be a violation of psychotherapy ethics and principles.

Chart by chart Nathan traveled through his colleague's early work with now more clear and identifiable information at his disposal. Some of the charts were quite thin but others appeared to contain separate volumes of distinct treatment episodes. Most of the records were also complete with the patients' hospital records from Metro, which Ben would have requested upon discharge, which now upon inspection noted the specific referrals by name and department. Nathan was able to see his name identified with numerous patients for consultation for psychotherapy and indeed Nathan as he scanned the chart could see his own transcribed notes from dictation outlining the initial consultation, developmental history, treatment history, working diagnosis, treatment recommendations, prognosis, and psychotherapy notes.

*Ah*, Nathan sighed thinking to himself, *if only we had computers back then to keep track* of *the data base of patients…my life today would be much easier.* Nathan also realized that he could make his task somewhat less complicated by quickly glancing at each case and see where Ben and he would have had contact with the same patient while treated at Metro or in the office. From what Nathan recalled however there actually were very few patients that the two shared in their practice together, as Ben tended to work with a much more severe group of clientele. Nathan typically worked with a much more stable and healthier group of patients. The early demise of their practice in that first year appeared to have that issue at the center with Ben's clients often crowding the waiting room in some disorganized fashion and as a result making Nathan's clients somewhat uncomfortable. Nathan was not very happy with this mix of patients in their Upper East Side practice which he envisioned, at an earlier point, would eventually become worthy of the reputation found with all the other offices on Analyst's Alley. Upon hearing from Columbia for an appointment as an assistant professor in the Psychology Department, Nathan was able to avoid any awkwardness with Ben and left under very good circumstances.

Nathan now noted about eighteen charts in which he was identified as the psychologist to consult and or treat as an inpatient at Metro which was conjointly followed by Ben. And, only one of these patients had continued with Nathan for a relatively brief period later in their office. As Nathan was looking through each chart he was very certain of the profile that he was searching for, in addition to the association that he and Ben had treated the patient together. The patient, Nathan recognized, would now be approximately in his or her fifties or sixties and perhaps older, looking to carry out a personal vendetta toward a previous treating provider. One by one Nathan spent considerable time reviewing each chart with no ostensible reason to suggest any particular patient with a specific motivation to inflict harm to Ben. Clearly, the group of patients were a high risk group hoping for some miracle treatment to eliminate positive symptoms for such illnesses like schizophrenia, major depressive disorder, bipolar disorder, obsessive compulsive disorder and borderline personality disorder. Some charts took only minutes to review based upon the treatment episode and other charts up to an hour. As the afternoon was approaching, a few charts remained, some of great volume which rivaled the size of a yellow pages directory. Nathan's eyes by now were a bit tired and as he was hungry, he walked through the empty house toward the kitchen to prepare lunch. Joanne, who was finishing up her morning office hours, agreed to join him for lunch and help out with the rest of the files.

***

It was rare to have an afternoon at home all to themselves so after lunch Joanne and Nathan very much aware that they haven't been together since the day before Ben's funeral drifted slowly to the bedroom and took turns undressing one another in the most seductive fashion. Joanne who was dressed more professionally, had on a seven button blouse which Nathan very slowly unbuttoned from

Joanne's neckline to just beneath her waist, untucking the blouse from her knee-high skirt and running his hands beneath her blouse gently sliding his index finger and thumb down and around the swell of her breast and stroking the sensitive area around the underside of her breast. Nathan proceeded to remove her blouse, unhooked her bra and ran his tongue ever so gently around Joanne's hardened nipples. As Nathan moved down with his tongue, Joanne arched her back slightly and seemed to enjoy every subtle movement by her partner. By now, Nathan had unzipped her skirt which gently fell to the floor and began applying some pressure from his mouth on the outer lining of her panties. She could feel the warmth from his breath which was incredibly arousing to Joanne. Nathan paused for a minute as Joanne pressed her body against his and began to slowly unbutton and unzip her partner's khakis and softly caressed Nathan's inner thighs, noting the heat and pressure building within his pants. Joanne slipped off Nathan's pants as Nathan removed his polo shirt at which point he felt the moist lips and tongue of his partner gently trace the firm shape of his penis beneath his boxer briefs. The two maneuvered each other somewhat side by side as they enjoyed the sensations delivered at first orally and then with gentle sensual touches. When the time seemed right, Joanne positioned herself on top of Nathan at first kneeling over and slowing rotating herself on and off his now fully erect penis and eventually sliding him slowly inside her pushing down with her pelvis and pressing up on his butt to allow a certain rhythm to ensue which allowed for the deepest penetration to bring both to orgasm within minutes. As Joanne continued to slumber on Nathan's body, she could still sense his post-tumescent hardness which she enjoyed for a few more moments and with several additional gyrations of her pelvis reached a climax again.

"That must have been a nice diversion," Joanne playfully said, as she cuddled next to Nathan.

"One hundred percent... got my mind off everything for a few minutes," replied Nathan.

As they rested side by side for a few more minutes, they were both mindful of the time moving closer to school ending with the boys coming home in about ninety minutes as well as the work that remained on Nathan's desk for he and Joanne to delve into. The couple freshened up a bit, dressed and met up in the office to look over the remaining charts.

***

Of the remaining charts to be reviewed, Nathan took half and Joanne took the other half.

"What are we looking for again?" inquired Joanne.

"Any patient who had both Ben and I as treating providers either during my year of post-doc or in our Manhattan office," noted Nathan. "Set those aside and I will take a closer look," Nathan noted further.

As Joanne was scanning over one of Ben's more voluminous outpatient records, which indeed met Nathan's first criterion point of Ben and Nathan treating the patient as an inpatient, she was distracted by an 8x10 yellow mailing envelope which appeared to be affixed to the back sectional divider labeled as personal writings. Joanne mentally noted that it would not be unusual for a chart to include a patient's personal recordings, reflections, and writings, as both she and Nathan would routinely ask clients to journal, record data and monitor certain symptoms or behaviors as part of the treatment process. As Joanne untied the thin string that attached to both fasteners and peeked into the envelope she could see a two inch stack of what appeared to be correspondences, essays and diary-like entries. Joanne set this chart aside for Nathan to look at as well as one other where Ben and Nathan both treated one of their patients only as an outpatient. Within an hour Nathan completed his review of the remaining charts without arousing suspicion for any of the patients' case histories. Near the end of this process, Nathan was not optimistic that he would find any particular pattern or connection to explain his enigmatic situation. One familiar pattern however which presented itself, that Nathan wasn't necessarily looking for or anticipating, was that several of his patients' interventions included the prevalence of using electroconvulsive therapy as well as certain medications prescribed by Ben and used in combination, including Prolixin, Mellaril, Lithium, Nardil and Anafranil. Nathan, although never studying pharmacology was quite knowledgeable of the major medications prescribed to a psychiatric population. Prolixin, Nathan knew was a medication used to stabilize patients presenting with acute symptoms of schizophrenia and offered in an intramuscular delivery system to deal with noncompliant patients. Mellaril was another anti-psychotic medication, and Lithium would be utilized primarily for bipolar disorder. Nardil, Nathan knew, was an MAO Inhibitor used selectively for patients with intractable or treatment resistant depression. Nathan also knew that Nardil was a difficult regimen to manage with serious adverse effects and required specific dietary restrictions when prescribing. Anafranil, a triclyclic antidepressant, Nathan was familiar with for treatment of obsessive compulsive disorder. When Nathan compared his small subset of patients compared to the larger group of Ben's total patients seen on the unit, the treatment protocols seemed invariably identical.

As Nathan now began looking over all the charts again, a second pattern of practice which was not unexpected was the utilization of psychological testing to clarify a diagnosis and offer treatment recommendations. However, what was surprising was the frequency of referrals to one particular supervising psychologist, Dr. Klein, and his post-doc residents, who typically used identical or interchangeable diagnoses in each evaluation and had recommended inevitably the most restricted treatment setting with longer treatment periods and the primary use of ECT and pharmacological intervention over psychotherapy. As Nathan read through a few of the psychological evaluations he found the language strangely coincidental. One of the residents' name appearing frequently on the last page of each report accompanying Dr. Klein's was interestingly, Nathans' and Bens' mutual colleague, Gerald Zwick.

Nathan thought to himself... *oh my old friend...what have you done* ... Nathan considered how alarming and unethical that was in terms of standards of practice, diagnostic integrity and efficacy of treatment recommendations. And for Gerald to sign off on those reports like that.

Nathan did not know Dr. Klein all that well and only had limited contact with him as an adjunct supervisor during his training at Metro. Gerald however had Klein as one of his primary and exclusive supervisors throughout the year as Gerald's specialization was in the area of psychological and diagnostic assessment. Nathan also recalled hearing through the residents' and interns' grape-vine as to how authoritarian and autocratic Klein was as a supervisor. Nathan noted that the majority of patients evaluated by Klein and Gerald carried diagnoses of Atypical Psychosis with Melancholia consistent with features of endogenous depression, Inadequate Personality, and Borderline Personality Disorder. The recommendations read in cookie-cutter fashion as: Continued commitment to an inpatient unit with a recommended length of stay of at least six to ten months with recommended treatment protocols of aggressive medication management as well as a series of electroconvulsive treatments. In referring to the use of psychotherapy, each evaluation recommended that psychotherapy in any traditional fashion would be ill advised and contra-indicated until the patient was stabilized on the correct levels of medication, and given the intractable nature of the course of symptoms, psychotherapy was not likely to impact favorably upon the patients prognosis.

As Nathan continued to backtrack over Ben's seventy or so cases, about two thirds of the reports were supervised by Klein, and Gerald and the team he was assigned to conducted the majority of these assessments. Nathan thought that was an unusually high percentage of patients assigned to one supervising psychologist and an unusually high percent labeled with the same diagnosis, recommendations, and treated in an identical fashion. Unlike the utilization review existing in psychiatry and psychology over the past decade, back in the 80's quality assurance- QA and UR – was just in its infancy and was not so well standardized as is currently to recognize such possible medical errors which may be coincidental or deliberate and red flagged for fraud, abuse and waste. Nathan who now read more specifically the actual psychological assessment in every chart had noted that the chief complaints and relevant background sections were well written and seemed to capture the unique histories of the patient. However, it was in the conceptualization and diagnostic section where the narrative seemed to be woven together with very similar jargon and phrases to support both the diagnosis and recommendations. As Nathan did not have the raw data from the test administrations it would be impossible to verify the scores from various indices and subsequent interpretations from the data to even see if there was some correlation between test data and what was reported. Nathan knew intuitively that in all likelihood the scores were either erroneously computed or simply manufactured to support the conceptualization and would therefore be the most egregious error tantamount to incompetence, fraud or malpractice which either Gerald or Klein as well as other staff committed on their own or complicit together.

Nathan now reviewed his most recent findings with an incredulous and speechless Joanne, and knew he would have a sobering conversation with Gerald next week on campus. When Joanne collected her thoughts she began to respond, "Can you imagine coming into treatment, especially as an inpatient with all those feelings of being out of control, arriving to a trusted psychiatric institution with impeccable credentials and then being evaluated by someone who delivered a report that may have been modified to fit a certain diagnostic conceptualization and support a specific treatment regimen. I can't imagine that the Gerald you know , would have done that unless he had no choice and caved to the pressure and demands of an abusive superior who had incredible power and control over him. How many lives were changed or impacted by this and how much weight did these reports carry in influencing treatment decisions about hospital stays, involuntary commitments, medication, ECT, therapy?"

"You know, from what I remember," replied Nathan, "some psychiatrists never gave the time of day to the evaluations, but docs like Ben used the psychologicals to help inform and complete their own clinical interview and I know for sure Ben relied pretty heavily on the diagnosis and recommendations section as a significant independent source of clinical data. It just doesn't sound like Gerald, and certainly Ben should have been suspect of any reports that read with very similar if not identical diagnoses and recommendations."

"Did you have any idea?" inquired Joanne.

"No, never. I didn't really have access to any other charts but the ones I would have been assigned... and most of the charts I had were assigned through a different team than the one Gerald and Klein were working on. During my rotation on that unit, if I saw one or two of Gerald's reports supervised by Klein that would have been a lot. After post-doc, I had routinely referred to Gerald for assessment and his reports were outstanding and nothing like what I have been reading today," Nathan noted.

"And you don't recall any of the other residents talking about Kleins' or Geralds' psychologicals?" asked Joanne.

"What came up is typically found in training programs as far as the amount of work and edits and third and fourth drafts of a report. If it specifically came up, I wasn't privy to that conversation and I think most would have been intimidated to say anything against a supervisor like Klein," replied Nathan. Nathan continued, "and as far as Ben, perhaps he looked the other way as it confirmed his need or gave him extra permission to treat aggressively and find the perfect combination of medications to help his patient recover more completely. As for Gerald, he was definitely more passive back then and could have felt threatened by the power that Klein had over him in terms of progress in his training, completion of the program, and eligibility for licensure and eventual success in the field in terms of connections and future referrals. I just don't know Joanne but I will certainly ask him on Monday and try to get some answers."

"Let's try to finish up with your cases," Nathan suggested, "as the afternoon was getting on and Jack and Erik will be home very shortly."

"Here are the two that you should examine," commented Joanne as she looked over some of her notes. "This one you had seen for a consult but Ben was the original psychiatrist assigned and only had seen the patient a few times as the case was transferred to a female resident. I took another look at the chart and sure enough the diagnoses were Atypical Psychosis with Melancholia and Borderline Personality Disorder. The patient was recommended to start a medication regimen of Prolixin, Lithium and Nardil but declined any medication and it looked like the hospital was waiting for an involuntary order to medicate but then the case was reassigned.

Subsequent to the transfer the psychological evaluation was completed by Zwick and signed off by Klein. Later in the hospitalization, apparently after the patient was placed either voluntarily or involuntarily on medication, the case was transferred back to Ben."

"Okay put that one off to the side," directed Nathan. "And the other?" Nathan questioned.

"Right," started Joanne. "This one is pretty thick as you can tell and seen by both you and Ben over your four month rotation, then continued as an inpatient after you left for the next seven months, and then followed by Ben as an outpatient on and off over the next several years. There were lengthy periods of active treatment followed by several months of a hiatus from treatment and then a resumption of care. And when I checked, evaluation by Gerald and signed off by Klein with the now familiar diagnoses affixed to her treatment record. Medication sheets reads like all the others you found along with several protocols of ECT. Your work seemed mostly to focus around assisting the patient's capacity to make good sound judgments and decisions primarily within her home environment and in her responsibilities as a young mother. A second psychological evaluation was later ordered through the Court to assist with determining the patient's competency as a parent and was conducted again by Gerald, who at that point was licensed and practicing independently."

"I vaguely recall that case," replied Nathan. "The patient had some very intensive treatment in the hope that she could be re-united with her child. She partially stabilized while in the hospital and months later I was asked to appear in an advocacy role with the Court to comment about her capacity to parent. I had seen her one or two times as an outpatient but it was clear that she had again decompensated, and fulfilling any parental responsibilities seemed to be quite a stretch for her and so I concurred with Gerald's opinion that parental rights should be terminated which permitted the child to transition from foster care placement to pre-adoptive placement. Is Gerald's Court ordered evaluation in Ben's chart?" asked Nathan.

"It is," commented Joanne who continued. "The report appears to be a standard psychological assessment for the Court and the Department of Protective Services when considering issues related to capacity to parent, parental re-unification or termination of parental rights. Gerald's examination seemed appropriate with the use of test instruments and collateral information. His opinion appeared to be well thought out with genuine concern for both the patient and ultimately for what was in the best interests of the child. Interestingly, Gerald's diagnosis was a little different from the inpatient diagnosis. The patient this time around was diagnosed with Major Depressive Disorder with Mood-Congruent Psychotic Features, Poly Substance Dependence and Borderline Personality Disorder."

As Nathan read through the evaluation he first noted Gerald's telephone interview with him in an attempt to collect collateral information regarding the patient's course of treatment. Gerald also included a statement from Ben, as well as an opinion from both Ben and Nathan regarding the patient's strengths and limitations with respect to responsible parenting, judgment and decision making. In the final analysis, both Ben and Nathan cautioned the Court in allowing the child to return to the mother and recommended that termination of parental rights would suit the child best. Subsequently, Gerald integrated all case and test materials and then delivered in the final bolded paragraph the quintessential expert opinion to terminate parental rights. During the next Court hearing, Charlene Yarborough's rights as a parent was terminated on October 3, 1986.

"So what became of the mother?" inquired Joanne.

"According to Ben's records like you said before, he had followed her for a few more years and then there were no further contact notes. The patient stopped her treatment with Ben and the case was closed with no additional follow-up," noted Nathan .

"And of the child?" added Joanne.

"Not much is written about the child. Ben's notes referenced the patient's increasing despair, following the Court's motion, with anergia, anhedonia and persecutory mentation. The patient appeared to be hospitalized several more times in a revolving door fashion with several additional medication trials as well as ECT trials. The patient never seemed to have any degree of stable functioning after losing her child. The only reference about the child was in terms of discontinuing all forms of visitation and that the child would remain in a pre-adoptive status until successfully placed with an adoptive family," replied Nathan. "Okay, then. So where is Charlene Yarborough now?" queried Nathan.

"Right, before you try to figure that out," Joanne noted, "you should look these over."

Nathan began to comb through a fairly dense array of personal writings, including poems, essays, and journal entries. Wedged between this material however and folded over in a smaller envelope were a stack of additional pages, and when unfolded, Nathan's facial expression with his eyes basically exploding out of his sockets was all the evidence that Joanne needed to be convinced that something very alarming was discovered by her husband. With his lips parted by an inch or so, a speechless Nathan gestured Joanne to move closer as both began to examine the several pages of prose which appeared to be the original writings of Charlene Yarborough, dated between 1985 and 1988. Beneath the first few pages, appeared several writings identical to the ones already familiar to and in Joanne's and Nathan's possession. Nathan with Joanne looking over his shoulder now began to read each page of prose:

## Trapped In A Web

Trapped and hands tied

Feelings frozen in the cold tundra

I see no way out of this turmoil

In the shadows of your frame

I find the urge to live on

Unmask me, reveal the true persona

Reaching deep for something, that may not be there

Now nothing to stop my demise

Although you may try to

see through my mask and free me from the web

Catch me as I fall. Catch me as I go by

Help me avoid smashing onto the cement ground

My eyes now closed tight

I am in a free fall waiting for your response

My eyes now open but I can see not a soul

No heroic effort, no magical cure

One more breath inside before I go


Truth and Lies


My universe has fallen apart

My ego crushed many times over

My life is empty and void

I scream out but there is silence... nobody listens

Can't recall the last time when I was heard

But it seems like decades when I last remember

that feeling

The chambers are now full

Look into it and cannot see that the end is near

Humpty Dumpty had a great fall

All the Kings horses and all the Kings men

couldn't put Humpty together again

At last, the simple Truth


## Warped


Can't remember when last I was free

It was some time ago when

I saw the beacons of light

transforming me into someone else

How can I crave to see such things that range

from angels to demons

I am no doubt warped as the next

Can't figure this out anymore, not even with you

Too much room for confusion

Now my cereal is getting stale

And my Rice Krispies say

Snap, crackle , pop


Restrained


I saw the sunrise one morning, and there you were

It was bright and cheery, a new vision inside

By night the stars were not out

You were gone

The planet now stripped of its resources

Mined for the elements…nothing left

But emptiness and void

I am tired of the cycles which persist forever

It would be nice one day to be free of the struggle

Healthy and fit and unrestrained by pleasure

But that is not perhaps in my future

Hope turned to sorrow

Depression, despair and despondent

Nothing to save me, not even you

You might as well give up too.


## Child's Play


How I miss the simple play of a child

Now the world is too complex with adults

who frighten and take advantage

How I yearn to be back at home

to be nourished and taken care of

Are you there for me, to supervise my journey

Or, perhaps like all the others you too will

Disappear from my existence.

How I miss the fun of the sandbox, the texture of the

sand, the childrens' laughter by my side

Take me back to a time of innocence

Life goes on and on, but for some we are just spinning

our wheels… frozen in time, going nowhere fast,

looking back only to a life lost.

Help Me, Heal Me, Stand By Me and Support Me

As I have lost my way.


"You must call Granger now and let her know what you found," Joanne firmly said. "No question about it, this former patient, Charlene Yarborough, who no doubt was very troubled even with receiving psychiatric care, was treated or better stated mistreated by Ben, Gerald and even maybe yourself, lost everything precious and is apparently out for revenge."

"Can I do that legally and ethically?" Nathan wondered out loud.

"Screw the law and ethics," Joanne expressed, slowly losing control and now speaking more loudly which was about to crescendo to a scream-level of intensity. She killed Ben, sent you letters which may make you the next target, and Gerald who may be most culpable here, based on his psychological assessments, is likely on her radar as well."

"If you don't call, I will Nathan," an out of breath Joanne firmly noted. Nathan now equally agitated with beads of sweat profusely falling from his brow which was already reddened from the flow of blood to his face was trying to wrap his brain around all of this as he reached for the phone to call Det. Granger.

Granger's phone went right to voice mail at which time Nathan left an extensive message insisting on a call back immediately. Nathan also left a message with the front clerk attendant who noted that Granger was out in the field but would call back as soon as she arrived back to her office.

Nathan also wanted to try to catch Gerald before the weekend but it was way after five and on a Friday, Gerald would certainly be gone for the day. Nathan subsequently emailed Gerald to schedule time Monday morning to discuss an urgent matter.

As the two calmed down a little, Joanne and Nathan seemed uncertain as to what to do next or even how to go on with any routine weekend plans that may be coming up. Although Nathan readily recognized that he wasn't quite sure as to what he was initially looking for or what he could find by reviewing Ben's records, now realized that what he had uncovered certainly was much more than he anticipated or could digest, and brought up several more questions without an immediate answer.

Nathan silently pondered… *Where is Ben's former patient, Charlene Yarborough…what state of mind is she in?…is she getting help?… is she medicated?…how long has she been plotting this personal vendetta?…how did she arrange Ben's death to appear as a suicide?…. is she here in Florida to settle a score with me and Gerald?…could she harm anyone else?…Joanne, Erik, Jack…will Granger be able to track her down?… will the police be able to protect us?* None of these queries left Nathan feeling good about the circumstances with so many variables outside of his control.

\*\*\*

# CHAPTER 11

"Dr. Stern, it's Det. Granger," the detective announced abruptly on the phone. "Sorry I missed your call. What's up?" questioned Granger.

"I think a lot. There's a lot for you to follow up on. A records search lead me down a path to a former patient of Dr. Solomon's and mine as well as another colleague who ultimately weighed in on her ability to be a parent. End result...her rights as a parent was terminated. It looks like the three of us, Solomon, myself and another psychologist, Gerald Zwick, all had varying degrees of involvement with her and she no doubt felt screwed by the system and is out to exact revenge," opined Nathan.

"How can you be so certain?" asked Granger.

"Here's the most crucial thing, this patient appears to be the writer of the letters I had been receiving. A complete set of poems were found in Solomon's files," replied Nathan.

"How long ago was this?" asked Granger.

"Back in the 80's," replied Nathan.

"Hmmn, after all this time you...doesn't make much sense that she would wait," suggested Granger.

"I know it just doesn't add up, but you just never know what may trigger someone into action, even after all this time," commented Nathan.

"Okay, so is there anymore to the story?" a curious Granger asked.

"I don't have the complete back story," as Nathan began to summarize, "but she was a relatively young mother, treated aggressively with meds and ECT and I don't think much progress was noted or if there was some improvement it was probably short lived. Followed by Solomon as an inpatient and then as an outpatient, seen by me for a few months as an inpatient and evaluated by the other doc, Zwick, whose report probably in the end convinced the Judge to terminate rights."

"Anything else?" asked Granger.

Nathan was a bit hesitant to share any more of the questionable and unethical aspects of psychiatric care uncovered in his review of the records until he spoke further with Gerald. "No , I don't have anything more at this time," noted Nathan.

"What's the patient's name?" asked Granger.

The question which Nathan knew would be coming and now was unavoidable placed Nathan's scope of ethical values and protection of a patient's identity directly up against the need to most likely protect himself and others. Nathan paused for a moment and then informed Granger of the patients name.

"Okay, then let me handle this from here," Granger replied. "Let me do some research and background check and locate Charlene Yarborough, set up an interview with her and proceed with my investigation. I'll keep in touch with any further information. I'm also going to again prioritize your security detail to make sure you and your family have suitable protection at home, at the office, at school and around the community. Report anything suspicious to me immediately."

"That sounds good . But I think you need to speak with Gerald

Zwick down at the University, because I think he is in danger too. If she is looking for some twisted sense of justice, she won't just stop at Solomon. Others are on that hit list too including Zwick and me," suggested Nathan.

"Yes I see that too. I'll get with Dr. Zwick also," Granger noted.

"Anything else?" Granger again asked.

"Yes , one other thing, I never had a chance to contact the last patient who may have seen Ben on that day. Can you call him as part of your investigation?" asked Nathan.

"Sure , what's the patient's name?" asked Granger.

"It's Giorgio Armis," replied Nathan who then proceeded to give Det. Granger Armis' phone number.

***

Granger was quick to contact her information tech specialist to plug in Charlene Yarborough's name and begin the search across all databases utilized by Granger's office. Although Granger had the technical competence to conduct her own search, police departments in most jurisdictions have set up a specific protocol to request a background check to avoid the misuse or abuse of power. "Just a name… nothing else…. no age, date of birth , social, address?" asked Sophia, a young, college-aged IT tech, of Columbian culture who was pursuing a Master's Degree in Forensics.

"That's all I got, possibly in her fifties or sixties if that helps," added Granger.

"Yep, that does," noted Sophia.

"How long?" asked Granger.

"Within a few…hang around or I'll call," suggested Sophia. "We have several search engines attempting to find your person."

"Interested in knowing which ones?" asked Sophia.

"Not really," replied Granger.

"Well then… we have the obvious, Google, and then there's Zaba, Pipl, PeekYou, Wink, YahooPeopleSearch, LinkedIn, Facebook, and of course we're linked to the FBI's National Crime Information Center," an enthusiastically Sophia piped in anyway. "Won't be long now," added Sophia. "Okay here you go," said Sophia.

A list of six hundred eighty four names appeared based on the limited information provided. "That's a long list of Charlene Yarborough's. Can you narrow it down if your search is limited to the metropolitan New York area including Long Island , New Jersey and Connecticut?" inquired Granger.

"Yep that would help," Sophia said. "Let's wait and…okay better, here's a list of three hundred twenty," noted Sophia.

"Okay, how about adding in a search with this name and all prior involuntary commitments to a psychiatric hospital. The mental health records are protected but I think the involuntary papers are public record," Granger added.

"I think we can access that unless the person was a minor at the time of commitment," replied Sophia.

"Okay, that narrows it down considerably," observed Granger.

"Anything else you want to add Detective?" Sophia annoyingly asked.

"One more fact…plug in court records, New York, termination of parental rights 10/3/86," Granger indicated.

"Okay. That's it… looks like we have a winner," Sophia jokingly commented. However, apparently you have a dead winner," added Sophia.

"Okay, not expecting that. Certain?" inquired Granger.

"Yes, most definitely based on the information you had me add…this Charlene Yarborough died quite a while ago," concluded Sophia.

"Any last known address back then?" asked Granger.

"Here it is," Sophia offered as she printed out Yarborough's address on Cloverdale Blvd in Queens, New York. "Apartment 3J," she added.

"Alright, thanks Sophia," a noticeably disappointed Granger said. "Let me have your complete list search as well for my records," added Granger.

\*\*\*

"May I speak with Giorgio Armis, please?" asked Det. Granger.

The scratchy older male voice with an Italian accent answered politely, "This is he, who's calling please."

"Mr. Armis, this is Det. Granger, I'm with a police department down in Florida investigating the recent death of a doctor in Great Neck. Do you have a moment to speak with me?" asked Granger.

"I do," replied Armis. "Awful thing the death of Dr. Solomon...suicide...go figure."

"Were you a patient of his?" asked Granger.

"Oh yes, for some time. I would see him once or twice a year," replied Armis.

"Well sir, I'm looking into the death of Dr. Solomon, and his appointment book indicates that you were scheduled to see him on that day," noted Granger.

"Is that right?" asked Armis. "Let me check my calendar. You know I have so many doctors' appointments it's hard to keep track of all of them. At my age that's my life...doctor to doctor."

"Oh, how old are you?" asked Granger.

"Well, I will be eighty-seven in April," Armis noted proudly.

"That's great, and about that visit with Dr. Solomon?" Granger reminded Armis.

"Yes, Okay. I see. Dr. Solomon was to see me but he had called a few weeks earlier to reschedule my appointment and we did for a few weeks later," Armis indicated.

"Alright, I see, thanks for speaking to me," Granger replied. "Oh, did he happen to mention why he needed to change the appointment?" added Granger.

"He just said a conflict in his schedule," said Armis.

With the conclusion of the conversation, Granger hit another dead end in her investigation.

\*\*\*

"Dr. Stern, it's Granger. Your patient, Yarborough, found her but she died mid-nineties."

"Are you sure?" asked Nathan.

"Certain, got it confirmed," replied Granger. "I'm gonna do some research on her anyway to see what comes up. I'll let you know in a few days. Oh, and Solomon's last appointment, that noon time appointment... didn't turn out to be that patient Giorgio Armis. He was scheduled but Solomon cancelled him out a few weeks earlier. What made you think it was Armis?" asked Granger.

"I'll double check the appointment book, but it did look like Ben had a new client Giorgio Armis on that date at that time. I might have missed something or mistaken something in his book, but what was clear was that Ben had a new patient on his last day around noontime apparently with the initials GA," affirmed Nathan.

"Okay Dr. Stern, I'll see what I can come up with when I speak with the New York police on that issue, but I don't think they have much of anything to share," noted Granger. "We'll be in touch," added Granger.

\*\*\*

The urgency of Nathan's email caught Gerald's attention over the weekend. Gerald's reply suggested that perhaps their conversation should not wait till Monday and the two agreed to meet over breakfast Sunday morning. In the meantime, Nathan gathered together Yarborough's chart, copied and de-identified several documents including Gerald's evaluations and then copied and de-identified a handful of Gerald's psychological assessments while at Metro under the supervision of Dr. Klein. Nathan also gathered some of Yarborough's personal writings as well as the letters that were sent to him. Nathan wanted to be prepared when he met with Gerald with the essential background information at his disposal.

***

Sunday morning in any breakfast establishment around town usually meant a long wait, a noisy atmosphere making conversation difficult and poor service. With this in mind Nathan suggested his home as Eric and Jack would be in Hebrew School at their temple and Joanne would be volunteering with the Women's Club who were actively engaged in a fundraising project.

"Good morning Nate," said Gerald.

"Morning Gerry," replied Nathan. "Come on in."

In all the time that the two knew each other, both probably found it odd that since Nathan's relocation from New York neither he nor Gerald entertained in one another's home. Nathan was very cognizant of that fact as it defined the two as mostly colleagues and as not having a significant friendship or relationship at this point in time.

"How's everything going?" asked Gerald.

"We're doing good. What about your wife and the kids?" replied Nathan.

"Also good. Michael has a high school graduation next year and we are looking at colleges soon and Tiffany is starting her sophomore year at Michigan State," replied Gerald.

Although both Nathan and Gerald completed their training around the same time, Gerald and his wife, Mindy, began their family while Gerald was still in graduate school. With the social pleasantries out of the way and a breakfast of French toast, fruit and coffee, Gerald inquired as to the purpose of the meeting.

"So, Nate what's this about?" asked Gerald.

"Not sure where to begin," replied Nathan, "but let me try." Over the next few minutes, Nathan carefully outlined recent developments starting with the letters he had received at his home and the tie in to Ben's death. Judging from Gerald's initial non-verbal reactions, none of the information shared by Nathan appeared to be familiar to Gerald. It wasn't until Nathan began to discuss Metro Psychiatric Pavilion that Gerald seemed to be more attentive yet fidgety. Nathan continued to link his information which associated Ben's pharmacological treatment protocols, psychological evaluations supervised by Klein and in part conducted by Gerald, and then highlighted the one case of Charlene Yarborough which seemed central to linking everything together.

"But you said she died some time ago," quickly responded Gerald.

"I did but it is confusing and brings up more questions, and I have the police down here looking into everything," noted Nathan.

As Nathan continued to press on, Gerald began to text Mindy and asked about any unusual letters sent to the home over the last year addressed to the two of them. Mindy responded back in a few moments with the text reading: *didn't want to trouble you. we get a lot of junk mail and it looked like some type of chain letter. just threw them away. why?* Gerald texted one more question: *how many?* Mindy responded: *hard to say, a dozen or so maybe. What's up?* Gerald responded back: *with Nate we'll speak later be home in about 2hrs.*

"Stop for a moment Nate," insisted Gerald. "Mindy tells me we got letters sent home as well but she didn't think much of them;

discounted them as junk mail and discarded them."

"The detective working on the case, her name is Granger, will need to know that as well," indicated Nathan. "And I think you should ask for protection for yourself and family."

"Is that really necessary, Nate?" asked Gerald.

"Gerry , I believe it is," replied Nathan. "Now tell me about Metro?" Nathan firmly asked.

"Look Nate, you basically fitted all the pieces together except the motivational part. You wouldn't know but after we all left within the next five years, the Insurance Commissioner in New York combined with Medicare and Medicaid regulators and auditors came to Metro and did a massive investigation on possible insurance fraud.

"I did hear something about all that," noted Nathan.

"You may have, but we were all told not to speak about it, gag orders were issued and Metro lobbied for closed hearings and got the media to back off from any coverage. In the end, it was a big story that got limited exposure," replied Gerald. Gerald continued, "subpoenas were issued and staff were called to deposition including Klein, Ben, myself and a handful of other adjunct staff, nurses and mental health technicians as well as the Medical Director and Board of Trustees. The Attorney General in New York and the DA brought criminal charges up on a few wrongful death actions which were ultimately dropped in lieu of a several physicians as well as Klein resigning and turning over their licenses to practice. Metro was fined several million and many of us who were subsequently licensed were placed on a probationary period due to failure to inform the appropriate agencies of medical negligence, impropriety, waste, and fraud. Klein committed suicide during the peak of the investigation. So yeah, there were probably plenty of patients who probably were quite angry with the care they received or the possible medical and psycho-social consequences from trials and trials of meds, ECT and lengthy hospital stays both on a voluntary as well as involuntary basis. Any one of them could have a gripe."

"What about your reports?" asked Nathan.

"Klein and the hospital board were padding their salaries with all types of kickbacks from the pharmaceutical companies, research protocols, and advancing their personal gain from tens of thousands of insurance dollars. Klein was very clear to his residents that the psychological assessments should emphasize the highest degree of pathology and the need for the longest length of stay in a hospital to allow for the patient to stabilize and recover completely," noted Gerald.

"What if your report didn't conform to Klein's edict?" asked Nathan.

"Well then I was fucked," replied Gerald. "Klein would make me edit and rewrite until the narrative conformed to his liking. The reports eventually were very similar as I'm sure you saw."

"And if you didn't?" inquired Nathan.

"Klein threatened first with poor performance evaluations, then suspension and eventually termination from the program and an unwillingness to sponsor me for licensure. Klein said he would destroy my career before it got started. And Mindy and I were just trying to get settled with the kids in our new home," replied Gerald. "I know I had a choice to make, and I regret making the one I did."

"Okay... so do you remember Charlene Yarborough?" asked Nathan.

"Yeah, I actually do," stated Gerald. "Really a sweet and bright, creative young person until the psychiatric community got a hold of her and from that point on she was probably never the same. Pumping her up with drugs along with countless series of electro-convulsive therapy, over time left her more emotionally crippled than when she started. There was no way she could have cared for an infant child and so later when I was asked to render an opinion regarding her parental capacity, I could only say at that point that she was not competent to perform any parental responsibility even with support. I don't even know if she understood the proceedings at that point."

"What do you think Ben had to do with all of this?" asked Nathan.

"You know, I guess we all wrestle with our conscience, but Ben somehow escaped at the time any legal or ethical consequence. He simply reported that he was following the recommendations from his learned scholars and in the end, Ben I'm sure believed that he was actually helping his patients to stabilize and live a more productive life. Whether he was blinded by his zeal to cure or simply looked the other way, Ben defended his interventions based on the evidence he had at that time," replied Gerald.

"Maybe it all caught up with him…the psychiatric liberties he and the field took back then. We just don't know, maybe he was in a way struggling with all that. But you're still suggesting Ben's death was not a suicide?" asked Gerald.

"The police up in Great Neck very quickly closed the case deeming a self-inflicted wound," a skeptical Nathan said. "Det. Granger is still looking into it and trying to re-open the case but she has been met with much resistance up in New York. And now, it doesn't help that one of our prime suspects, Charlene Yarborough, is no longer living," added Nathan.

"That's definitely true but there could be someone acting on her behalf," offered Gerald. "Any thoughts?" added Gerald.

"Not anything specific, but could be familial or friend," replied Nathan. "The only other lead we have is that a few weeks back when Joanne and I were up in New York attending Ben's funeral, one of our boys was approached by some guy who gave him a condolence card. Jack didn't think much about it but the police are investigating.

Spooked Joanne and I. However, nothing has come up yet."

"This is all very alarming to hear," Gerald said. "Retribution again being doled out after all these years for legal and ethical violations some of us had committed who were complicit in one way or another in providing disgraceful psychiatric and psychological care."

"How did you get caught up in this matter?" asked Gerald.

"I had worked with the patient for about four months as an inpatient and then later saw her for a few visits as an outpatient. The critical thing here is that you consulted me and asked for my opinion and recommendation with regard to parental capacity. My opinion along with Ben's was part of the Court evaluation you performed," Nathan replied.

"I'm sorry Nate that you got pulled into that evaluation," Gerald replied.

"No, I understood then and now, you were just including collateral sources to cover all bases. Most any psychologist when charged by the Court to perform competency evaluations or custody evaluations would do the same," noted Nathan.

As the two parted, Nathan reiterated his concern for Gerald and insisted that Gerald contact Det. Granger as soon as possible and to request protection. Gerald was next heading home to review his morning with Mindy.

***

# CHAPTER 12

John Donnelly, a former NYC Detective from the Midtown North Precinct, worked private detail for some time before retiring with a sizeable pension and a dream to start up a private investigation firm. By the time a young, grieving eighteen year old Veronica Fitz-Morris found him, his store front walk up office on 38<sup>th</sup> and Seventh Avenue, just a few blocks from Madison Square Garden, was one of three offices owned in the greater metropolitan area. Over the next several years, Private Investigative Services would expand its presence across the Hudson to Hoboken, Newark and Fort Lee.

"You've done an incredibly good job," said Ronnie. "Whatever my request you always delivered the information in a timely way and more importantly the material was spot on. Not sure how you obtained the information and I probably don't want to know, but thank you John."

"You're very welcome, I hope everything turned out okay for you," replied John.

"Oh, I think it will," noted Ronnie, as she gave an envelope containing ten thousand dollars to John. "I think this should cover all your fees and expenses up to the present," said Ronnie.

The initial work Mr. Donnelly conducted for Ronnie, a little over ten years earlier, was a fairly simple request to find her biological mother which he was able to do rather quickly only to find that she had died years earlier. Ronnie's next request about a decade later, which was framed with more broader parameters, was to have at a her disposal everything that her private investigator could find about her mother.

Several weeks before Ronnie decided to relocate to Florida, she met with her private eye and over the next several hours followed John's rather complete presentation of Charlene Yarborough, who was born September 16, 1963 and died July 7, 1995. Ronnie recognized the date of July 7, 1995 as being the date for the final proceedings of her adoption.

"So, here is everything I have on your mother," began John. "Your mother, Charlene who was nicknamed Charlie, was born in Harpers Ferry, Iowa, a small town about three hours east of Des Moines. From what I can tell she had an older brother, Janson, who died in a freak incident on a baseball field and a younger sister, Kate, who died a few days after birth. Your mother's mom, your maternal grandmother, Helene, lived in Harpers Ferry her whole life, married your grandfather, Harold, in 1957, who later died in Viet Nam in 1965. After your grandfather's death, Helene struggled terribly both financially and emotionally. When Janson died at age fourteen your grandmother never rebounded from the loss. Your mom was eight when Janson died in 1971. Three years later when your mother was eleven your grandmother committed suicide. Your mother was taken in by a maternal aunt for the next several years, until she was eighteen at which time your mother left Harpers Ferry for the first and last time and traveled to New York via Chicago and Philadelphia. It's not clear how she supported herself but my sources suggested that she performed at local clubs, sang and danced, and wrote ads for local theaters. When she got to New York, she worked retail by day but at night apparently she made her real money by accompanying men of significant stature from the business world around town to Broadway openings, fancy restaurants, gala openings and movie premiers. She was mistress to several men who took care of her, set her up with a prestigious upper east side address and bankrolled her ever expanding life style. By 1985 however, between the drugs and alcohol, she apparently crashed and required substantial care in an attempt to recover. Although she had several abortions, she decided to keep this last pregnancy and delivered you in late 1985 at Roosevelt Hospital. Your biological father was not identified and your mother either never knew or never disclosed who the father was. Shortly after your birth, your mother was diagnosed and treated for postpartum psychosis and anaclitic depression. She was in and out of hospitals, sometimes for weeks but spent the most time on a psych unit at Metro Psychiatric Pavilion. Throughout most of her time in treatment as there were no family or relatives to care for you, you were placed in foster care from a few months old where you remained a product of foster care over the next nine or ten years. Your mother did make several attempts to reclaim you with various legal maneuvers, but the Department of Protective Services had their attorneys and fought harder to maintain your status in foster care. Eventually your mother stopped trying, her rights were terminated and years later you were successfully placed for adoption."

"Before you go on," Ronnie interrupted, "how did she pay for all that treatment and legal work?"

"Good question," replied John. "No records of having any type of private or government insurance and from what I could tell all bills, and I mean everything, paid out by cash. Even back then, the bills were enormous, not hundreds, but many thousands."

"Do you know if she had bankrolled her care by herself or had help?" asked Ronnie.

"Still looking into that aspect of the case," said John.

"What kind of psychiatric treatment did she get for that money?" asked Ronnie.

John continued, "there were very few staff around still to speak to who were actually willing to discuss with me the ins and outs of psychiatric treatment on an inpatient unit. Those that took the time all shared the same impression... long stays, intensive treatment including meds, testing, therapies including individual, group and milieu, and ECT. Your mother was treated for the longest at Metro, spent the most money there and apparently complied with her doctors in the hope of a cure to win you back from the State. We know that she never did and by all accounts the "cure" did more harm than good."

"Outpatient care?" asked Ronnie.

"Yes," replied John. "Continued for the most part with the same psychiatrist over several years, a Doctor Solomon, who treated your mom as an inpatient and in his office in Manhattan."

"Do you know who else treated her?" asked Ronnie.

"It looks like Solomon was primarily it over the long haul, but she saw a psychologist at Metro, a Dr. Stern, and another psychologist, Dr. Zwick, who performed all the assessments recommending treatment at Metro and later conducted your mom's competency evaluations to see if she was fit to be your mom," noted John.

"Are they still practicing?" asked Ronnie.

"All are. Solomon practices mostly in Great Neck, Long Island but still maintains an office in the city. Stern moved a while ago to Florida and Zwick is a Dean of a Florida graduate school in psychology," replied John.

"Okay good. I think I would like to meet them. They all knew my mother, treated her and could tell me about her. Make sure I get their addresses and phone numbers," said Ronnie.

"Will do," John indicated.

"Do you have more?" inquired Ronnie.

"Sure," suggested John.

"What happened when she left the hospital? Where did she go?" asked Ronnie.

"She had her place in the city, but after a while it looks like she moved to Queens to a less desirable address," John noted.

"Do you know why?" asked Ronnie.

"Remember, that city apartment was apparently your moms' as long as she fulfilled her job as mistress. My guess is with all the hospitalizations, medications, and ECT she lost a lot of her marketable qualities and became less desirable. She probably was moved out but still taken care of as part of the original agreement," John suggested.

"Can we find out who that guy was?" asked Ronnie.

"Difficult, but I don't think impossible, I'll need more time," indicated John.

"Did she work ever?" asked Ronnie.

"Odd jobs in clerical... stenographer and typist but all short-lived," noted John. "Lived out the rest of her life in a small apartment in Queens. Bills always paid on time. I spoke to a few neighbors who were around that time... their memories somewhat fading...who recalled your mom as a very quiet person who kept to herself. They couldn't recall visitors. One remembered your mom as being a babysitter as she was always taking care of a young child over the years. The neighbor added however, that the child would be around for a few months and then not seen for a while and then your mother would be taking care of him again. I was told it was the boy who found your mother dead in her apartment in the bath tub with a plastic bag over her head and her wrists slashed. Also, the toxicology report found multiple drugs in her system."

"How old?" asked Ronnie. "Didn't really say," said John, "but I guess around seven or eight."

"Can you look into that some more for me?" asked Ronnie.

"Will do," John said. "Anything else?"

"Any pictures?" asked Ronnie.

"Sorry, none that I found," John said.

"Okay John, thanks again. This was a big help for me. Stay in touch and when you have something new give me a call," Ronnie replied.

\*\*\*

# CHAPTER 13

"Nate, its Mindy…Mindy Zwick, is Gerry still there?"

"No Mindy, I'm sorry, he left a while ago, maybe ninety minutes or so," replied Nathan.

"Oh… Okay, maybe he stopped off to run some errands," Mindy said. "Thanks Nate, let's all try to have dinner out one night, and catch up…just the four of us. Take care Nate."

"Okay you too Mindy," replied Nathan.

***

The tire pressure indicator on the Mercedes touchscreen dashboard alerted Gerald to a grossly underinflated left rear tire which required immediate attention. As he was slowing his vehicle down and looking for a good place to pull over to check out his tire he began to hear the wobble-like sound of a flat tire. Gerald wasn't quite sure how much more he could drive but the upscale community he was riding through was comprised of narrow winding streets mostly bordered by canals on either side with a lush beautifully landscaped hedge of sea grapes intermixed with coconut palm trees. Gerald was looking for a safe enough place on a shoulder to pull over and thought he found one.

"Hi there Mindy, it's Gerry, going to be a while… have a flat… calling road side assistance." Gerald's call went right to Mindy's voice mail. Gerald's next call was to road side assistance to obtain an estimated time to have someone to attend to his flat. Not having to change a tire for some time, Gerald opened his trunk and wondered if he would be up to the task. As Gerald was fiddling around with the spare, a white paneled van pulled up by the side of the Mercedes, brought the passenger window down half way and the driver had asked in a soft voice if Gerald needed some assistance. Before Gerald could complete his sentence that he was waiting on road side assistance, the driver was out of his van and stepped over to the side of Gerald's car and offered to help. Within another moment as Gerald was lifting the spare out of the trunk and bending down placing the tire next to his car he experienced a sudden pulsating jolt of immobilizing energy which was delivered from a Taser sending approximately 50,000 volts of electric current through his body. Twitching briefly for a moment or two, Gerald's body collapsed to the ground and his world next went black.

The driver quickly opened the side panel of his van and within one sweeping movement placed Zwick's body into the van. The driver promptly returned to his van and the entire kidnapping occurred within thirty seconds. As the van pulled away from the stranded Mercedes there were no apparent witnesses to report the incident. With the trunk of the Mercedes still open and Gerald's cell phone on the front passenger seat, it would be only a matter of time before someone would approach the vehicle and call in the stranded, unattended car to the police. It was actually the Road Side Assistance attendant who was at the scene within forty- five minutes who would eventually make the call to the police.

The van drove around for a minute or two before pulling into a shopping center parking lot and from the front drivers section the driver could see that Gerald was still unconscious. The driver straddled slowly into the rear section of the van and began to securely restrain Gerald's hands and legs with zip-ties which were then adjoined together with rope so that Gerald's body when positioned on his side was in a curled up fashion. Gerald's mouth and eyes were duct-taped shut. The driver checked Gerald's pockets for phone, keys, wallet and anything found was placed in a garbage bag.

A few more minutes had passed and Gerald now was beyond the twilight level of consciousness that he had found himself in previously. He was alert enough to know that he was taken while waiting for Road Side Assistance and greeted by his now captor.

"Okay... good you're up and ready for the next step Dr. Zwick," said his captor.

The muffled and muted sounds coming from Gerald were not coherent, however Gerald's captor responded as if he was holding a conversation. "Yes, you were kidnapped for reasons which will be made clear shortly... We've never met but I know of you and your work...and I guess you can call me Li'l G... Okay, I think that's enough sharing for now." A few additional muffled sounds were made by Gerald.

"That's right I know all about you and all your mental health buddies who supposedly know how to treat and help others with sensitivity, compassion and understanding." As each term was verbally emphasized starting with sensitivity, Zwick experienced a sharp stabbing sensation delivered from the steel tip boot of his captor.

"Shortly we will be driving over to your school and I imagine one of these keys will open your building, the lobby and your office. It would be most helpful if you let me know which key in advance, if not I guess I will figure it out somehow. Then we'll get comfortable and being Sunday I don't think anyone will be bothering us. I also figured out the campus security pattern for each building and I think we will be just fine. No need to worry about the police. If they check your office on campus I think they will be gone by the time we get there. Okay Dr. Zwick, we'll have a good talk later. But now we're on the move," indicated Li'l G.

The police began to canvas the immediate area within a half square mile in a grid like fashion which also included both canals to the north and south side of Zwick's vehicle. Within a few hours with no signs of Gerald the lead investigator on the scene, Detective Paulson, temporarily suspended the search within the immediate vicinity. A BOLO was put out by the police using Gerald's physical description and his recent dress and appearance. Mindy had already been contacted as her number and road side assistances' number appeared in Gerald's recent calls directory.

The second principal investigator, Detective Granger, was already sitting with and interviewing Nathan on the disappearance of his colleague. As Nathan was reviewing several pertinent details with Granger, which now included Gerald's involvement with the case, he could clearly sense how quickly the detective escalated her own concern with the matter before her.

"Your wife and children…where are they?" asked Granger.

"They've been here since one," replied Nathan.

"No one leaves the home today," insisted Granger.

Granger also had asked for the morning report from the patrol vehicle which was situated diagonally across the Stern home. Nothing unusual was noted in the report from Patrolman Jackson other than Zwick's black Mercedes coming and going from the Stern home at 9:35 A.M and departing at 11:45 A.M.

"No suspicious activity…no other vehicles pulling up?" asked Granger.

"No nothing," Jackson replied.

"The guy had a flat , a slow leak, something disabled his vehicle. I want to know about that now," demanded Granger.

***

As Zwick's captor was preparing for the drive over to campus, Gerald could hear the movement of containers and equipment being moved around the small quarters of the van. Gerald was unable to see that Li'l G was dressed in painters' overalls and that the outside of the van which he recalled was nondescript was detailed with the name and logo of the university along with the label identifying the vehicle assigned to the Physical Plant Operations Division.

"I don't think I will be needing this again," Gerald heard Li'l G mumble, referring to a pneumatic nail gun which was used to puncture the steel belted tire. With a sharpshooter's acumen, Li'l G was able to maneuver the van behind Gerald's Mercedes, at the first red light, within close enough proximity to fire a few nails toward the rear tire. From that point on it only took a few more minutes for the tire to go flat.

***

Before impounding the car, the forensic team carefully collected any evidence to assist with the investigation. From what Det. Paulson observed, there was very little at the scene to move the investigation any further from this point. Fingerprints would only be Zwick's as his prints would be in the car, on the jack and spare. The soft shoulder where the vehicle was parked had the impression of the spare tire and what appeared to be Zwicks' shoe, hands and knee impressions. Forensics did however take photos from all different perspectives and did bag the spare tire which later would show the cause of tire failure as coming from a two and one-half inch carpenters nail.

\*\*\*

"Mindy, it's Nate, I can't believe this. Any word from the police yet?" asked Nathan.

"No nothing, Nate , what is this all about ?" replied Mindy. "The police told me that you have been given protection for a while, what for?" questioned Mindy.

"Look… those letters Gerald was asking about earlier…," started Nathan.

"Has something to do with this," completed Mindy.

"Yes and may be linked to a former patient from a while ago and Ben Solomon's death," Nathan said.

"How long have you known about this?" asked Mindy.

"Not too long," replied Nathan, who deliberately omitted some information regarding the time line. "Just the other day, I learned that Gerry was somehow involved and may need protection as well from the police," noted Nathan.

"And when were you going to get around letting Gerry and the police know," an angered Mindy replied.

"It happened so quickly…there wasn't time too…," Nathan hesitated.

"What… make sure my husband was going to be safe," added Mindy. "Nothing better happen to him Nathan or I will never forgive you," Mindy said. With that last remark, Mindy abruptly discontinued the call and hung up on Nathan.

Joanne who overheard most of the conversation, as Mindy's near hysterical voice was bellowing over the phone speaker, could do very little to console Nathan who recognized that Mindy had a legitimate complaint over how he was managing the information.

\*\*\*

Li'l G's van approached the open, sprawling university campus without raising any level of suspicion. On any given weekend day, maintenance trucks and vans would be routinely seen around the school as large and small jobs were being completed when classes were out. Li'l G pulled up to the graduate psychology building and parked next to another maintenance van.

"Okay Doc, I need to know which keys open the building, lobby and office?" asked Li'l G. "So I am going to remove the tape from your eyes and you are going to point to the keys," Li'l G suggested. With the tape removed, Gerald saw his captor for the first time. His eyes gradually adjusted to the dim light of the interior of the vehicle. Nervously squinting for a few seconds and then within a minute nervous blinking was replaced by active visual scanning with Gerald focusing in on the details of the van and of his captor. Gerald noted that Li'l G was over six feet tall with a muscular build weighing about 200 lbs. with black short hair. Several tattoos appeared on his forearms and neck with Li'l G inked on the back of each hand. He was wearing overalls and a NY Yankee baseball cap.

"Okay Doc, make this easy and tell me which keys?" Li'l G asked. Gerald shook his head no which upset Li'l G.

"Don't be like that Doc, I don't want to hurt you right now over these keys, but I will if you make me," implied Li'l G. "So which keys open the building?" again asked Li'l G. Gerald again nodded and mumbled the sounds of a resisting no.

"That's not being helpful at all," said Li'l G. "Last chance before I practice with my new toy," as Li'l G was pointing in the direction of his nail gun. Li'l G leaned over and grabbed his nail gun and took aim in the general direction of Gerald's calf. With his index finger on the trigger, Gerald could see that Li'l G was beginning to apply pressure to the trigger and nodded his head in the affirmative and vocalized a sound to convince Li'l G that the information would be given.

"Okay good , so point which key is for the building and which for the lobby and your office," Li'l G asked again. Gerald indicated quickly to each corresponding key and for the moment Li'l G was pleased with the response. "Thank you Dr. Zwick, that's a big help…I hope that's right." Gerald's defeated expression was obvious to Li'l G who then indicated his apologies in advance as they were about ready to move to the building.

"Sorry Doc, I need to subdue you again to transport you and my things to your office," Li'l G indicated. With that said, Li'l G rendered his prisoner powerless with another jolt of electricity from his taser.

Li'l G was able to place Gerald's limp small statured physique in a medium sized industrial drum container which was subsequently wheeled into the building on a cart containing various smaller containers of paint, painters equipment and a tool case. The keys which Gerald identified opened all doors respectively and within a few minutes Li'l G went up the elevator to the second floor and wheeled Gerald into his office. Dusk was approaching and as planned Li'l G had the night ahead to complete his work.

\*\*\*

By the 5 P.M. news hour, all the local channels and some affiliates throughout the state had covered the disappearance of Gerald Zwick. Upon hearing from the police public liaison officer, local authorities were asking for the community's help in coming forward with any and all information that may help in locating Zwick or in identifying those involved in the kidnapping of the Dean and leading to his safe return. Within the next news cycle, Gerald's disappearance would get national attention.

\*\*\*

When Li'l G opened the container he could not have anticipated Zwick's lifeless body appearing before him. As he carried the body to the couch, Li'l G repeatedly was shaking and slapping Gerald's face hoping to get a response. However, there was none. Li'l G listened for a breath and checked for a pulse, but there was none. "Wake up, wake up," Li'l G forcefully yelled a few times. "You're messing this up for me." After no movement or response , Li'l G began mentally reviewing his research on the use of his Taser and the effects that 50,000 volts would have on an adult. *"Only neuromuscular collapse, involuntary movements and temporary loss of consciousness,"* Li'l G recalled. *"Very little evidence for fatal cardiac arrest or stroke in the literature."* Li'l G was unable to anticipate however that Zwick had a pre-existing congenital heart condition which upon being tased for the second encounter in such a short time frame, resulted in a condition called cardiac capture followed by ventricular fibrillation and eventual sudden cardiac death. *"This was not how it was supposed to be,"* Li'l G reflected to himself. *"Zwick now would not be tried in front of me for his crimes. He would not hear the story, hear the evidence or know why he was being sentenced to death."*

With a few hours left before his planned departure from Zwick's office, Li'l G took care to clean up Zwick's body, remove any remnants of tape residue on his face and tidy up his dress and overall appearance. *"Casual but neat, fitting of a Dean visiting his campus office on a Sunday,"* Li'l G amusingly thought. Li'l G's intent all along was to stage a suicide with Zwick personally composing a letter whereby he would acknowledge professional wrongdoings and an inability to continue living with the shame and guilt. Now, with Zwick gone, Li'l G either could compose a letter himself, which Li'l G knew he could easily do, or select a symbol of great significance which Zwick or any professional would value and let that symbol serve as the statement. As Li'l G looked around the room, he noted the plaques of diplomas on the far wall adjacent to a bookcase of volumes of books, journal publications and various reference materials. *Perfect... what better symbolism,* Li'l G thought. Li'l G walked over to his tool case and took out a thickly gauged rope long enough to loop over the lighting fixture which suspended from the twelve foot ceiling. Li'l G quickly made a noose and slipped the rope tightly around Zwick's neck and then temporarily propped Zwick's body on a sturdy oak chair. Li'l G next went over to the bookcase and began to empty out shelf by shelf placing the books and references beneath and around the chair where Zwick sat. Finally, Li'l G removed each diploma from its frame and created a necklace-like design linked together by nylon cord. Before draping the necklace over Zwick's neck, Li'l G took a red marker and placed a large X on the doctorate diploma and wrote across I HAVE FAILED and on the other diploma DISGRACED PHD. Li'l G then began to position Zwick's body in an upward fashion until the body was raised high enough to remain hanging once the seat was removed from his feet. Li'l G without hesitation then kicked out the chair which rested at an angle on top of the books. Zwick's body swung back and forth a few times and then remained motionless. Before leaving the office, Li'l G cleaned up the room attempting to remove any evidence that he was there. He closed the office door having left Zwick's keys and other personal belongings on the desk. Li'l G left quietly through the building with his materials being carted off to the van, which disappeared into the early morning darkness.

***

The Dean's graduate assistant, Alysa, started her Monday morning, especially early arriving around 7:45 A.M. Alysa therefore was first on the scene and while her impressively voluminous scream could have been heard throughout the building, there would be no one in the Psychology Building to alarmingly react. After seeing Dean Zwick hanging there in his office, Alysa ran to her desk and called security. Within a few minutes, campus security had taken Alysa's statement, the building had been secured, and local police and ambulance had arrived. As the academic day was about to begin, the growing campus traffic was being detoured away from the Psychology building, and faculty, staff and students who had business in the building were not given access. Local media, monitoring official police activity, also were soon to arrive on campus and began to set up on the perimeter road to begin their newscast. Nathan who was en route to the campus also got caught up in the traffic and knew intuitively that the police presence suggested that the investigation of Gerald's disappearance had now somehow moved to the University. Nathan also had that hollow, pit in the stomach feeling that something awfully wrong happened to Gerald.

At first, the news about Zwick launched the rumor that following his disappearance, the day earlier, he had travelled to his office where he subsequently committed suicide as he was being investigated by the University for sexual harassment. The group of reporters however quickly disowned the story and indicated that any conjecture of inappropriate behavior was unfounded and unsubstantiated. The news reporters although indicating that Zwick's death was a result from an apparent suicide quickly added to the story and suggested that his disappearance may indicate otherwise and that information would shortly be presented from the police investigating at the scene.

Detective Paulson was joined by his forensics team which began surveying the grounds and entry point to the building. The team slowly progressed to the elevator and up to the second floor and again slowly canvassed the hallway leading to the Dean' s office. Half the team remained investigating the crime scene outside the office and the other half began processing Zwick's office and eventually his body. "Any video from surveillance cameras on campus... I'll need immediately," Paulson indicated.

"Doesn't look like it. The university was in the process of finalizing connections with their monitoring system, but hasn't gone live yet," noted a tech.

"Okay then, gather up any video from the community, from traffic intersections...you know the drill, anything that may be useful," added Paulson.

Upon the medical examiner's arrival, the forensic team was just about finished with processing the scene and taking final photos of the body, which had not been brought down yet. The medical examiner, Dr. Margaret Findley, a twenty year veteran with the department, asked that the crime scene remain intact until her presence. She approached Zwicks' limp body and focused for several minutes on the whole gestalt. As she approached the body, she had raised Zwicks' pant leg on both sides and folded over his socks. She removed her camera and took several photos from different angles. Findley then looked carefully at the hands and again took photos of Zwicks' wrist and fingers. Next, she proceeded to stand on a ladder and gently lifted Zwick's button down shirt and in circular fashion examined his torso and again took several pictures. She went up two more rungs of the ladder and leaned in carefully to note Zwick's neck and head position and again took a few photos. Findley also took note of the length of the rope and the precise drop from the lighting fixture to Zwick's neck. Findley then dismounted from the ladder and asked that the body be brought down and bagged. "Okay, my work is done here, I will finish up at the morgue," Findley indicated to Paulson.

"What do you think?" asked Paulson.

"All preliminary until my autopsy, but I'm fairly certain this was staged and not a suicide. This man probably did not die from asphyxia strangulation," noted Findley.

"How can you tell?" asked Paulson.

"A few things stand out which need to be confirmed but here are some of my initial impressions," commented Findley. "First, the ligature mark did not leave any bruising as there was no venous congestion about the ligature. There also did not appear to be any violent compression of the neck and my guess is that there were no or very few turns or twists of the body which typically would be consistent with someone in the process of hanging. My guess also is that there is no fracture of the larynx and look no tongue protrusion. Finally, look over here on his hands and ankles. There appears to some type of ligature mark as if he was tied up. And look here, not sure what these marks on his torso are but here you have some redness, inflammation and a welt-like mark. This could be from a blunt force object or something like a stun gun. I'll figure that out later when I can match these marks up to the instrument. This guy died from something else and then he was hung to give the appearance of a suicide," Findley said with some certainty. "You'll have my final report in forty-eight hours," Findley added.

"Any idea of the time of his death?" inquired Paulson.

"Recent enough. By the temperature of the body, maybe six to twelve hours," suggested Findley.

Paulson and his team continued to work through the morning into the early afternoon and had advised campus security that the building would not be cleared until around 3 P.M. By mid-day, the media were getting increasingly nervous that they were going to miss another news cycle and began encroaching more on the University's spokesperson to convince the police to release information or at least a statement on the current status of the investigation.

Detective Paulson was not so gently reminded by his superior to get to the podium and brief the media. Paulson although a very seasoned detective was not comfortable with any role interacting with the news people. Paulson readily would admit to his colleagues that he found the media to almost always interfere with an investigation, as the reporters inevitably would position themselves in the role of investigator and in turn would add significant roadblocks to the police investigation. Paulson stepped to the podium and began. "I have a few brief remarks regarding the ongoing investigation of the death of Gerald Zwick, who is, sorry, was the Dean of the School of Psychology here at the University. Dean Zwick was found approximately at 7:45 A.M. this morning by a student employee of the university who promptly called campus security. Given that this is an ongoing investigation, there will be no further details shared at this time," said Paulson.

"How was the Dean found?" the questions began by the local media.

"As I said, he was found by a student employee," replied Paulson.

"What is that students name?" asked another reporter.

"Sorry, I'm not at liberty to release the students name," Paulson said.

"Was he in his office and what condition did he appear in?" asked the same reporter.

"Yes he was in his office. I can't say more about that… so as to preserve the integrity of the investigation," replied Paulson.

"An unnamed source told me that the Dean was found hanging in his office from an apparent suicide, any comment Detective Paulson?" asked another reporter.

"No comment. This is an ongoing investigation pending an autopsy. The medical examiner's report will be released in a day or two. I can't say much more until then," an increasingly frustrated Paulson commented.

"Was there a letter left by Zwick?" asked the reporter.

"No comment," Paulson said.

"There was a rumor that Zwick committed suicide as a result of a pending university inquiry regarding inappropriate sexual conduct between himself and a student. Any truth to that?" inquired another reporter.

"Not aware of any such inquiry," replied Paulson.

"Can you comment about any connection between the Dean's death and another death of a psychiatrist in New York earlier this month?" asked a reporter.

"Where did you hear that?" asked Paulson to the reporter.

"A high level source in the police department investigating the death of Benjamin Solomon, a psychiatrist in New York, who apparently worked at some point with Dean Zwick and another local psychologist on staff here at the University," expanded the reporter.

"I have no knowledge of this connection or any association between the two you mentioned," commented Paulson. "This briefing is over," Paulson emphatically stated as he abruptly left the podium in an agitated state. Paulson was on his phone within a few seconds checking with his office as to who might have been speaking to the media.

"Couldn't say for sure Detective Paulson," the front desk officer said, "but there is another detective who caught a case several months ago which may be related to yours. You should contact Det. Granger. I'll transfer you to her cell. Hold on."

The two detectives, separated by a generation, never worked a case together and would seem as dissimilar to one another as possible. Granger, a second year detective on the force for five years and Paulson, twenty-five years on the force, who earned his detective shield after paying his dues, managed their police work and interactions entirely different.

"This is Bev Granger," as the detective answered her cell phone.

"Granger, this is Paulson...I'm working my case which looks like a homicide at this point..." "Zwick, I know," commented Granger.

"Yeah, exactly," replied Paulson. "What are you doing in the middle of my case and speaking to media."

"No idea what you're talking about," Granger replied firmly but calmly.

"Some reporter indicated speaking to someone on the force who referred to some psychiatrist up in New York and linked the two deaths," griped Paulson.

"Okay... and you think I'm that someone?" asked Granger.

"Yep, you couldn't wait. I've seen you with the reporters talking about transparency and all," Paulson note.

"Again, don't know what you are talking about," Granger commented.

"Okay... so we are done here," Paulson said.

"Not quite," Granger said.

"I don't know who's talking with the media but the two cases are very connected. I've been researching this and getting information from another psychologist, Dr. Nathan Stern, who also worked with Zwick and Solomon a while back. It looks like all three are on this killer's hit list. With Zwick and Solomon gone, Stern remains in grave danger. I've been interviewing him and we're providing round the clock protection for him and the family.

"Sorry Granger, I got carried away," Paulson said apologetically. "So we got one case here. We'll work together. I'll continue with the Zwick homicide. What are you working on?" asked Paulson.

As Granger briefed Paulson on the relevant details, both agreed that Zwick's death should remain as an apparent suicide until the final autopsy report comes out.

"So, I need to speak to your Dr. Stern as soon as possible, probably later today as he was the last one to see Zwick," indicated Paulson.

"That would be a good idea," replied Granger, who provided Paulson with Nathan's telephone contact information and home and office address. "I was heading up to New York tomorrow morning to look into some things about the case and will be back by Thursday," Granger indicated. "And, oh, I'll look into that leak when I get back," Granger added.

"Okay, so we will get together when you come back," Paulson said.

***

With having no access to his campus office, Nathan continued around the University's perimeter road and completed three circles before realizing what he had done. Nathan pulled over and surmised that he likely dissociated on some level and had been in deep thought over Gerald's disappearance and now death. He had heard on a radio news channel that the body of Dean Zwick was found earlier in the morning. His hand grip was so tightly embracing the steering wheel that his hands which now felt cramped appeared locked onto the wheel. As he looked up to the rear view mirror, he could identify his police detail which was within a few yards of his car. Nathan relaxed his hands, took a few deep breaths, and proceeded to make a u- turn and began to travel north to his office, letting Joanne know that he was on his way.

***

Nathan and Joanne revisited the issue earlier in the morning as to whether they could both continue to function professionally with everything that was going on. Neither wanted to suspend their work schedule or movement around the community. Both felt that as long as the police would provide twenty-four hour coverage, at their home and at work, that they could continue close to a normal routine.

Upon arriving to the office, Nathan could see one patrol car stationed outside the office and the one traveling with him was soon to be relieved. Joanne was vocal in asking the police detail to remain outside their office so as not to alarm any patient or potentially intrude upon any privacy issues. However, Det. Granger was unable to agree to that request as the office had two point of entries and Granger wanted one officer , in plain clothes, situated somewhere in the office during hours of operation. Joanne and Nathan understood the safety concern and acquiesced to Grangers' request. Before Joanne's next patient, Nathan and Joanne had a few minutes to talk and reassure each other that they would be okay even though the evidence was mounting to prove otherwise.

\*\*\*

"Dr. Stern, this is Det. Paulson. I'm investigating Dr. Zwick's death and circumstances related and would like to meet with you…I have some questions to ask you. How would later be?" asked Paulson.

"I've told everything to Det. Granger," replied Nathan.

"I know. Det. Granger and I spoke earlier and we are now working on the case together. It will take only a few minutes, I suppose. How about within the hour at your office," Paulson suggested.

"Okay, Det. Paulson , see you shortly," Nathan replied.

Before Nathan and Paulson met, Nathan began to review a few patient charts that were prepared by Myra. Especially on this date, Nathan found it helpful to get his mind off things. When Det. Paulson arrived, Nathan however, appeared distracted and had some trouble focusing on Paulson's questions.

"How long did you know Gerald Zwick?"

"How long…oh… since the 80's…we trained together up north," replied Nathan.

"I see… and how well did you know him?" asked Paulson.

"How well… better back then… but we were colleagues more recently," replied Nathan.

"You worked together at the University?" asked Paulson.

"That's right. I actually just started in August," Nathan replied.

"When you saw him on Sunday, were you visiting with him as a friend or were the two of you discussing university business?" asked Paulson.

"As a concerned friend," Nathan said.

"How do you mean?" asked Paulson.

At which point Nathan reviewed for Paulson the recent history and development of his ongoing situation.

"That's quite a story Doc…so when your friend left on Sunday, did you feel that he was in some type of imminent danger?" asked Paulson.

"Imminent danger," echoed Nathan, who thought to himself, *so the reports of a suicide are not correct.* How the question was asked gave pause to Nathan as he was reminded by Mindy's comment as well and wondered as to how responsible he was for what happened.

"Doctor Stern…," Paulson cued Nathan as a reminder to respond.

"No, if you mean did I believe something would happen as soon as he left my home… no not at all, but I wanted him to be aware of what's been happening and to speak with Det. Granger about it and to get some protection," Nathan replied defensively with some pressure to his speech.

"Okay, Dr. Stern, take it down a little, no one is suggesting that you should have done more," Paulson said.

"Was it suicide?" asked Nathan.

"Did Dr. Zwick talk to you about anything that would make you think that he was depressed or suicidal?" replied Paulson.

"No, never crossed my mind," replied Nathan.

"Did you know about any University investigation looking into a sexual harassment charge between Zwick and a student?" asked Paulson.

"No never heard about that in the month that I have been there," Nathan replied.

"The information you shared on Sunday morning and the discussion you had about his work at Metro Psychiatric Pavilion and those evaluations about that patient…do you believe that could have caused Zwick such emotional distress that he feared he would be exposed…and he took his life instead," suggested Paulson.

"So you are saying it was a suicide?" asked Nathan.

"No, I'm not suggesting that, just exploring all possibilities here," Paulson noted.

"I don't think Gerald would have done that. He just wasn't expecting that after all this time, something like that would come up from his past and that somebody would be looking to retaliate," Nathan replied.

"No I guess not, we just never know what may surface from our past," Paulson noted. "Okay Dr. Stern, thanks for your cooperation. Det. Granger and I will be working on the case together, so if you need anything contact one of us immediately."

\*\*\*

During the interview, Paulson's phone vibrated a number of times with several corresponding voicemail messages. One message had informed Paulson that a white van, a university service vehicle, which was reported as missing from the transportation depot, was located about a mile from campus. Not knowing yet how this information was related to the case, Paulson returned the call and indicated that he was on his way back to campus and asked for part of the forensics team to meet him at the garage.

\*\*\*

The van, which was parked in a mall parking garage, apparently went missing late Friday afternoon. The facilities director had filed a report at that time and noted that the employee operating the vehicle had been disciplined as he had left the keys in the vehicle during one of his service calls.

"Let's catch a break here," Paulson said. "Any video from the garage?"

"Yep, the garage is wired up, we'll have that surveillance video for the last twenty-four hours very shortly," a technician commented.

"Check the van, inside and out, and see what comes up," Paulson indicated. "I want to know who drove that van and whether or not if Zwick was in there," impatiently added Paulson. "He got from his stranded car to the campus somehow and my best guess is that van was involved."

An hour or so later, forensics came up empty. No prints on the door, steering wheel, signals or shift gear. Nothing helpful from a forensics standpoint. "The van was wiped down pretty good and cleaned out. Nothing in the rear. Whoever was in the van, did a really good job," noted the forensics specialist.

"We got lucky with the video surveillance in the garage," added another tech. "Take a look," Tina added as she narrated further. "3:35 A.M...the van pulls in, parks. A few minutes pass, the driver exits the passenger side, hoody on looks like over a baseball cap, about 6 foot, strong, angular build, walks out the south east side of the garage."

"Check for video outside the garage," demanded Paulson. "We need something more."

Within a few more minutes, one of Paulson's forensic techs would disappoint him further with the information that there was no additional video from outside the garage. However, the tech did improve Paulson's disposition when suggesting that the van was caught on video at an intersection half a mile from campus on a traffic signal violation. The video stream which was uploaded to one of the tech's laptops was brought to Paulson.

"Let's take a look," Paulson said. "4:05 P.M. Okay, we have a working hypothesis... kind of time line for that van. Arrived on campus around 4:10-4:15 P.M. and left around 3 A.M. Let's keep looking for any other surveillance data out there... people let's get a face on this guy," added Paulson.

Before leaving the garage, Det. Paulson stepped into the rear of the van and appeared to meditate there for a few moments before scanning the inside of the vehicle. His forensics people were right... *pretty clean, nothing left.* As Paulson was beginning to exit the vehicle, the pen he was holding had slipped through his latex covered finger tips and rolled off to the corner of the inside panel where it rested. Upon retrieving his pen, only the angle at which he was approaching allowed him to see a corner edge of what appeared to be paper nestled into a crevice behind his pen. Paulson gently scraped at the surface, using the point of his pen to excavate the paper out, and then tugged further at the corner at which time he was able to free from its position a business card that was folded over twice. Upon carefully unfolding the card, the name of Gerald Zwick, Ph.D. was embossed on it along with the university name, address and logo.

"Hey, Einsteins," calling over his forensic team. "How did you miss this?" Paulson shouted angrily. "Bag it and check for prints. Zwicks' should be all over it. He was here and he wanted us to know that," added Paulson.

\*\*\*

# CHAPTER 14

Nathan's schedule for the afternoon was unfortunately beginning to open up as a few patient's had either cancelled or rescheduled their appointments. The time afforded to Nathan was not however welcomed as Nathan was hoping to remain busy with his clinical work to draw his attention away from today's dreadful circumstances. "Myra, please no interruptions over the next hour. I'm going to rest my eyes for a while," noted Nathan.

"You got it Dr. Stern," said Myra.

As hard as Nathan tried to rest and free himself from all the weight of the day's residue, he could not relax. Ironically, from an intervention standpoint, although not being a fervent advocate of cognitive-behavioral therapy, Nathan attempted to employ breathing exercises along with progressive muscle relaxation as well as mindfulness exercises to unwind . Floating around within his consciousness were intrusive thoughts about Ben and Gerald, Charlene Yarborough, the letters, his work at Metro, his kids and Joanne. Mixed between those thoughts were also recent conversations he had with Granger and Paulson. The hour flew by for Nathan with no apparent gain from his respite.

"Dr. Stern, your next patient is waiting," indicated Myra who first had knocked on Nathan's office door and then opened the door slightly.

"Okay. Thanks Myra," replied Nathan. Myra then reminded Nathan that she would be leaving for the day shortly.

Nathan's 4 P.M. session was with Justin who had returned following his last session with news that he had indeed discussed his sexual orientation with his parents.

"Dr. Stern, you were right about sitting down with my parents and talking with them. It went better than I expected," stated Justin.

"We always anticipate the worse in conversations like that," replied Nathan. "So, tell me how did you decide to bring it up?" asked Nathan.

"My mom, I think kind of knew already. She said she was happy for me that I wanted to share that part of my life with them. My dad though at first said nothing and just looked down at his phone and then all of a sudden he looked up, stood up, and gave me a great big hug," Justin noted. "Never said a word though until the next day and then expressed that he is one hundred percent with me but recognized that it would be very difficult on the field should I come out in school. My dad said he'll be with me every step of the way, but just make sure that I wanted to take that next step with my coach and teammates. He talked about how police officers are not quite there in coming out and how players in the NFL and NBA are just first disclosing their sexual orientation, but high school is very different. In the end he said he didn't want me to get hurt."

"Surprised by your dad's reaction?" asked Nathan.

"Very much so. I figured I would get the silent treatment forever, but I'm glad to see that didn't happen," replied Justin. "Now what?"

"Well, you continue to discuss things with your parents and develop the emotional infra-structure you need in and out of family, and then get a game plan together for your team," suggested Nathan.

"Sounds good," replied Justin."Can I ask you something Dr. Stern?" asked Justin.

"Sure, what is it?" replied Nathan.

"So why is there a police vehicle out front and who is the cop in the waiting room?" asked Justin.

"Well that's an interesting question, Justin. How do you know he is a cop?" asked Nathan, buying just a little time. The last thing Nathan wanted to do was to impose his issue onto any of his patients, thereby burdening them with any outside distractions. "After all he's not in uniform," Nathan added.

"Oh, give me a break, I live with one. You just know," replied Justin. "And, I think I've seen him on the job with my dad," added Justin.

"Well this is an interesting dilemma. You're probably thinking that he is a patient of mine or my wife's… and if so, you then know I have to take a further step to protect his privacy. But by doing so and saying nothing more, you will leave thinking he is indeed a patient. When in fact, he's not a patient here. He's just waiting out front to speak to me about some events in the community, not professionally, definitely not a patient," commented Nathan.

"Okay great, if that's your story," Justin smiled. "See you next time Dr. Stern."

As Nathan peeked out into the waiting room and greeted his next patient, he also glimpsed over in the direction of the officer and passively noted that Justin was right as he did look like a cop. Nathan's next hour was a new patient, Emanuel Alvarez. Over the last week, Nathan had temporarily relinquished some of his practice responsibilities and had asked Myra to begin calling new patients and arranging their initial appointment. Nathan wasn't totally pleased with this arrangement but it was necessary to make some concessions as he was feeling overwhelmed. Myra who became pretty skilled as an intake coordinator had scheduled several new patients for Nathan over the next two weeks, with Mr. Alvarez being the first. Emanuel Alvarez, who was recently discharged from a local psychiatric inpatient unit following thoughts of suicide, arrived to Nathan's office seeking a second opinion regarding treatment.

Emanuel, fifty-six and married with four children, recently confronted significant financial hardship and was forced to sell his business and list his home for sale before the bank initiated foreclosure proceedings. Emanuel appeared to be a proud man of Brazilian culture who travelled to the states ten years ago bringing his import-export business to Florida.

"Thank you for seeing me Dr. Stern," Emanuel started the conversation. "Dr. Johan from the hospital wanted me to start some medication for depression and sleep, but honestly I don't want the pills. I think therapy would be enough," Emanuel expressed in his heavy accent. Nathan began his standard intake interview which included discussing with Emanuel any language and communication concerns he may have.

"How is it speaking with me?" Nathan asked.

"It's fine," replied Emanuel.

"Okay, that's good, but at some point if you think you would feel more comfortable with speaking to a bilingual therapist who speaks Spanish, I could make the referral," Nathan said respectfully.

"No that won't be necessary. Actually, I don't speak Spanish, but Portuguese," Emanuel clarified.

"Oh, Okay, sorry….," Nathan said.

"No problem, common mistake made," suggested Emanuel. "So tell me what's been going on and what led up to your hospitalization?" asked Nathan.

Over the next forty-five minutes, Nathan learned most everything he needed to know about Emanuel. Most importantly, Emanuel convincingly denied the presence of any self-harm plan. Nathan listened as Emanuel detailed his family history including high achieving, well-educated parents who expected nothing less from their children, especially the eldest. Bridged by perfectionistic traits and obsessive-compulsive features, Emanuel's personality coupled with his intelligence and creativity propelled him further toward a successful career. His makeup however, made him feel more vulnerable when suffering any type of personal or business failure. Upon visiting with his primary care physician and relating some of his circumstances, Emanuel's doctor likely misunderstood his English and confused a statement or two with suicidal intent and subsequently committed him to an inpatient unit.

"How long were you in the hospital for?" asked Nathan.

"I was in for three days before I was able to convince the staff that I wasn't about suicide," replied Emanuel. "Still the psychiatrist wanted me to start an anti-depressant, Celexa, and Restoril, for sleep."

"What are your concerns about the medication?" asked Nathan.

"I've seen too many people depend on their pills and lose track of their own personal responsibility in addressing things that need to be fixed in their life," replied Emanuel. "Anyway, in our country, psychotherapy and especially psychoanalysis is simply the way of life," added Emanuel.

"So you are interested mostly in therapy. But what if I am of the opinion that you should consider medication," Nathan stated.

"Well, then I guess I will listen to see why that is so important to my treatment," noted Emanuel.

As the hour concluded, Nathan and Emanuel agreed to meet again in a few days and continue their conversation. Nathan's final hour was with Ronnie who had called earlier in the day and spoke to Myra to see if she could come in sooner than Wednesday's appointment. Myra, sensing some urgency, scheduled Ronnie into one of the hour slots that had opened up from the morning. Upon greeting Ronnie in the waiting room, Nathan could sense her upset.

"Thank you for seeing me early and squeezing me in this afternoon, I just couldn't wait till Wednesday," voiced Ronnie.

"Come on in," replied Nathan, as Ronnie walked briskly to the office. "Were you on campus too this morning?" asked Ronnie excitedly even before sitting down in her usual chair.

"I was but couldn't get to my office," Nathan noted.

"Yeah, that Dean was from your school, wasn't he?" Ronnie indicated.

"What were you doing on campus today?" Nathan curiously asked.

"Well, I would have had that interview, but like the whole campus was in lock down mode so I couldn't get over to Human Resources," Ronnie said.

What was it like for you to be there today?" asked Nathan.

"I think anyone would have been nervous and worried about their safety," replied Ronnie.

"That's probably true, but I was asking what it was like for you Ronnie," Nathan firmly asked again.

"For me…I was mad that it interfered in my job interview. I wasn't worried… so many police there. They looked in control," Ronnie noted. "You know I think I was going to meet with him this week if things went well with HR. My job was going to be in the Dean's office," Ronnie added. "Did you know the Dean, Dr. Stern?"

"I did, he'll be missed by the school," Nathan replied.

"By the school I'm sure, but what about by you?" Ronnie inquired in a curiously odd exchange of questions.

There was something about the way Ronnie had phrased the question that had provoked Nathan into a deeper level of thought and emotion. Nathan suddenly became aware of his growing irritation with his patient's response style and of her interest in his reaction to the loss of a colleague. It was however, not only Nathan's initial countertransference toward his patient which concerned him. Nathan also was overpowered with a simultaneous growing curiosity coupled with an uncomfortable feeling over a certain degree of familiarity with the content of Ronnie's life story that eventually provoked Nathan into an analysis over the flood of information he recently had come into contact with. Nathan certainly did not want to respond in a defensive tone and thus, reflected and paused, and then shifted the conversation appropriately away from himself, while mulling over mentally the layered information delivered by his patient and the information in his possession about Charlene Yarborough.

*...given up early to protective services in NYC... a mother with a history of psychiatric disturbance... placed for adoption... ... birth mother dead...too many coincidences...is it possible that I'm sitting across from the biological child of Charlene Yarborough, a patient I treated nearly thirty years ago...too many similarities...come on, how many kids are given up each year by troubled parents who lose their parental rights and then do away with themselves...if Ronnie is the child then she is the one behind all of this and I am sitting across from her...maybe there is some other logical explanation...how do I approach this with her as she is still my patient and here for help... how do I keep safe in this situation...*

Nathan continued the session after a few moments of silence. "I appreciate your concern, but let's focus more on yourself...," Nathan replied. "Were you feeling anything more than anger when your interview had to be rescheduled?" asked Nathan.

"Why do you ask that?" replied Ronnie.

"Well there could be a range of feelings you might have directly experienced given some of your history," Nathan said.

"A range of feelings….what are you a mind reader?" commented Ronnie. "Well it was like this…as I was approaching the campus I saw all these police cars speed by me and then saw the blockade and the police presence around the campus and especially around the buildings. I think I kind of froze up for a moment or two and flashed back to the day of 911."

"That would make sense," Nathan noted. "Go ahead and continue, where did your mind race to?"

"I was in Manhattan walking to school, a few minutes from the World Trade Center. My parents already at work in the Towers. Of course no one knew what was happening, but the sounds, the pillars of smoke, the hysteria. I knew I was safe, but somehow instinctively knew that my parents would not be. Chalk it up to my history but I knew I was going to be all alone again. I thought about my mother and not having a family again. I thought about all those years in foster care," described Ronnie.

"I can see how today's events could have triggered your flashback," Nathan noted.. "It's interesting though when something pretty big occurs like 911 or this morning on campus, you very quickly focus on the immediate impact on yourself and not on the impact on others," Nathan suggested.

"You must think I'm very selfish and only thinking about myself. But that's who I have become…just trying to survive on my own," Ronnie replied.

"I understand that. It's a coping strategy, a survivor tool," noted Nathan.

"Ronnie, can I ask why you needed today's session with me?" asked Nathan.

"Everything was coming apart and I needed a place, a safe place to go, and I thought of you," replied Ronnie.

"I'm glad you think of this as a safe enough place to bring your thoughts and feelings to," noted Nathan. "Ronnie, do you think of me as someone that can assist and help you?" asked Nathan.

"I do. I know we only recently met, but I see that you are a good person and would be there for me," Ronnie said.

All throughout the discussion, Nathan was attempting to size up if his patient presented as a potentially dangerous individual, but he wasn't getting that sense from sitting across from Ronnie. In fact, Nathan was better appreciating Ronnie's need for security and her fear of abandonment. Nathan opined that if Ronnie could tolerate the therapeutic environment, he felt somehow reassured that she would not be seen as a threat. "Can you maybe tell me something more about your mother now?" asked Nathan.

"I think I told you mostly everything that I heard from the private eye," Ronnie replied.

"You may have told me most everything from what you learned, but very little about any feelings you have about never knowing your mom," Nathan noted.

"What do you want me to say…it feels empty," Ronnie quickly replied.

"Is that what you are feeling?" asked Nathan.

"Yes. I'm feeling horribly empty… not knowing about her, not feeling her touch, not knowing her likes and dislikes, her favorite color, her favorite movie, restaurant… you know there is no one I know that can tell me about her…I don't know my father, I have no older brothers or sisters, living grandparents, uncles or aunts to provide the context to her life," Ronnie indicated.

"I understand that. You're right, it's like you need someone to be a historian for you, to chronicle your mother's life or at least parts of her life," suggested Nathan. Nathan was maneuvering through the interview rather intuitively without realizing how close he was to the truth about Ronnie Fitz-Morris.

"So Ronnie, I want to ask again why are you here to see me? Why did you find me of all the psychotherapists out there?" asked Nathan in a firm and inquisitive way.

"I thought I covered that before," replied Ronnie.

"You did, but I don't think that was the full story," Nathan commented. Nathan was now very much aware that he was crossing the therapeutic boundary in attempting to confirm his hypothesis that Ronnie's choice of psychologist was not based on a referral but upon her interest to meet someone that knew her mother in a professional sense. Someone, in effect, that had treated her mother and that could share with her what her mother was like. Nathan knew he was taking a risk here, as potentially he could be inaccurate in aligning the information and lose a patient or possibly open himself up to some type of complaint to the Department of Quality Assurance or to expose himself to a possible malpractice suit.

"I don't understand," replied Ronnie.

"Oh, I think you do and I'm sorry to take this tone with you, but I'm simply trying to clarify what you are doing here," Nathan said.

"You don't understand, don't be angry with me, don't send me away… you're the only one left to talk to," implored Ronnie.

"I'm the only one left to talk to? What do you mean?" asked Nathan.

At this point, Ronnie was shaking and crying and the words from her mouth were barely audible and coherent.

"Take your time, take some breaths and calm yourself; try grounding yourself…feel the floor beneath your feet, look around see where you are, feel the texture of the chair you are sitting in, feel your back as it presses against the cushion," Nathan directed calmly and confidently.

As Ronnie became better organized, she sighed and stated, "Okay,

I'm okay, just give me a minute, Dr. Stern, just let me sit here, don't send me out or call anyone in."

"I won't. I promise. Take as much time as you need," Nathan replied. Ronnie took a few more minutes of trying to collect herself emotionally and then began. "I wanted to speak to Dr. Solomon, but first he had no appointments and then he was gone. I read about his suicide in the paper," Ronnie noted. "I never got the chance to ask him…"

"Tell me why you were trying to see Dr. Solomon?" asked Nathan, still attempting to confirm his hypothesis with the last few pieces of the puzzle to make the picture complete.

"He would have known for sure," Ronnie softly replied.

"He would have known what for sure?" asked Nathan.

"He would have had some answers about my mother," Ronnie replied.

"Why would that be?" asked Nathan as he continued to test what he already knew intuitively.

"You see…Dr. Solomon was the first to treat my mother, he would have known her and could have told me about her," replied Ronnie.

"I think you're right, he would have been able to answer some of your questions," Nathan said.

"How do you know that?" Ronnie asked in a coy like fashion.

"Oh, I think you know the answer already," Nathan replied. "Just like you knew that you needed to meet with Dr. Zwick as he too would have been able to talk to you about your mother. Isn't that correct, Ronnie?" Nathan added.

"That's right, and now he's gone too and you're the only one left to talk with to make some sense of all this for me," affirmed Ronnie.

"That's a pretty tall order as I'm trying to make sense of all this too," Nathan started to respond with his own anxiety level increasing.

"It would seem as you have been on a fact finding mission to become better acquainted with who your birth mother was, and, the very people you have been trying to connect with have become unavailable due to their untimely demise. And now you are sitting before me which frankly is very troublesome."

"Are you afraid of me, Dr. Stern?" asked Ronnie.

"I'm not sure, should I be?" replied Nathan.

"Do you want me to leave, because I can get up right now and march out of here," Ronnie said.

"That would concern me as well," suggested Nathan.

Nathan and Ronnie sat for a minute or two in silence. Nathan also became aware that the session was running way over, but with no next patient scheduled he was willing to spend as much time needed in an attempt to better understand Ronnie's circumstances, and his own situation and vulnerability. Nathan did suggest to Ronnie that he needed to step out for a moment to let his next patient know that he was running late. Ronnie however did not need to know that Nathan was simply referring to the plainclothes police officer sitting in the waiting room. "Sorry, I'm running late. Please wait a few more minutes," Nathan commented.

As Nathan returned to his office he could see that Ronnie was pacing back and forth. "Okay Ronnie, have a seat, we have a few more minutes now," Nathan noted. "Now let me understand this better. You wanted to meet face to face with Dr. Solomon, Dr. Zwick and now myself, and explain to us that you are the daughter of Charlene Yarborough and that you wanted to spend some time asking questions about your mother. And this was a way you thought would bring some peace to you and that you finally would get some closure," Nathan indicated.

"Yes that's right," replied Ronnie.

"Were you at all concerned when you heard about Dr. Solomon

or today about Dr. Zwick?" asked Nathan.

"Only in that I missed the opportunity to speak to them both," related Ronnie.

"Okay, there's that self-involvement tactic you routinely use," noted Nathan. "Do you worry that the police may want to interview you as it is just a little suspicious that both Solomon and Zwick are dead and that both were people you wanted to meet with. You can easily see how you can become a person of interest to talk to," Nathan noted.

"Why, both committed suicide didn't they?" asked Ronnie.

"That may be the case, but the police are investigating both deaths and you may have some information to help further the investigation," Nathan replied.

"How do you mean?" asked Ronnie.

"Well I'm not quite sure now, but here you were searching and locating a few providers who were involved in treating your mother and both providers are now dead and the third provider is sitting with you right now," reviewed Nathan. "I understand that you were simply trying to learn more about your birth mother, but the police, sometimes they don't think like that and might think that you had a personal vendetta against these doctors and had something to do with their deaths. Who knows why but it would be in the realm of possibility, don't you think?" Nathan concluded.

"Preposterous that anyone would think that...," Ronnie confusingly replied.

"Maybe so, but I think the police would be interested in your story," Nathan indicated.

"Or maybe not, they don't know about me and you can't say anything. Everything I talk about is privileged and confidential. Right?" asked Ronnie.

"That's correct, unless it becomes my ethical obligation under the duty to warn statutes that allows me to breach privilege and report a clear and immediate probability of physical harm and or danger to a patient or to others or to society," Nathan described.

"Well, that's not happening here. You're not seeing me as a danger, are you Dr. Stern?" asked Ronnie.

"No, I don't think so. But remember how I said I want you to think about how others are doing or feeling... well you might want to think about that a little bit and see why it may be important to speak with the police," suggested Nathan.

"Because of your safety, right?" Ronnie said.

"That's right. So I am going to encourage and strongly recommend that you speak to the police. I have the name of two detectives who would be interested in speaking to you," said Nathan. Nathan proceeded to jot down Det. Paulson and Granger's names and numbers and had circled Granger as the best contact.

"I don't know...I will have to think about this," Ronnie indicated.

"Okay, but try not to think about it too long," Nathan replied as he was trying to manage his own level of anxiety and fear. "Ronnie, we are going to end now but when you come back on Wednesday, I will try to respond to some of your questions about your birth mother. Keep in mind, I only have some limited first-hand knowledge about your mother but whatever I have I certainly will share with you if it brings some comfort and closure for you," Nathan indicated.

***

"Everything okay?" Kevin Myers, the plainclothes officer asked as Nathan was finishing up and preparing to go home for the day.

Nathan hesitated for a moment, but then used his best clinical judgment to protect Ronnie's privacy and simply indicated "Yes, all considering, we're good."

"That's good…so I'm going to follow you home at which point I will be relieved by the night detail," Myers noted.

Upon returning home, Nathan picked up the mail and there appeared one more letter similarly addressed to Nathan and Joanne. Nathan's fatigue from the day no doubt had influenced his critical judgment, which perhaps on another day, would have allowed him to take further caution and allow the police to first process the letter. However, on this early evening, within a moment, Nathan had ripped open the envelope and began to read the prose.

Once upon a time, the three Musketeers

surrounded by their mentors, considered healing their

small world.

Once upon a time, the three Musketeers

surrounded by their books, considered studying their

small world.

Once upon a time, the three Musketeers

surrounded by their tests, considered evaluating their

small world.

One down, two down, one to go, oh my, how can

this Musketeer prove himself a worthy foe.

Should the sun not rise, will the world be cold

and desolate.

**Cold... Cold... Cold... Desolate... Desolate... Desolate**

When I wake , who will keep me warm,

who will keep me safe and away from danger,

who will me mine to hold.

Like all the others, the content of the letter now provoked Nathan into deeper thought as to the particular meaning given the events over recent weeks. Later, Nathan placed the letter in a plastic zip lock and walked the package over to his security detail to forward to Det. Granger.

\*\*\*

# CHAPTER 15

The medical examiner's final report completed by Dr. Findley was due out any moment. Det. Paulson was anxiously awaiting Findley's report as he fully expected the autopsy to confirm that the case he was working was determined to be homicide. Findley, a physician and trained forensic pathologist, had a reputation of being meticulous to the point of being obsessive during her medical review. Within the county and across the state, Findley had the least amount of challenges in Court in an attempt to overturn or discredit her determinations.

"Okay, here it is," Paulson said out loud to himself as he began to read only the summary section of the report:

> Cause of death is conclusively consistent with sudden cardiac death due to a progression from cardiac capture to ventricular fibrillation. It should be noted that based on this examiner's autopsy, the deceased had a history of aortic stenosis, with apparent aggressive use of beta blockers, which would have required cardiac catheterization in the very near future to preserve adequate cardiac functioning. Based upon my examination, Gerald

Zwick had already expired prior to any attempts at staging a suicide via asphyxia strangulation. The ligature marks are post mortem. There were only superficial abrasive bruises about the ligature. There was no venous congestion about the ligature . There was no violent compression of the neck, although the neck did show evidence of a slight elongation due to the simple process of hanging over a several hour period. It would also appear based upon my study, that the deceased was tased at least once if not three times as two welts appear on or beneath the surface of the skin. The taser, exact voltage unknown but believed to be in excess of a standard charge from a commercial taser product, was not only strong enough to render the deceased at least immobile from a neuromuscular standpoint, if not temporarily unconscious, but also impacting his cardiac functioning and predisposed cardiac history. Although not typical, there is only anecdotal evidence in the literature to suggest the possibility of sudden cardiac death secondary to an episode of being tased. Also noted were the use of restraints placed securely around the hands and ankles, which were subsequently removed. Further noted was the presence of some adhesive residue very likely from the underside of tape which was placed over the victim's eyes and mouth. The use of a taser and restraints would clearly suggest that the deceased was rendered at least temporarily incapable of defending himself, likely transported from one venue to another venue and then left in the positional state in which the deceased was subsequently found. There were no defensive wounds which suggests no struggle and there was no DNA material under the victim's fingernails. The victim's hands and fingers were somewhat soiled with dirt and ground residue which was consistent with the crime scene by the victim's vehicle as he was in the process of perhaps changing a tire. I am ruling this as a homicide with a time of death somewhere between 5 P.M. and 7 P.M. this past Sunday.

Detective Paulson, nodding multiple times in agreement as he was scanning the report, was pleased to see that the medical examiner's report lined up very well to his own investigation. Paulson was quick to email a copy to Granger as he wanted to comply with her request for total cooperation and transparency in sharing of information. Paulson was now awaiting any further evidence gathered from his forensics team from the three crime scenes to see if Zwick's kidnapper and murderer left anything behind at the car, the university, or in the garage to assist in the investigation. He would be speaking with Granger later in the day who was in New York proceeding with her end of the investigation.

***

Det. Granger, with her chief's approval, had informed the Great Neck police department of her interest to again speak with the detective and officers involved in their preliminary investigation with regard to the death of Benjamin Solomon earlier in the month. Upon her arrival to New York, Granger rented a mid-size car which was within her departments' budget, and took the forty minute drive from LaGuardia to Great Neck. On her way east to the Island, Granger took note of an exit on the Long Island Expressway which she would take to travel to Yarborough's last known address.

As Det. Granger entered the Great Neck P.D., the desk sergeant directed her upstairs to the second floor where Det. Munson would be waiting. Munson, who was more like a peer to Paulson given their ages, waved Granger over to his desk station in a less than enthusiastic greeting.

"Okay, let's make this quick, I have little time to process a closed case," Munson commented in a hoarse voice.

"Hello to you too," Granger stated. "The case may be closed to you, but down by us, we have a very open case which has today been deemed a homicide and we have an interesting association which has developed between three mental health professionals, two of which are now dead. We're trying to move fast on this to avoid a third death," Granger replied. "If you can free up some of your valuable time, I need to see what you have on the Solomon death, the medical examiner's report, any photos, items secured from the home…everything you have, and then I would like to go head out to Solomon's home to take a look," Granger indicated.

"Okay, give me a moment," Munson replied. Munson stepped away from his desk and retrieved a box labeled with Benjamin Solomon's name, file number and date of death. "Here is everything you should need," Munson said. "When you called the other day, I figured you would need all this," added Munson.

"Is that it? There's not much here," Granger commented.

"Yeah, not much of a case. Investigated as a suicide and signed off by the medical examiner. The family wanted an expedited processing of the body so as to inter the body soon after the death based on religious custom," Munson stated.

And the autopsy report?" asked Granger.

"It's in there. Single gunshot to the head, his prints on the firearm," Munson said.

"Was it his gun?" asked Granger.

"No, not registered to him or to family. Appeared to be unregistered, not quite sure how it came into Solomon's possession," replied Munson.

"Don't you think that's strange," noted Granger. "Is that still being investigated?" asked Granger.

"No I don't think so," noted Munson. "Look, lots of people have guns which are not registered. Maybe he wanted it for protection, maybe he took it away from one of his suicidal patients, or maybe he got it sometime after his wife died and knew that he couldn't go on and turned it on himself," Munson opined.

"Possibly, but I'm asking because our murder down in Florida of the psychologist was staged to appear as a suicide, but our medical examiner did her job and the forensic evidence and pathology report said otherwise. I'm only saying that you may have another staged suicide up here and your forensics team and medical examiner might have been too quick to rule the death a suicide. Now that we have a possible connection with the case you may want to take a second look at the information," suggested Granger.

"Look, it's not my case anymore but I will send it over to the chief to see if he wants to reassign and reopen the case. That's the best I can do now," Munson replied.

"I think I'm ready to go to the house," Granger noted.

"Okay then. Let's go. Solomon's house is a few minutes from here," Munson replied.

When Munson and Granger arrived to the house, they were met by a neighbor, Judy, who was looking after the home. Granger wasn't clear if she would be meeting family but Judy explained that Ben's children were currently residing with an Uncle who lived further out on the Island.

"I haven't been in the house since the shiva call," Judy said, as she waited in the foyer as the detectives walked through the house to Ben's office.

"Can I see the photos of the office taken by your forensics team?" asked Granger. Granger carefully glanced over the photos and then scanned the room, as if she was re-enacting the scene. As she walked slowly around Solomon's desk and chair and then looped around to the arrangement of sofa, arm chair and recliner, she turned about and noticed something strangely out of place. Granger took another look at one of the photos and then approached a wall which held all of the doctor's diploma plaques and certificates. Again, Granger held the photo up to the wall and compared it to the hanging plaques.

"Look at this, Solomon's diplomas are hanging very precariously upside down and his medical school diploma is missing," noted Granger.

"Look here and here in the photo and see on the wall," Granger directed Munson.

"Mother of Mary...how did they miss that," Munson commented referring to the forensics team.

"The diplomas hanging that way and the medical school diploma missing is very interesting as the killer in our crime scene got involved with the doctor's diplomas as well. I don't think any were missing but I will need to double check," Granger noted. "Can you check with the family to see if anyone grabbed Solomon's medical school diploma?" added Granger. Granger wrapped up this part of her investigation pleased with her finding which now was beginning to convince Munson to look further into the case as a possible homicide.

On the ride back to the precinct, Granger looked over the autopsy report which indeed declared Solomon's death as a suicide. As she read on however, Granger compared a few comments to Findley's report which she now had in her inbox on her cell phone. Granger noted that the medical examiner for Solomon's autopsy referred to slight abrasive marks on the wrists and ankles which were noted to be apparently preexisting. The examiner also referred to unidentified residue around the victims mouth and lips which were perhaps associated to lip balm. *How did she miss that...restraints and tape,*

Granger thought. However, the next sentence which commented about burn marks or welts on the torso, also noted as preexisting, convinced her that the medical examiner was grossly incompetent. *Welts from a taser* , Granger again silently thought.

"Munson, I think your medical examiner took some liberties and short cuts with his work and concluded prematurely that Solomon's death was a matter of suicide. Maybe he had a lot on his plate that week," expressed Granger. "But he certainly took the expedient route or he is just plain incompetent," added Granger.

In his defense, he was looking at a single case here and had nothing to compare his findings to, like you are," Munson replied.

"If this is not enough to open up the case again, I don't know what is," implored Granger.

Munson tacitly agreed and indicated that he will coordinate on this end. Before Granger left Munson's office, she sent off an email to Paulson to discuss Solomon's autopsy and then to inquire if any of Zwick's diplomas were missing. Paulson emailed back within seconds: *Interesting autopsy, ME must be incompetent. I'll check on the diplomas.*

"I'll get you that information on Solomon's medical school diploma asap," Munson noted. Munson and Granger parted with both having a little more respect for one another.

***

Granger's ride back from Great Neck to Bayside to find Charlene Yarborough's old neighborhood was an approximate ten minute drive. She found the street address on Cloverdale Blvd and pulled up to a group of townhomes in which Yarborough's building address would be found. Granger's city driving was a bit rusty as she was out of her element when it came to parallel parking a car. As she angled and maneuvered her vehicle into the spot she was momentarily distracted by a ping which alerted her to an email. Having parked the car she then checked her email. Paulson's email responding back to Granger's inquiry regarding the diplomas read: *Still checking into this. Comparing photos of Zwick's body and the diplomas hanging from his neck and any other diplomas or certificates in the office. Asking around his department, his receptionist, other faculty and checking with Stern as well. Will get back when I have an answer.*

As Granger walked toward the cluster of townhomes she was hopeful to find someone during that time period who remembered Yarborough. Granger approached the exact address and not finding anyone home began to canvass the other units. As she proceeded systematically, and rang the last doorbell, an elderly woman easily in her eighties and perhaps nineties opened her door and through the outer-door screened in section she greeted Granger. Granger took out her badge, identified herself as a detective from Florida, and explained that she is trying to find anyone in the neighborhood who may have known Charlene Yarborough.

"I'm sorry but I can't be of any help," replied Ann Margolis. "I moved into the area after that time," she added. After a pause, Margolis continued. "However, you may want to speak to the previous renters who lived here during that time," Margolis noted.

"Oh, okay. Thank you very much," replied Granger. As Granger began to step back from the door, she had asked without much confidence, "Mrs. Margolis…you wouldn't happen to know where they moved to?" Mostly expecting a reply that they both were deceased, Granger was relieved to hear that she was only half correct.

"Well after her husband died, Mary took a smaller unit and became a snowbird between here and down where you are. You may be in luck. I think she is still up here. She usually leaves in mid-October before the weather cools down," Mrs. Margolis explained at which point she directed Granger across the street to Mary Franco's townhouse.

"Thank you so much Mrs. Margolis," Granger said politely.

"Oh, that was no bother, I told the same thing to that other nice detective a few months ago," Margolis noted.

"Another detective?" Granger inquired. "He was asking for similar information about Charlene Yarborough?"

"Oh yes, he too spoke to me and a few others. I sent him across the street as well, I think I still have his business card. Wait here for a minute," Margolis suggested. "Here it is, you can have it if you like." Granger looked down at the card and read: *John Donnelly Private Investigative Services* "I would like to hold onto this if you don't mind," replied Granger and again thanked Mrs. Margolis.

"Sure you can keep it. I have another. I think Donnelly came back again and left another card for me to get in contact with him," noted Mrs. Margolis.

"Did you speak to him again?" asked Granger.

"I was planning to, but forgot about it . All these questions about Charlene. What's this about after all these years?" asked Margolis.

"Can't say for sure, but it's part of an ongoing investigation," commented Granger. "Thank you for your help and time," Granger added. Granger proceeded to walk across the street hoping to find Mrs. Franco home and available to speak with. Granger who was now on the front porch and about ready to ring the doorbell, heard a voice from the side of the house.

"Can I help you with something?" the fragile and soft voice asked.

"Yes, I'm looking for Mrs. Franco," replied Granger.

"Well you found her. I'm Mary Franco," as the voice and tone got stronger. Granger could see that Franco was in one hand holding her cell phone and in the other a small pruning shear. Sensing Franco's apprehensiveness, Granger quickly introduced herself and showed her badge.

"Thank you for showing me that, I was about to call 911. Isn't that funny," commented Mrs. Franco. "Let's sit here," directing Granger to a small seating arrangement on the front porch. Would you like something to drink?" asked Franco.

"That would be nice, thank you," Granger said.

Franco returned with a pitcher of iced tea, two glasses and a plate of vanilla wafers. As Granger explained her visit, Mrs. Franco confirmed as Margolis did that a private investigator was inquiring about Charlene. However, Mrs. Franco indicated that she chose not to speak with Mr. Donnelly. "I don't talk to P.I.'s…budding into other peoples' business," added Franco. "He called a few more times but I never called back."

"Do you remember Charlene Yarborough?" asked Granger.

"Of course I do, she would be difficult to forget," Franco noted. "I was her next door neighbor for quite a while. She moved from the city to here. These were rental apartments back then. The community back then was changing in so many ways, but mostly this community was going from a rental community to ownership. The management was remodeling everything and some stayed and others moved. I moved to this unit a few weeks before she died. I remember her telling me that she had nowhere else to go. Those that stayed had to put down a sizeable down payment and get qualified for a mortgage and she didn't have that kind of money. She told me that she and her son would have nowhere to live and would end up on the street. The day she killed herself was the day she was going to be evicted."

"Thanks for telling me about the neighborhood's history," replied Granger. "Can I ask a few more questions?" inquired Granger.

"Sure, at my age I love to reminisce, although this memory is very sad to talk about," Franco noted.

"You said she had a son. I wasn't aware of that," commented Granger.

"He was a cute little boy when they moved here... let me see... probably about two. His given name was Victorio but I called him Victor," Franco noted.

"What was Charlene like?" asked Granger.

"She really kept to herself for the most part. Didn't come out much. Didn't socialize much," Franco noted.

"Did she work?" Granger inquired.

"I don't think so. If she did she didn't keep a job for very long," replied Franco.

"Did she have any relationships?" asked Granger.

"For all the time she lived here I only remember one man who stopped by once a month, I think to pay the rent," Franco noted.

"Boyfriend?" asked Granger.

"You know he was much older, but maybe a boyfriend, but more like when a man keeps a mistress," noted Franco.

"Occasionally, I saw him with the boy," added Franco.

"Father of the boy?" asked Granger.

"Maybe, but again he was so much older than Charlene, but maybe," replied Franco.

"What do you remember of the boy?" asked Granger.

"Oh, well like I said the boy was really cute when I first met him. Victor though changed over the next few years, I think mostly because of his mom's health. She was in and out of hospitals over the years for depression and you can imagine when a mother is not available either physically, or there for her son emotionally, that the child will suffer dearly. You could see it on his face and know it by his behavior. He became sullen and angry. When Charlene was hospitalized or just not herself, Victor would be taken and placed in foster care and when I would see him next he always seemed so much older and more bitter. Never really got along with the other kids in the area. Occasionally, Charlene would ask if I would tutor him in reading and math because he fell so behind in school. She knew I was a teacher and she would drop him off a few times a week for about an hour or so. She couldn't pay much but wanted to give Victor a chance in school. He was so far behind and I think he had some type of learning disability, that the little time I had with him wasn't going to make a huge difference," related Franco.

"Where did the child go after his mother died?" asked Granger.

"Well he was around ten at that point and I think he was placed again in foster care but then I heard he was being looked after by that man who may have adopted him," Franco replied. "All their things were boxed up and shipped over to an address by the Whitestone Bridge," Franco added.

"Thank you Mrs. Franco, you have been a big help," Granger indicated. "By any chance did you ever get to know the name of Charlene's male friend?" asked Granger.

"No, I'm sorry I don't think I ever heard Charlene mention his name," replied Mrs. Franco.

"Okay, no problem. And just one other thing... you wouldn't happen to remember the name of the moving company?" inquired Granger.

"Oh sure I do. It was the same company that moved me across the street. A bunch of local guys... Five Guys Moving and Storage. Charlene asked for the name a few weeks before she committed suicide," replied Mrs. Franco.

"You've been a big help," Granger noted appreciatively. "Thank you for talking with me," Granger added. Bev Granger didn't become the astute detective at such an early stage of her career without asking the right questions, following her intuition, and then following up on any potential leads. As she walked away from Mrs. Franco's home she already knew that she could track down the name of Charlene's male friend through the property management company, if records were retained over such a long period of time, and that she could contact the moving company and see if their invoice statements were retained which would reveal the address to where Charlene's possessions were delivered to. Granger also knew that she had an outside shot with the Department of Children and Family Services to locate Victor and his adoptive family. That is, if the Department's records were not sealed and protected.

On her way out of the complex of townhomes, Det. Granger stopped off at the Cloverdale Property Managers' Office and inquired about any records and documents retained, such as leases and rental agreements during the time that Charlene Yarborough rented her apartment.

"I don't think I can release that kind of information," said Megan, the office manager. "Who did you say you were with... what police department...don't you need like a subpoena?" Megan questioned. "I told the same thing to that private eye a few weeks ago... he too was snooping around for some information," added Megan.

"This is very different than that private eye. This is official police business of an ongoing investigation of someone's murder... and I guess I can get a subpoena but it's really not necessary as it involves information from over a decade or two ago... you know statute of limitations and all," Granger replied as she distorted the truth somewhat.

"Oh yeah , that sounds right, the limitations," Megan agreed. "Anyway, all that information has been archived and it will take several hours to locate and we are closing up for the day. What was the tenants name and apartment number and for what year?" Megan asked. Granger gave Megan the necessary information and thanked her for her time. "Give me your cell number and I will call you tomorrow," Megan suggested.

"Okay that sounds good," Granger said, as she now realized she needed to make arrangements to stay at least another day in New York. Granger's next day already seemed pretty full as she anticipated tracking down the moving company to locate the address in Whitestone, speaking with the private investigator, John Donnelly, and, waiting on a return call from Megan.

\*\*\*

With the medical examiner's report signed off by Findley, Det. Paulson now had his team in place to continue to move forward on all aspects of the homicide case. Paulson again sifted through the evidence collected which was now arranged on a large display board in time line fashion across crime scenes with a partial image of the alleged perpetrator's photo affixed squarely in the center of the arrangement.

"Let's get an ID on this guy and find him," Paulson commanded his team with a degree of forcefulness in his tone. Later in the day, Paulson was heading back to the University campus to revisit Zwick's office with the intent to follow up on Granger's question if anything was taken from the scene, specific to academic diplomas. Paulson requested several of Zwick's colleagues and support staff, including Dr. Stern to join him.

\*\*\*

For the small group which gathered outside of Zwick's office, this would be their first time back to their place of work since the gruesome discovery of his body. "Thank you for coming on such short notice," Paulson commented. Paulson unsealed the crime scene tape from the door and permitted entry to the group of five. "I would like everyone to take a look around and see if anything in particular is missing. Dr. Stern please come with me for a moment," directed Paulson. "Dr. Stern you may be in the best position to help out here as I am trying to determine if any of Zwick's diplomas might be missing. So I know this can be upsetting to you, but I need for you to look at a photo of the Dean when he was found and identify each diploma in the photo."

Paulson slowly took out the photograph from a folder as Nathan prepared himself before he viewed the picture, but in actuality no amount of preparation would have been sufficient. Nathan, at first staring beyond the photo, eventually focused and noted several diplomas were placed around his friend's neck and then identified each for Paulson as requested.

"It looks like all his diplomas are accounted for," Nathan noted as he identified the doctoral diploma, masters' diploma, undergraduate diploma, and internship certificate . Nathan then proceeded over to the wall where Gerald had placed his diplomas and noted that in the batch of discarded diploma frames, he had counted five but only four diplomas were identified. As Nathan pointed this out to Paulson, Nathan blurted out, "residency certificate is missing for the fifth frame".

"What is that Dr. Stern?" asked Paulson.

"His certificate of completion from his post-doctoral training at Metro is missing," replied Nathan.

"Is that one of some significance?" asked Paulson.

"Well certainly, it's one further recognition of a higher level of specialty and its relevant to the case as both myself and Gerald completed our training there along with Solomon," Nathan added..

"Why do you think the killer would want that?" Nathan asked.

"I think he's collecting gifts or trophies along the way," Paulson noted. "He also left with Solomon's medical school diploma," added Paulson.

With Paulson obtaining the information he was looking for, he escorted everyone out of Zwicks' office and again sealed off the door with the crime scene tape. Paulson emailed Granger shortly after leaving the campus to inform her that the working hypothesis was indeed correct as a certificate from Zwick's office was taken by the killer. *Perp collecting trophies, you were right,* the email read. Later that night, Granger's hunch was further substantiated when Munson left her a voice mail to confirm that the family had no knowledge as to what may have happened to Solomon's medical school diploma.

***

Granger who spent the night at an airport hotel started her day with a call to John Donnelly who after hearing about the nature of the call, reluctantly agreed to meet with Granger mid-morning in his Manhattan office. In the meantime, Granger got back onto the LIE and traveled a few minutes to Forest Hills to meet up with the owner of the Five Guys Moving and Storage Company. After explaining her request, Sal, a husky, bearded individual in his thirties explained that the business is a family owned company over a generation or two, and that he only in the last few years got his company modernized with computers and electronic billing systems. As such, Granger was not optimistic that Sal could be of assistance.

"However, before I re-vamped our way of doing things," Sal began, "I catalogued all our business transactions by year and boxed everything away. So perhaps, I might be of some help here if you can tell me roughly the month, year and name of the customer," Sal indicated.

"June or July 1995 and the name was Yarborough...Charlene Yarborough," replied Granger.

"If you want to join me in our storage facility I could use the extra hand," Sal suggested. Sal escorted Granger outside the office and proceeded to walk around the corner to a larger facility which housed the company's trucks, moving equipment and what appeared to be storage cartons of unclaimed and damaged furniture. "Over here," Sal directed Granger. Sal opened up another door which revealed a closet full of wall to wall boxes. "It should be in here," Sal suggested. Granger could not help to notice how meticulously arranged the storage closet was which in many ways appeared to resemble how a moving truck is loaded with all the containers and storage cartons placed in an organized system.

"More recent invoices would be up front but we're going back quite some time," Sal noted, "so we are going to have some shuffling around to do. I can't believe I kept all this paperwork around," added Sal.

Sal located the storage box for the year that Granger was looking for and carried the box out and rested it on a desk. Granger began to flip through month by month the various work orders and invoices until she came to June and July. Granger carefully filed through the next several invoices until she found Charlene Yarborough's invoice, dated 7/6/95, one day before she died.. Granger further noted her signature and that the invoice was stamped cash payment in full with the inventoried furnishings shipped to an address in Whitestone, New York. "It looks like you found what you came for," Sal stated.

"I certainly did," replied Granger. "Just one question…is the invoice date the same as the shipment date?" asked Granger.

"That's correct," Sal replied. "On a local shipment like this one, the company would have invoiced, been paid and delivered all on the same date," added Sal.

"Okay, great. Thanks Sal for meeting with me," Granger indicated. "By the way, how far am I from Whitestone?" Granger asked.

"This time of day not too bad, maybe twenty minutes or so. Let me print out the local directions for you," Sal suggested.

"Thanks. That will be a big help," Granger replied. Granger took the directions but didn't think she had the time to first travel to Whitestone and then make her 11 A.M. meeting with the private eye.

***

Once declared a homicide, Det. Paulson had been coming under stronger pressure from his command to solve the case and find the individual responsible for Zwick's murder. The command post was also receiving significant pressure from the University President who too wanted the homicide cleared as the school was getting unusually negative media coverage since Zwick's death. Paulson's forensic team had been spending hours and hours combing over all the evidence a second and third time in the hope that something new may come up to help move the case along.

"Detective, come on over to my cubicle," one of the lab techs called out to Paulson. "So we have this video from the garage and here we have this guy in the hoody and we really can't make out his face, but when I slow it down a little, we can see that the sleeves from his sweat jacket are rolled up slightly above the hands... and let me stop it. Right here, we get a pretty good look at his hands which appear to have some writing on the back of both hands, some type of tattoo. I took the image and have a photo of just the hands now magnified 150 percent. Take a look. We got some initials...looks like LG, can't make out the rest but we are working on the resolution."

"Okay, that's good. Let me know when you have the rest," noted Paulson.

***

Granger's drive into the city went better than expected as she followed Sal's traffic advice to take the Mid-Town Tunnel right into Manhattan as she was told that traffic after 10 A.M. always appeared lighter through the tunnel than on the 59th Street- Queensboro Bridge. Finding a parking spot though proved incredibly frustrating for Granger who eventually pulled into a garage off of 7th Ave and 31st and then paid an obscene amount for an hour or two. Before meeting with Donnelly, Granger knew that the history between private investigators and the police department had not always been very favorable. Of course for Granger, compounding the history was another elder colleague set in their ways and reminiscent of a failed relationship with her own father, a police officer himself who retired within the last two years, who always questioned and criticized his daughter's decision to become a cop and then a detective.

"Detective Granger, come on in," Connelly greeted and motioned her into his office. "Like I said on the phone, I'm not sure how I can be of some help given that I'm not at liberty to talk about any investigation without my client's consent," Connelly stated.

"Well I might suggest after we talk that you may want to speak with your client to inform your client that he or she may be involved in a larger investigation that involves two murders. And while you are advising your client you may want to retain an attorney for yourself because your name has come up once or twice in my investigation as well," Granger replied.

Granger then proceeded to review how she came by Connelly's name as part of her investigation. Connelly appeared to be very attentive and interested in how the two covered the same ground out by the Cloverdale townhomes. However, Connelly admired that Granger learned so much more on her visit and could see that the detective in earnest was attempting to solve a double murder.

"Look, is there a way for you to tell me what the nature of your investigation is about?" asked Granger.

Connelly reflected for a moment and thought he can discuss the scope of his work without bringing the client into the conversation.

"It's mostly a family matter," Connelly vaguely replied.

"Okay good that's a little helpful. So it's a family matter involving Charlene Yarborough," Granger indicated.

"That's correct," replied Connelly.

"Is it about Charlene's son?" asked Granger.

"Her son!" echoed Connelly. "I'm not aware of another child until you just mentioned it," added Connelly.

"Another child. I didn't mention anything about another child," replied Granger. "Charlene had two kids?" Granger asked surprisingly.

"Look, I don't think we should talk anymore," Connelly stated.

Granger knew that she was now approaching the abrupt ending of this nearly one sided conversation with Connelly. "What do you know about Yarborough's past psychiatric treatment and her doctors... Solomon, Zwick and Stern, and you do realize two of those docs are now dead?" Granger emphasized.

"I don't know anything about this. We are done here," Connelly indicated.

"I can see that," replied Granger. Granger knew that she could petition the Court for a motion to compel Connelly to disclose information. However, being out of her jurisdiction and not wanting to play that legal card at this time, Granger declined any further inquiry.

"Well then you go get with your client and give your client my name and number so that we can talk real soon. The longer your client puts off speaking with me, the more your client becomes my main person of interest in this case to interview," Granger noted as she placed two of her business cards on Connelly's desk. On her way to get her car, Granger took a call from Megan, from Cloverdale Property Management, who was responding back to her inquiry. Granger listened as Megan indicated that the initial lease and all subsequent renewals were signed by Yarborough and each month's rent, including any deposit and security payments, were without exception paid in cash. Granger had asked again if any of the lease agreements were perhaps countersigned by another party, but again Megan indicated that this was not the case.

Granger's ride out of the city was fraught with more traffic with a lane closure and construction through the tunnel. As Granger came out of the tunnel on the Queens side she checked her rear view mirror and noted the skyline of the city behind her and realized that Connelly had much more to share but that she would have to wait a little longer to appreciate the content of his material.

***

"Det. Paulson," the technician said as she brought over several photos. "This is the best it will get," referring to the photo from the garage. "After I magnified and inverted the image, take a look."

Paulson held the photo and tilted it first left and then right and then brought it closer to his face. Paulson was now able to clearly see not only the initials LG tattooed on the back side of the right and left hand but now with better definition was able to see L'il G. Paulson first spelled out and then pronounced "L'il G." "What's that a gang name or nick name?" asked Paulson. "Let's run this photo up to Sophia, our information specialist, and have her scan it into the various data bases to see if we get any hits or matches in terms of identification."

Within minutes Paulson got an email back from Sophia who offered several interesting variations to the L'il G search but no real assistance in identifying their guy in the photo: *Sorry those tattoos do not come up in any criminal identification search but loads of hits in social media.* Sophia went on: *First consider the original comic strip L'il Abner who was actually tall and muscular, so maybe a play on words your perp is using. Maybe more relevant, the urban dictionary refers to lil'G as a little gangster or criminal. Also, Rap artists, like Lil Wayne and King LIL G have become overnight celebrities in the music world and there is an R&B artist Gary "Lil G" Jenkins. Also there is a Lil G's Cajun restaurant in Belle Chasse, Louisiana, if you care to know. Hope some of this helps in your investigation, Sophia.*

Paulson nodded his head and had a perplexed look as he was unable to clearly tie the arrangement of letters to anything specific to the case as of yet. Paulson reflected to himself...*what is this guy a comic strip reader, a huge rap fan or a gang banger who likes spicy food.* Paulson decided to let his team work on the initials symbolism through the day to see what they would come up with. Paulson also decided to email the photo along with Sophia's research to Granger with the subject line reading: *Help, maybe you can decipher better than I can.* Also Paulson asked Granger how her investigation up there was going.

Granger's email response arrived to Paulson's inbox within a few minutes: *Will look at the photo later. Interviewed one of Yarborough's neighbors with some leads to follow and met up with a PI who was hired to do a background on Charlene Yarborough. Not sure why yet. Wouldn't give the client up but I think I rattled him enough to reach out to his client to come forward. Check back with you soon, Bev Granger.*

***

# CHAPTER 16

Attending two funerals, occurring within a months' time, would be somewhat unexpected for anyone to experience. Two funerals of colleagues within a months' time would also be most improbable, and statistically the only explanation to be found would lie in an association between both. Though, this is what Nathan was confronting now as he again reached for his black suit in his closet.

"Are you certain Mindy would want you in attendance?" Joanne questioned believing she already knew the answer.

"I'm really not sure, but how could I not go the Gerald's funeral," replied Nathan. "Are you about ready to go?" Nathan asked Joanne.

"In a minute," Joanne replied as she was mostly attending to give support and comfort to her husband, as her relationship with Gerald and Mindy never really launched into a substantial friendship after the early years of sharing time together.

The two drove first separately to the office as Joanne was planning to return to the office after the service. The drive over to the chapel was about an hour ride south to Miami and then east across the intracoastal waterway. Nathan and Joanne remained rather quiet with their conversation consisting of several mundane family events as they were deliberately trying to avoid any discussion about the circumstances which have preoccupied all of their time. The Port of Miami, with none of the large cruise liners in on this date, appeared to mirror the void both Nathan and Joanne were experiencing. Periodically, Nathan looked toward his rear view mirror to see if the security detail were following close behind.

Upon entering the Miami Beach chapel off of Alton Road, Nathan and Joanne were directed to the guest book so as to recognize their attendance as well as to convey a written condolence message. Both were next ushered toward the vestibule which served as a sitting room for the Zwick family who were receiving their guests' prayers and condolences. As Nathan approached he could now see Mindy sandwiched between her two children who were trying their best to comfort her.

"I'm very sorry for your loss," Nathan expressed in the direction of Mindy, but both Nathan and Joanne could tell by her demeanor that she was not planning to accept their condolences at this point in time.

"You could have done much more to have prevented this Nathan," Mindy commented with a controlled angry tone about her as Nathan and Joanne passed by. You should leave now," Mindy suggested.

Nathan and Joanne however chose to move on with the other mourners toward the sanctuary where the service was about to begin. Both sat toward the back with several other faculty members, staff and students who were in attendance. At this point, Nathan knew that he and Joanne would only remain for the chapel service and would not make the trip to the cemetery where Gerald would have a graveside service before he was interred.

"What was that about?" asked Priscilla Hickman, who as executive administrator worked pretty close with Gerald.

"You know…Mindy is naturally overwhelmed with grief and she

knows I was the last one to see Gerald," Nathan replied attempting his best to avoid any further explanation.

"Did you hear anything more about his death?" inquired Priscilla.

"No, not really. The police have been talking to me to get some more background information, but honestly there's not much more I can say," replied Nathan again deliberately being vague.

"That was so weird the other day....stepping into his office and looking for things out of place or missing. I think you were right about the missing certificate. I used to admire all his plaques hung up on the wall so proudly showcasing his achievements," noted Priscilla.

As the service continued, several family members, including Gerald's daughter and son, brother, and sister, and the most tenured professor of the graduate psychology program, eulogized Gerald with very moving and kind words. Under different circumstances, Nathan realized that he too would have been asked to share his thoughts and feelings about his colleague. Anyone in the room cognizant of their relationship probably was very confused over the noticeable absence of Nathan's eulogy. As the service ended, Nathan and Joanne inconspicuously left before others gathered outside in their cars to line up for the processional to the cemetery.

"Well, that was overall incredibly unpleasant and awkward as funerals go," Nathan expressed to Joanne.

"Considering everything, we probably should have not attended and just sent a sympathy card," Joanne replied.

"I know in retrospect you are right, but I'm not sure now how to grieve Gerald's loss, which is complicated by my own guilt and questioning of my own behavior," noted Nathan.

"Give it some time and you will find the right path to mourn the loss," Joanne said supportively.

The two drove generally in the direction of their home, with the same relative silence as the drive over, however Joanne wanted to be dropped off at the office before Nathan went toward the campus.

*\*\*\**

Joanne was surprised that she had to open up the office as that was a responsibility typically performed by Myra at the start of each day. *That's unlike Myra not to be here*, Joanne voiced out loud. However, when Joanne turned on her cell phone, which was powered down before the funeral had started, she saw Myra's email and heard her voice mail message that she had some car trouble in the morning and in all likelihood would either be in very late or not at all. Joanne then looked over her appointment book of scheduled patients and got ready for her first patient.

*\*\*\**

Returning to the campus, after the building was cleared by the police and approved by the University to reopen for classes, was very unsettling for all. Gerald's position was to be temporarily filled by the Associate Dean for Academic Affairs until a suitable candidate could be found. Some of the more senior and tenured faculty were likely to consider the position, but given all the University and department politics, most insiders knew well enough to pass on this opportunity. Nathan was of the opinion that another outsider, like himself, would be a fresh start with a new outlook for the program.

With Nathan back on campus, some faculty and staff, who were somewhat tuned in to Nathan's relationship with the Dean, had approached Nathan to offer their sympathy, concern and support. Most however had inquired uncomfortably about the circumstances of Gerald's death seemingly aware that somehow Nathan may have been more plugged into knowing somewhat more than the average person in the building. In general, Nathan was appreciative of their concern but in the end voiced that he was feeling overwhelmed by it all and was trying to limit the amount of conversation over the next few days. This approach seemed to work for the most part as concerned parties or curious and intrusive individuals eventually got the message.

As Nathan's day continued, one of his responsibilities as Director of Training was to meet with students who were cited for various ethical, legal or compliance issues related to patient services. Waiting outside his office was a very anxious third year student, Timothy Kubic, who was referred by one of his practicum supervisors for late and potentially altered documentation regarding one of his therapy cases who attempted suicide over the past month. Fortunately, the suicide attempt was not completed and the patient was involuntarily committed under the Baker Act to a local psychiatric facility. Timothy entered the office and sat across the desk as Nathan reviewed the chart.

"Timothy, can you tell me about the case and then be more specific about the last session when you conducted your risk assessment and what you may have initially documented," Nathan requested.

Timothy then proceeded to discuss the patient as well as the patient's report of suicidal ideation. Timothy noted that he unfortunately did not completely evaluate if the patient was a danger to herself and now realized he should have called in a licensed supervisor to assist with the assessment. Timothy explained that he had failed to do so and simply documented that the patient expressed passive thoughts of suicide which were fairly typical for the patient to discuss during session. After learning about the suicide attempt and subsequent hospitalization, Timothy noted that he went back to the chart, removed the initial documentation of the session and completed a second progress note which described conducting a full risk assessment during the session in which Timothy noted that the patient convincingly denied the presence of any thoughts of self-harm and that the patient did not meet the criteria for involuntary hospitalization nor was a recommendation for voluntary hospitalization seen as necessary.

"Timothy," Nathan began, "I hope you can appreciate the gravity of the situation that you find yourself in and that you have placed our training program in."

"Yes, I do Dr. Stern," replied Timothy.

"On multiple dimensions, involving falsifying documentation, destroying documentation, negligent professional conduct, professional incompetence, and failure to take appropriate steps to protect a patient, you have exposed us all to potential litigation, fraud charges, audits, and regulatory agencies coming in and making our lives very difficult," Nathan noted.

"Yes sir, I understand Dr. Stern," Timothy replied.

"And as far as you go, we will continue to conduct an internal review of both your academic and practicum standing to see if you can continue with our program. As for now, I am suspending your clinical privileges here with us until further notice," added Nathan.

Nathan was trying to be as constrained emotionally and as objective as he could be given some of the egregious behaviors he recently learned of that occurred with his colleagues during his own training period. As Timothy was leaving the office, Nathan reflected on what it was like to be a student in clinical training and how overwhelming the whole experience can be. Everything under scrutiny, under a microscope, supervisor evaluations, looking within and questioning yourself. Sometimes that overwhelming feeling once in a while could lead to a breakdown in how someone may problem solve a situation. Nathan knew though that students learn so much about themselves and in their interactions with their patients, that the whole experience will eventually result in professional growth and maturity. Nathan already learned from years of experience that mental health professionals can play a significant role in an individual's life and can have a huge impact on a person hopefully in a positive way. What Timothy did not have a perspective on yet was how certain errors in judgment or certain clinical decisions or even things a clinician may say to their patient or write about their patient, in an effort to help, can later cause grave harm and result in a catastrophic outcome.

At this point, Nathan realized he was becoming consumed by several negative thoughts, attitudes and beliefs, some rational and accurate but others mostly irrational and distorted. The events from earlier in the day certainly was a force impacting Nathan in a dramatic fashion which convinced him to take a break. Nathan cleared his schedule on campus for the rest of the afternoon and decided to get a bite to eat at a favorite restaurant before traveling back to his office.

***

Nathan's afternoon appointments with Marla Phillips and Natalie Klingel, who initially were two patients on a short list of possible individuals to have sent the letters, went by uneventful. Both appeared to be in a stable place with regard to any borderline phenomena being acted on, and at least for this week, seemed well aligned to working on their therapeutic goals and maintained positive energy in working with their therapist. Nathan's last appointment of the day with Ronnie, which was much anticipated, was scheduled for 6 P.M. During a brief conversation with Ronnie a day earlier, she seemed to still be on the fence as to what to do regarding speaking with the police. Ronnie suggested that she needed a little more time and would discuss this during her next session. With each day,

Nathan's growing impatience over Ronnie's hesitance to reach out to the police was quite alarming. Nathan knew that he would likely be speaking with either Det. Paulson or Granger over the next day, and was constantly deliberating and agonizing over breaching privilege to share his information about Ronnie to assist in any way with the investigation.

Upon Ronnie's entry to the waiting room, she waited only a minute before coming into Nathan's office. "So who's the guy always out there?" Ronnie asked. "He's not finishing up a session with you or waiting to see you, and, I think your wife is already gone for the day when I see you," Ronnie added.

"Given the situation, he's here to provide protection in the office if necessary," replied Nathan.

"Does he know about me?" asked Ronnie.

"No, of course not, but he could put you in touch with the two detectives working the case," Nathan noted.

"Well... we'll see about that," Ronnie stated. "If I decide to speak to them, will you like be my advocate and make sure nothing goes wrong?" Ronnie asked.

"I don't think I can represent you like that. However, you may want to look into retaining a lawyer to protect your interests," Nathan suggested.

"That's a good idea, but if I sign a release allowing you to speak with the detective, then you could, right?" Ronnie asked.

"Technically and ethically yes, but I'm not sure if that's such a good idea," Nathan responded, "but let me think that through," Nathan added.

Nathan recognized that stepping into that arrangement would be quite unorthodox for a psychologist, but in the matter of time and interest, especially his own interest, he was weighing the pros and cons to doing just that and subsequently acquiesced to Ronnie's plea.

"At the end of our session, if you still would need me to, I will have you meet the officer outside or we will call the detective and discuss the matter further. But, I would still highly recommend that you seek out legal counsel to cover yourself," Nathan noted. "If that's agreeable, let's move on a bit with your session," Nathan added.

As Ronnie began the next segment of her session, Nathan could tell that she somehow transformed herself into a more childlike state with her posture, language and mannerisms. "Can I ask you anything about my mother?" questioned Ronnie, as she sat curled up in her chair.

"I suppose so, although I may not have all the answers you are seeking, but I will try," noted Nathan, who prior to Ronnie's session had reviewed Ben's psychiatric admission note, treatment notes and discharge summary as well as outpatient notes of Ben's contact with Ronnie's mother. Nathan also again reviewed Gerald's evaluations of her mother as well reviewing some of his own therapy notes which were part of the original hospital record kept in Ben's possession. Nathan wanted everything fresh in his head when he met with Ronnie. "Okay, so when did you first meet my mother?" asked Ronnie.

"I think it was probably the first week of her hospitalization at Metro Psychiatric Pavilion. I was training there along with Dr. Solomon and Dr. Zwick. It was 1986. Your mother came to our facility a few months after giving birth to you," Nathan replied.

"Did you ever see me?" asked Ronnie.

"No. By the time your mother was hospitalized I think Protective Services had already removed you from her custody and placed you into foster care," Nathan replied.

"What was she like?" asked Ronnie.

"You know it was a long time ago...I don't think any of us really got to know what she was truly like given the severity of her condition. I think her psychiatric status quite drastically masked her real self and genuine personality. No one got to know her and I think she probably didn't even recognize herself," Nathan suggested.

"What was she being treated for?" asked Ronnie.

"Keep in mind psychiatric care was different back then and things that we may diagnose or treat now would be different than how they were managed back then. But I think she was being treated for post-partum depression possibly with psychotic symptoms and borderline personality disorder. And then there were the street drugs. She was in a terrible way," noted Nathan.

"Did you see her for therapy?" asked Ronnie.

"I did over several sessions to help her figure things out," Nathan replied, "but in the end I don't think she was either ready for the help or stable enough to be receiving therapy," Nathan suggested.

"Was she there voluntarily or involuntarily?" asked Ronnie.

"I think over a few hospital periods she was at times committed and at others times voluntary. I remember participating in one of her involuntary commitment procedures with Dr. Solomon," Nathan indicated.

"Did she get better?" Ronnie asked.

"Ups and downs, sometimes she looked like she was becoming stable but then would spiral emotionally out of control. Dr. Solomon I think was trying his best to treat her with a range of medications and she also had a few trials of ECT. Sadly, I don't think any of his efforts worked beyond a few weeks, a month at best," Nathan replied.

"Did you see her after her hospitalization?" Ronnie inquired.

"Once or twice for an interview regarding child custody issues," Nathan commented. "At that time I saw her at her worst and she was in no place to take care of you and I think she knew that. I've worked with several young parents who ultimately gave up their child for adoption placement. As difficult a process that is for a mother, most know at some level, that giving up their child is a final act of love. In the end, most recognize that they are actually being a good mother realizing that the child will be in a better situation," Nathan replied.

"What was Dr. Zwick's role?" asked Ronnie.

"He was called in to evaluate your mother during her hospital stay and later during the custody phase. He did the psychological testing," Nathan explained.

"And it was his report which convinced the Court to terminate my mom's rights to me?" asked Ronnie.

"Yes in part. The Court gathered as much material to make an informed decision and then rendered an opinion," Nathan explained..

"Do you think it was the right decision?" Ronnie asked.

As Nathan began to respond he was mindful that his next choice of words would be very difficult for his patient to process. "Ronnie, as difficult as it is to hear, at that point in your mother's life she couldn't manage her own affairs let alone an infant child's needs. So yes Ronnie I think it was the only decision any of us could have made at that time." Nathan paused for a moment to allow Ronnie to comment, however not a word was uttered by her. Nathan continued, "maybe it would be handled differently now a days with so many other support programs in place to bolster a mother's capacity to take on parental responsibilities. And maybe the medications and therapies offered now would have been more effective in helping your mother. And maybe the Courts would take more time before reaching a determination about terminating a parents' rights." Nathan again paused to see if Ronnie had any response. But again there was silence. "Please realize, that we have always been far from a perfect profession and I know errors in clinical judgment are often made, most unintentionally, and others due to incompetence. Ronnie, I'm very sorry for your loss at such a young age. I wish things would have worked out differently for your mother and for you, but unfortunately that wasn't the case," Nathan added. At the conclusion of his comments, Nathan felt exhausted and concerned for his patient who sat curled up before him. Nathan felt a combination of relief discussing Ronnie's mother as well as a duty to safeguard his patient and provide nurturance and protection. As he looked toward Ronnie, Nathan saw her sad, glum expression which was followed by heavy sobbing in response to what she had just listened to. As Ronnie continued to sit in silence, Nathan gently asked her to try to put some words to what she was feeling. After a minute or two, Ronnie took a deep breath and thanked Nathan for sharing what he had.

"It helps putting things in perspective for me. I can now see that for whatever reasons, my mother was very troubled and must have felt very much alone and couldn't see her way past her immediate difficulties to think of anyone else," commented Ronnie. "Did she ever say anything about a relationship or about who my father was?" Ronnie asked.

"No she never did," Nathan noted.

"Did you have any further contact with her?" Ronnie inquired.

"No I never did, but Dr. Solomon had seen her over the next few years but then he too lost contact," Nathan replied.

"You know she killed herself around the time that I was adopted," Ronnie stated.

"I know you mentioned that she committed suicide but I didn't know it was close in timing to your adoption," Nathan replied. "What's that like to know?"

"Yeah, it was like she lost me forever and probably she felt like she had no reason to live," expressed Ronnie.

"Perhaps, but we just don't know what went through her mind or even if she knew about the adoption. Your mother lost you years earlier when you were placed in foster care and then when she had her rights terminated. Remember Ronnie that I mentioned earlier of working with many young parents who had their children taken by Protective Services and placed for adoption. Many are haunted by their actions which resulted in their child being taken. They feel angry, guilty and ashamed but eventually realize that their child was in a better family and would be safe, taken care of, and healthy. Certainly, if they would be able to go back in time and do things over, maybe they think things would be different but that's never a possibility. They grieve the loss but are comforted by knowing that their decision was the best plan at that time and knew better than to intrude upon the new family relationships. Perhaps, if she was still living, you might have met her eventually and had some type of rapprochement, especially after your adoptive parents died," commented Nathan .

"You're probably right," Ronnie noted.

"I think I might be," replied Nathan. Nathan then reached by his desk to retrieve a folder in which contained several copies of the letters he still had in his possession. "Look I want to show you something of your mothers. These letters were sent to Drs. Solomon and Zwick and to myself over the past year by someone who had access to your mother's belongings. The letters have become the beginning point of the police investigation, and while I first may have thought you had something to do with mailing the letters, I can now see that is not the case. But the letters may give you some insight into how your mother was functioning back then. Take your time as you read through them," Nathan indicated.

"And these are all my mother's writings?" Ronnie asked.

"They certainly are," Nathan replied.

Ronnie then took the next fifteen minutes reading each letter in a way which suggested that she was for the first time feeling closer to her mother and appreciating a part of her mother's life through her writing. "Thank you for letting me see these. I know you didn't have too, but it really helps me," Ronnie commented.

"I thought they might," Nathan noted.

"Most of them are very distressing to read and borderline threatening in nature. I can see she was so troubled," expressed Ronnie..

"Yes they are very disturbing to read. So you can see why I and the police have been very concerned. Someone got a hold of these and sent them to get our attention. And now with the deaths of Drs. Solomon and Zwick, you can see the need to move on any possible information related to the case," Nathan indicated.

"Dr. Solomon and Zwick's deaths were not suicide, were they?" questioned Ronnie already knowing what Nathan's response would be.

"I'm afraid not," replied Nathan.

"So Ronnie, can you help me here and speak with the police?" Nathan gently but assertively asked.

"Okay, Dr. Stern.. I will. Can you call the Detective and we will set something up?" Ronnie asked.

"Sure. Let's have you complete the release of information giving me permission to contact Det. Granger and to discuss broadly the ongoing investigation. I think we can accomplish this via a conference call but again I do recommend you getting an attorney before the two of you meet," Nathan noted. Once Ronnie completed the paperwork with her signature to execute the release of information form, Nathan took out his cell phone and went through his contacts to find Bev Granger's number and put the phone on speaker. Detective Granger answered on the third ring and greeted Nathan in a business-like fashion.

"Hello Dr. Stern. Everything okay?" Granger inquired.

"I never know what to say to that now," Nathan replied. "Just so you know I have you on speaker."

"Why is that?" Granger probed.

"There's someone in my office sitting across from me who I want you to meet as soon as possible," Nathan answered.

"Well that's going to be late tomorrow when I get back from New York. If it can't wait contact Det. Paulson," Granger suggested.

"I think it can wait till tomorrow. Say hi to Ronnie," Nathan said.

"To who?" Granger asked.

"Ronnie is a patient of mine who agreed to speak with you about the investigation," noted Nathan.

Granger then asked for Nathan to take the call off of speaker. "What's this about Dr. Stern?" asked Granger.

"Look I have limited disclosure in terms of a release, but Ronnie is someone you definitely want to interview. She is the daughter of Charlene Yarborough," explained Nathan.

"Are you safe right now?" asked Granger.

"Yes. That's not a concern. Ronnie poses no danger. But I convinced her to speak with you about the investigation. Can I put you back on speaker?" Nathan asked.

"Yes, go ahead," Granger said.

"Okay we're both back," Nathan clarified.

"Ronnie, this is Detective Beverly Granger. I understand from Dr. Stern that you are the adult child of Charlene Yarborough and would like to speak with me."

"Yes that is correct," Ronnie replied tentatively.

"Ronnie, what is your full legal name, age, phone number and current address?" Granger asked. Ronnie then provided the information to Granger who then proceeded to inquire as to what kind of information Ronnie may have about the investigation into the deaths of Drs. Solomon and Zwick.

Ronnie replied, "I'm really not sure, but Dr. Stern thought it would be a good idea to speak to the police."

"Do you have specific information about the homicides of the two doctors?" Granger inquired.

"No I don't," replied Ronnie.

"Do you have any specific information about the letters that were sent to Dr. Stern?" questioned Granger.

"No… no information about the letters either," replied Ronnie.

"Again, do you have any knowledge as to who might have committed the two homicides or sent the letters?" asked Granger.

"No I do not," again replied Ronnie emphatically.

Granger was beginning to wonder as to the usefulness of meeting with Ronnie who didn't seem to have much to offer to further the investigation.

"Just one further question at this time," Granger suggested. "Did you hire or retain a private investigator by the name of John Connelly to look into Charlene Yarborough's history?" asked Granger.

"How did you know that?" a surprised Ronnie questioned.

"Was that a yes?" replied Granger.

"I did," noted Ronnie.

"Okay then. I need to know what Connelly found out and to see his report. Can you help me out with that?" Granger inquired.

"I guess I can," Ronnie said.

"Have you heard from him over the week?" Granger asked.

"No why?" Ronnie replied.

"Well, I met with him a few days back as part of my investigation and all he would say was that he was hired by a client to learn more about Charlene Yarborough's life. So you are that client, aren't you Ronnie?" explained Granger.

Ronnie was taken aback by how thorough the detective's investigation had become. "I'll assume your silence is a yes," Granger further noted. "Please contact your private eye and give him permission to speak with me as he may have additional information about my investigation which he is holding onto. Can you do that for me Ronnie before I leave New York, and then you and I will meet late tomorrow," Granger suggested.

"Okay I'll try," Ronnie indicated in a soft tone.

"Do a little better than try Ronnie. It's important… understand," Granger urged.

As the conversation ended between Det. Granger and Ronnie, Nathan took the phone off of speaker again and spoke briefly to the detective and suggested to meet up over the next day or two. Ronnie's session also was coming to an end as the two agreed to continue the session in two days. "Ronnie, I am very proud of you in the way you stepped up and managed the conversation with Detective Granger," explained Nathan.

"Do you think she believed me about not knowing anything about the deaths or the letters?" asked Ronnie.

"I think so. What matters though is that you know you are telling the truth and that I know that you have nothing to do with all of this. The police though have their ways of investigating and typically consider everyone guilty until innocent. So be prepared for another line of questioning when you meet with Det. Granger," Nathan suggested. "In any event, I will speak to the detectives about you to help them understand that you had nothing to do with all of this," added Nathan.

"Are you sure you believe that Dr. Stern?" Ronnie asked apparently still not fully convinced.

"Absolutely, Ronnie, no doubt in my mind," Nathan said with a reassuring tone.

"Okay…thanks for taking the time today in helping me deal with this," Ronnie said appreciatively. "I'll see you in a couple of days,"

Ronnie added. As Ronnie exited the office a forced smile seemed to mask the tension in her face as she said goodbye to the officer sitting outside. Nathan followed a few minutes later having closed up the office and was looking forward to a quite night at home with his family.

\*\*\*

# CHAPTER 17

Detective Granger's morning drive to Whitestone from her hotel was quicker than she expected. It appeared to her that any early morning traffic was mostly heading in the opposite direction toward Manhattan. Whitestone, bordered by the Bronx-Whitestone Bridge and the Throgs Neck Bridge, was touted to be one of the few elite enclaves in Queens, New York. As Granger pulled into the community and approached the street address that she was looking for, she noticed that the property was set off from the street in a way which offered the home a near panoramic view of the Long Island Sound and both bridges. The house, large by any standards in Queens, was a two story Old English Tudor design, which had an extended walkway to the front door.

As Granger approached the front door she admired the perfectly landscaped and manicured yard which was appointed with several ornamental statutes and a gazebo toward the side of the house. At first Granger did not believe that anyone was home as there was no response to the doorbell chimes. Just as Granger was about to depress the doorbell for a second time, the door was opened by a woman in a nurse's uniform.

"May I help you?" the woman with an Jamaican accent asked.

Detective Granger introduced herself and inquired as to the owner of the house and if she could speak to the owner. Granger also offered her identification and business card. "Wait here for a moment , please," the woman said.

The door was closed and locked as Granger waited for what seemed like an indefinite period of time before the nurse came back. When the door reopened Granger had seen an old man sitting in a wheelchair before her with his nurse providing assistance.

"Detective Granger, you didn't have to come all the way up here to continue our conversation," the man said trying to prop himself up in the wheelchair to a standing position. Granger was totally caught off guard, although if she would have done her homework and had performed a property records search for the address, Granger would have known in advance that she was visiting the home of Giorgio Armis, who she spoke with a few weeks ago.

"Mr. Armis… hello…it's nice to speak with you in person," Granger said, making her best attempt to conceal her personal embarrassment over not doing her homework. "I'm following up on my investigation of the Solomon death and had a few more questions to ask. If this isn't a good time, I could come back later," Granger indicated.

"No that won't be necessary. No time like the present time," Armis noted and invited Granger into the house. Walking side by side with Mr. Armis, who was now back in the wheelchair, the nurse directed Granger to follow to the living room.

"You have a beautiful home," Granger said to Armis.

"Thank you. It's been in the family for a very long time, built in the 1920's before the Great Depression, remodeled a few times, but the original architecture has never been modified. One of a kind in this area," Armis noted proudly. "I grew up in this home and I will probably die here," Armis pragmatically noted. "Okay, so now that we are both sitting, you may ask some more of your questions about my appointment with Dr. Solomon," Armis suggested, not realizing yet that Granger was primarily on a different fact finding mission.

Over the next few minutes Granger proceeded with some general follow up questions for Armis about his contact with Dr. Solomon and then eased her way into her agenda of questions about Charlene Yarborough. "Mr. Armis, while I am still interested in your appointments with Dr. Solomon, I'm going to take a slight detour and ask you about another part of my investigation involving some furnishings that were shipped to your home back in 1995 belonging to Charlene Yarborough," Granger explained.

"Charlene...you mean Charlie," Armis indicated . "There's not a day that goes by without my thinking about Charlie," Armis added. "What does Charlie have to do with your investigation?" Armis asked with a confused tone and puzzled facial expression.

"Well, I'm not quite sure yet, but maybe you can help," Granger suggested. Granger then asked if Armis was residing in his home during that time and if he accepted a delivery of furniture.

"Yes I was here and yes I signed for the delivery," Armis indicated. "Charlie was going to move into the mother-in-law cottage behind the house, and then...well you probably know she ended her life a few days before she moved here," Armis noted.

"Yes, I heard about that," Granger indicated. Granger's next question for Armis then opened the door to a lengthy story about Charlene Yarborough's rather short life as narrated by Mr. Armis.

"Mr. Armis...can you tell me how you came to know Charlene...I mean Charlie?" asked Granger..

Armis' personal assistant, who brought in a pot of coffee and some water for his medication, left the room and closed the door behind her which afforded the two more privacy. As Armis delicately, with a steady tremor, began to pour a cup for Granger, he began to respond to the detective's question.

"Charlie was a beautiful young woman, smart and spunky who came to the City from a small mid-west town. She stepped into my supper club one night with her date but she was really looking for work. At that time I owned a restaurant but also operated a club downstairs with singers and dancers. She convinced me she had some talent and I hired her on to work some nights. I didn't realize until a few weeks later that she also was moonlighting with some of our patrons. She apologized for her transgression and pleaded for her job. I could tell she was desperate and I kept her on, and from there, I realized she was seeing me in like a father role but one thing lead to another and we got seriously involved. I told her she had to clean up her act, no drugs or heavy boozing, and no other men, and if she could do that, I would take care of her, and put her up in a nice apartment off of Park Avenue. My kids were all grown up and my wife had died a few years earlier so Charlie also served a purpose in my life. Some months later, she came to me letting me know that she was pregnant and I insisted that she take care of it or our relationship and everything before her would end. I told her I didn't want to see her until she was no longer pregnant. Months passed and then she turned up again in really bad shape both physically and especially emotionally. She started to use again and drink again. Several more hospital stays, which I financially took care of... drugs, ECT, therapies, none seemed to make a difference in the long run. I helped her get back on her feet, weathered several psychiatric treatments and for a while it looked like she turned the corner but that wasn't to be for long. She got pregnant again and insisted it was mine and this time she said she was going to keep it and that I couldn't make her get rid of the baby. That was it for me. I eventually ended our relationship but felt responsible and set her up out in Queens in that apartment," described Armis, as he completed his last sentence with a sigh and a sip of coffee.

"You continued to take care of her financially?" inquired Granger.

"Yes, I felt responsible for her. Paid her rent, bills, made sure she had a budget to work with to take care of herself and her child," Armis replied.

"You mean your child?" Granger noted.

"Yes that's right. I felt committed to making sure her child, Victorio or Victor for short, would be provided for," noted Armis, "but it didn't quite work out that way during the early years of Victorio's life."

"How do you mean?" asked Granger.

"I could have done much more back then, but simply giving her money obviously wasn't sufficient. The child from early on was removed several times by child welfare for neglect and abuse allegations. I regretted not being involved in his life at an early age, it might have made a difference for him. It wasn't until after Charlie's death that I took Victorio in as my own, but by then it was too late. I couldn't make up for all the lost time. Even till this day, Victorio doesn't know that I am his biological father. He was told I adopted him after his mother's death," Armis explained. "He found his mother dead, you know. That kind of image in anyone's mind, let alone a child of seven or eight, does something wicked I imagine," Armis added.

"I suppose so," Granger replied. "How's your son doing now?" asked Granger.

"I'm really not sure. Like his mother, I tried to get him the best care. Victorio spent two years in a residential facility when he was thirteen followed by boarding school. Got his GED later than most and really has not had any steady work, mostly day labor kind of work," Armis noted.

"Has he been around recently?" asked Granger

"You certainly ask a lot of questions, Detective Granger," said Armis.

"Just trying to be thorough to avoid bothering you again," Granger replied. "So when did you last see him?" Granger asked again.

"Oh, I don't see much of him now. At this point at his age, he's on his own. I financially support him, you know, but haven't seen him for about a month," Armis indicated. "He used to live in the cottage out back, and now he comes and goes," Armis added.

"Can I take a look?" Granger asked.

"I guess that would be okay," Armis replied.

Mr. Armis called for his aid who accompanied the two through the home toward the back of the house. Walking through the hallway, Det. Granger noticed the gallery of photographs arranged meticulously on one of the glass console tables. "What a beautiful family. These are your boys?" asked Granger.

"Yes and grandchildren and great grandchildren," noted Armis.

"And this is you and your wife?" asked Granger.

"Our wedding picture," replied Armis.

"Do you have a picture of Victorio out here?" inquired Granger.

"Let me see, there must be one here," suggested Armis. Armis however was unable to find one amongst the gallery. "I know I have one upstairs and I think there are a few in the cottage," noted Armis.

Granger and Armis exited the home through the back door and continued down the path to the cottage at which time Mr. Armis gave the key to Granger who entered the small efficiency unit. "You can go in by yourself, the steps here are too much for me," noted Armis.

The interior of the apartment was scantily furnished with mostly storage boxes lined up against the walls which Granger noted were from the Five Guys Moving Company. As she walked through to the rear of the unit, a photograph of Victorio and his mother was standing on the night table and another more recent picture of Victorio which appeared to be a selfie was pinned to a bulletin board. Granger took a quick look and placed the photo in her pocket. As she approached the kitchen area, on a small round table, scattered around, were highlighted psychiatric reports about his mother, a Diagnostic and Statistical Manual of Mental Disorders, and various professional publications in which several names were circled including Ben Solomon, Gerald Zwick and Nathan Stern. Off to the side of the table sat a PC and printer and beneath the table and resting on a Meriam-Webster dictionary, a thesaurus, and several phone directories, Granger saw an Olivetti typewriter as well as a folder of letters and poems identical in content to the ones that Dr. Stern had received. Granger realized at this point she needed to step outside the cottage, secure the door and obtain a warrant for a legal entry and search of the premises. Although she was given permission and entrance to the cottage, Granger already wondered if she had compromised the investigation and evidence found within.

Upon leaving the cottage, Mr. Armis was waiting at the bottom of the steps sensing that something was amiss. "Is everything alright?" Armis asked.

"I have a few more questions if I may Mr. Armis," Granger expressed.

"Okay, but I have one for you. Do I need an attorney?" Armis asked.

"I don't think you do, but your son Victorio might," Granger replied. "But if you do not want to speak with me anymore, I understand, but I will be back with a warrant later to go through everything in your home and on the premises including the cottage," Granger indicated.

"What did Victorio do? What did he do?" Armis said emphatically.

"Right now he is a person of interest that I would like to speak to as I believe he was involved in at least some of the planning and maybe in carrying out the murders of two doctors, one being Dr. Solomon," Granger indicated. "Did he know about his mother's psychiatric treatment?" asked Granger.

"Unfortunately yes … His mother… I told her many times not to burden such a young child with that kind of material…she had poor boundaries and overloaded little Victorio with all of it," Armis noted. "Later after she was gone, I tried to balance out the information but he kept on asking about her, her doctors, her treatment. He seemed obsessed with it all and tried to understand," Armis explained. "I even suggested for him to meet with Dr. Solomon to perhaps get a better perspective on his mother's psychiatric difficulties and even to get some help for himself," Armis added.

"That was the appointment you told me that was cancelled and rescheduled by Dr. Solomon. Did your son Victorio keep that appointment with Dr. Solomon on that date?" asked Granger.

"He did. Dr. Solomon did it for me as a favor. He said he would just meet with him, no formal records maybe just some notes but all discrete and private. What did I do? … What did I do?" Armis cried out in disbelief.

"Mr. Armis, I think you said before that you hadn't seen or heard from your son Victorio for some time?" asked Granger.

"That's right. It's been a few weeks now," noted Armis.

"No idea as to his whereabouts?" Granger inquired.

"I wish I did," Armis replied.

"A cell number or email address?" asked Granger.

"Sorry. I don't have either," noted Armis

"Mr. Armis, what is Victorio's full name?" asked Granger.

"It's Victorio Yarborough-Armis," noted Armis.

"Any other names he may go by?" asked Granger.

"Mostly Victorio, but Victor sometimes, and often we used a nickname...we called him Little G... short for Little Giorgio as he looked a lot like me when I was a kid in my teens," Armis related.

"Any distinguishable birthmarks, scars, deformities, earrings, or tattoos?" asked Granger.

"Yes. About three months ago he got two identical tattoos on his hands...letters spelling out L'il G, here and here," as Armis pointed to the back side of his hand.

"Would these be like the tattoos on Victorio's hands?" Granger inquired as she now opened her email message from Det. Paulson with the attachment displaying the photo of two hands with the tattoos of L'il G inscribed on the back," Granger asked.

"Looks just like them and that looks like Victorio. Where was this taken?" Armis asked.

"Down in Florida, last week on the night that another doctor was killed," Granger replied.

"Oh my god...what has he done!" shouted Armis.

"Mr. Armis, did you know that Victorio apparently has an older sister, Veronica...Ronnie for short?" asked Granger.

"How can that be possible, I'm not aware of any other child of Charlie's," Armis noted.

"No that's right. As part of our investigation we learned of another child who was looking for her mother and the doctors who treated her," Granger noted. "I'm interviewing her when I get back to Florida," Granger added. "In your story earlier Mr. Armis, you told me that you demanded Charlie "to take care of it" referring to the pregnancy, and I was thinking you were referring to an abortion. My information tells me that Charlie kept the baby but the child was ultimately taken by Protective Services and placed in foster care and then placed for adoption. You didn't know about that?" Granger inquired.

"No. I never knew about that. As I informed you, I didn't see Charlie for some months after she told me about the pregnancy, so remaining pregnant and delivering the child certainly could have been a possibility," Armis suggested.

"And she never spoke about the baby or adoption or anything related to this child?" asked Granger.

"No never," Armis indicated.

"Is it possible that Victorio knew about his sister?" asked Granger.

"Anything is possible with Charlie, who knows what she told Victorio, but he never mentioned anything about a sister to me," Armis indicated.

Not quite accepting everything coming out of Armis' mouth, Granger was now drawing to the conclusion of the interview. "Okay Mr. Armis. Here's the next few things that will happen. Mr. Armis…no one can enter the cottage, even yourself at this time. I am directing another detective from Great Neck, Det. Munson, to obtain a search warrant and remove all relevant materials and contents from the premises to assist with our investigation," Granger indicated. "And should you hear from your son, as difficult as it may be… call me," insisted Granger.

***

Det. Granger spent the next half hour coordinating with Det. Munson who was en route to the Court house to meet with one of the assistant district attorneys to obtain a Judges' order. After obtaining the search warrant, Det. Munson suggested that he would meet up with Det. Granger in Whitestone to execute the warrant. In the meantime, Granger contacted Det. Paulson to update him on the investigation, and to share with him the identification of Victorio Yarborough-Armis, aka Victor and or L'il G, which subsequently would be distributed to the respective departments in Florida.

"Terrific work Detective," Paulson commented. "What do you need me to do?" Paulson added.

"I'll be sending a photo of the suspect shortly along with Mr. Armis' statement. Go ahead and circulate both. This is our guy. Also, pick-up Veronica Fitz-Morris, aka Ronnie Fitz-Morris, aka Veronica or Ronnie Yarborough. She is a current patient of Dr. Stern. I was told by him earlier that she is the biological daughter of Charlene Yarborough. Stern doesn't think she is involved but pick her up. I'm not buying into his thinking that she has absolutely nothing to do with this. Have her ready for interrogation when I get back," Granger indicated.

***

By mid-day the quiet street in Whitestone was temporarily displaced by two police vehicles and two crime scene unit vans. The warrant was served to Mr. Armis, and this time, Det. Granger accompanied by Det. Munson entered the cottage with the full legal force behind them from a Nassau County Judge. An IT specialist sat in front of the computer and began examining files, documents, web sites visited, searches conducted, and an email account which was de-activated over the past month. Amongst the most incriminating evidence were searches about how to stage a suicide via a gunshot wound, short term effects and medical consequences from taser application, methods of strangulation and how to stage a hanging. There were several pdf's on psychiatric nomenclature and diagnosis, treatment for borderline personality disorder and post-partum depression, ECT, and medication. Also located were journal publications in which either Solomon, Zwick and Stern were contributors with accompanying curriculum vitae's documenting the most current professional work of the three. "There's a lot here to nail the guy. Impound everything," Munson announced.

Within an hour or two, technicians from the Great Neck P.D. were seen carrying out boxes, a computer, a typewriter and articles of clothing. A search of Victorio's bank and credit statements alerted Granger and Munson that the suspect had closed out all accounts three months earlier and had taken cash advances on three of his credit cards including Visa, American Express and Mastercard. According to Mr. Armis, Victorio also had asked for a larger distribution from a trust account over the past month which amounted to approximately ten thousand dollars.

"The guy is going cash only. He's off the grid if that's the case," Granger noted.

Although Victorio's license came up in the Department of Motor Vehicles for Queens County, the detectives also found materials in the cottage which suggested the production of falsified documents including driver licenses and various employment badges. Granger asked that the typewriter be inventoried as evidence but then released to her in the chain of command so as to bring it with her to Florida to compare the key strokes in the carriage to the typed material sent to Stern. Granger also impounded a few sheets from the open ream of paper found in the cottage so as to compare the weight, bond and color. Granger expected that there would be a perfect match with typewriter and paper. Granger was attempting to be as thorough as possible at this stage of the investigation to insure that the case would be air tight.

"Now we just have to find this sick bastard before he hurts someone else," Granger commented to Munson as she thanked him for all his assistance during her trip.

Just prior to departing to the airport, Granger and Munson compared notes on their respective homicides and agreed to stay in contact until Victorio was located and apprehended.

\*\*\*

# CHAPTER 18

"What's this all about?" Ronnie impatiently demanded from outside her condo door.

"As I was saying Ms. Fitz-Morris, before you interrupted me, I was asked by another detective, Det. Granger, to bring you in to talk with us about the Solomon-Zwick investigation," Paulson indicated.

"To bring me in… am I being charged with something?" Ronnie asked.

"No, nothing like that," Paulson responded.

"I can't believe this…my doctor got me involved in this mess the other day…to do the right thing and speak with the police," Ronnie commented.

"That's all it is Ms. Fitz-Morris…to have a conversation with us about what you may know about the deaths of those two docs," Paulson reiterated.

"Wait here," Ronnie directed, "I need to put these bags inside. Can I follow you in my car?" Ronnie inquired.

"Sorry Miss, that won't be an option. I was instructed to accompany you to our department," Paulson noted.

After a few minutes, Ronnie exited her condo and proceeded with Det. Paulson to his car. Just prior though, Ronnie had left a voice mail message for Nathan which had a rather angry tone to the message in which she conveyed that she was being brought in for questioning by Dets. Paulson and Granger and that she was pissed that she had listened to him the other day.

Upon arriving at the police department , Ronnie was asked to wait in the lobby until called in by either Paulson or Granger. Ronnie, who was getting nervous and a bit paranoid in the waiting area, was under the impression that the detective had asked the police officer sitting behind a glass impaneled security window to keep an eye on her.

***

Det. Granger's flight from LaGuardia was delayed an hour and a half which resulted in her getting back to her office, later than expected, in the early evening. After freshening up and having a bite to eat, Granger walked out to the reception area to find that Ronnie was sprawled out on the couch, sleeping with earbuds from her iphone dangling around her neck. Granger couldn't help but notice the incredible resemblance to Giorgio Armis as well as to the photo she had of Victorio. There was no way to mistake the three as being from the same gene pool.

"Ms. Fitz-Morris," Det. Granger stated as she gently tapped Ronnie's shoulder to awaken her. Ronnie opened her eyes slowly at first squinting and then yawned and sat upright on the couch. "Ms. Fitz-Morris, I'm Bev Granger. I'm very sorry to have kept you waiting. My plane got delayed this afternoon. Thank you for staying," Granger indicated.

"Oh, I didn't think I had a choice. That other detective told me to wait here," Ronnie said.

"Yes I know, Det. Paulson can sound very forceful at times," Granger replied."Please come back with me. Would you like anything to eat or drink?" Granger asked.

"No, I'm good… but maybe some water," Ronnie indicated.

Ronnie was escorted by Granger through a secure door which was opened via a keypad entry system and taken to an interview room. "This looks a lot like one of those interrogation rooms," Ronnie noted.

"I guess it could be called that but we call it our interview room. Detective Paulson may join us a little later to process his part of the investigation. Do you know why we asked you to speak with us Ms. Fitz-Morris?" asked Granger.

"I do. My doctor, Dr. Stern, suggested that I come forward to speak with you," Ronnie replied.

"And how do you know Dr. Stern?" asked Granger.

"He's my treating psychologist for the past month," replied Ronnie.

"And why did he recommend that we speak?" asked Granger.

"This investigation of yours it seems to trace back in some way to my birth mother, Charlene Yarborough. I don't know why but it does," Ronnie related. "All I've been trying to do is track down her doctors so that I could speak with them to learn more about my mom," Ronnie added.

"And you've been doing that? Searching for each provider like Dr. Solomon, Dr. Zwick and Dr. Stern?" Granger inquired.

"That's right," Ronnie agreed.

"Do you know what a person of interest is Ms. Fitz-Morris?" asked Granger.

"I do. It's when someone has some valuable information about a case or investigation that may help the police solve it," Ronnie indicated.

"That's correct. It's a term used in law enforcement when identifying someone involved in a criminal investigation who has not been arrested or formally accused of a crime," Granger clarified.

"Would a person of interest need an attorney Det. Granger?" Ronnie asked.

"Usually not, but sometimes," Granger ambiguously noted. "If you think you want one present, we can end this interview and wait some more before an attorney is retained by you. But… I don't think it's really necessary to have one here with you," Granger related.

"It's okay. I've done nothing wrong and certainly I haven't committed any crime," Ronnie replied.

"Well then, with that said…tell me about why you hired that private eye, John Connelly?" asked Granger.

Ronnie then proceeded to give Det. Granger the background story culminating with the information that Connelly shared with her prior to her move down to Florida.

"I see. And you never got to meet Dr. Solomon personally or speak with him?" asked Granger.

"No never," replied Ronnie.

"And when you relocated down here, you were planning to meet with both Dr. Stern, who you did, and then to meet with Dr. Zwick. And you knew that both had treated your mother years ago?" commented Granger.

"That's right. I learned that from Mr. Connelly," Ronnie noted.

"Did you let Dr. Stern know that when you initially contacted him or when you first met with him?" Granger asked.

"No not at first. I wanted to get comfortable with Dr. Stern first and slowly bring this up to him," Ronnie noted.

"And why was that?" Granger asked.

"I'm not sure why, but I wanted to get a sense of who he was first and I wanted him to understand who I was before I brought that up. You know… I didn't want him to think I was some type of crazed family member trying to exact revenge or anything like that," Ronnie stated.

"Precisely," Granger agreed. "And Dr. Zwick?" asked Granger.

"Yeah, he too was gone before I had a chance to speak with him," Ronnie noted.

"When were you planning to meet with Dr. Zwick?" asked Granger.

"Actually…," Ronnie started and then hesitated.

"Please, go on," Granger encouraged.

"Actually I had a job interview with his office on that day that he was found. I know that sounds pretty bad, but I was on campus that morning with the Human Resources Office," Ronnie noted.

"Well it only sounds bad if you did something wrong on that day," suggested Granger.

"Exactly, and I didn't do anything wrong," Ronnie clarified.

"Okay that's right, but quite a coincidence being on campus and having a job interview in the building. And the person who you were hoping to meet and speak to about your mother ends up dead," Granger suggested. "It's almost as if someone knew about your interest to speak with your mother's doctors and was out to make sure that didn't happen," Granger speculated.

"Hmmn… that's interesting but the only one to know about this was Mr. Connelly," Ronnie noted.

"For the moment, I guess that's correct, but Mr. Connelly is not being considered as a person of interest at this time," Granger indicated.

"Well then there is no one else who would know about my intentions," Ronnie added.

"That's right and you're not like…what did you say before, oh, "not a crazed family member looking to exact revenge or anything like that," Granger indicated.

"Precisely," Ronnie replied.

"Because if you were I don't think Dr. Stern would still be around treating you. You certainly would have had many opportunities to "exact revenge" right?" Granger indicated. At this point, Det. Granger placed several of her mother's letters on the table . "Have you ever seen these letters before?" asked Granger.

"Yes in Dr. Stern's office," replied Ronnie.

"Have you ever seen them before that?" Granger inquired.

"No never," Ronnie said.

"Do you know they were written by your mother and that several were sent to Drs. Stern and Zwick and most likely Dr. Solomon?" Granger noted.

"I was told that by Dr. Stern," Ronnie commented.

"Do you know who might have sent them?" asked Granger.

"No clue about that," Ronnie replied.

"Okay then let's move on. Ms. Fitz-Morris, have you ever heard of a man named Giorgio Armis?" Granger asked.

"No. Who is that?" replied Ronnie.

"This is the man who looked after your mother over some years. He was involved with her romantically when she came from Iowa to New York and paid for most of her expenses over a significant period of time including an apartment in the city and out in Queens. But you may already know that from the private eye," related Granger.

"I knew some of that but never had a name to the man that was with my mother," Ronnie noted.

"Okay then. So when I was up in New York I located Mr. Armis in Queens to interview him about your mother. Would you be interested in what I learned?" asked Granger.

Ronnie at this point had never expected that she would be hearing more about her mother or her mother's relationship history from a police officer during an investigation about two murders. Ronnie felt her heart beginning to race and the tension building on either side of her face up by her temples. She began having trouble controlling her breathing and knew she was a moment away from a panic attack.

"Are you alright?" Granger asked noting Ronnie's physical appearance.

"This is all very overwhelming, just give me a moment. Can I get that water now?" Ronnie asked softly.

Granger came back with two bottles of water and passed one over to Ronnie. Ronnie took several short, frequent sips and then took out a few tissues from her purse and poured some water onto the tissues in an effort to create a make-shift compress which she placed to her forehead and then to the back of her neck.

"Are you ready to proceed?" Granger asked.

"I believe so," Ronnie replied.

Granger then went on in a somewhat abridged fashion to share with Ronnie her conversation with Armis from earlier in the day. However, when she arrived to the part about Victorio, Granger paused and tried to anticipate what Ronnie's response may be. "And there was one other piece of information which Mr. Armis shared with me," Granger stated slowly, "which had shed more light on my investigation."

Ronnie appeared to wait with some degree of anticipation. "And what was that?" Ronnie asked hurriedly.

"Mr. Armis it seemed not only tried to look out for your mother but also was looking out for a child… Victorio. This boy as it turned out was his child. I think he knew it all along but only got more involved with the boy after his mother died. After your mother died," Granger repeated. "After your mother was gone, Armis took Victorio in and tried his best. He was around seven or eight but it seemed like Victorio was already spiraling out of control behaviorally and emotionally," Granger added.

"I have a half- brother," Ronnie stated with great surprise. "He's what …mid-twenties now?" she added.

"Have you ever been contacted by him?" Granger asked.

"How would that be possible, I just learned about his existence moments ago," Ronnie replied.

Granger at this point placed a photo of Victorio in front of Ronnie and asked her to take a close look at the picture. Ronnie knew that the photo had far greater significance than just a photo of someone that she wouldn't recognize. Ronnie who was prepared to look at a photo of someone she was just told was her half-brother, was totally caught off guard when she actually recognized the person.

"Have you ever seen this person before?" Granger asked again.

"Where did you get this?" Ronnie screamed out as she studied the photo carefully. "You say this is some guy Victorio who is my half-brother. That's all wrong. This is an ex scum bag. A real loser. His name is George and when we were together his hair was blondish-brown and George had a beard and George had no tattoos," Ronnie explained.

"Ms. Fitz-Morris... you went out with this man Victorio?" asked Granger.

"No not Victorio...George, this is George," Ronnie attempted to correct Granger.

"When?" asked Granger.

"Oh about a year ago... briefly we were together. He was scary and controlling. I ended it and it didn't go well," Ronnie noted.

"What was George's last name?" asked Granger.

"It was Sanchez," Ronnie indicated.

"How did you meet?" asked Granger.

"In a recovery group, Narcotics Anonymous," Ronnie indicated. 'You're not supposed to get involved with any members like that, but we did and I seriously regretted it after a short while," Ronnie related.

"Did he ask you about your past or your mother?" Granger asked.

"I talked a little about it but mostly that I was adopted," Ronnie noted.

"Did he talk about himself or his family?" asked Granger.

"No not really. He was quiet in that way. He said one day I will meet his family," Ronnie added.

"Did he know the name of the private investigator or did he ever see any information from your private eye or get ahold of any type of reports from him?" Granger asked.

"I don't think so. I didn't keep anything like that out in the open," Ronnie noted.

"But you had things like that in your place?" asked Granger.

"Sure that's right," Ronnie noted.

"Were there times when he might have been alone for a while to look for something like that?" asked Granger.

"A few times perhaps," Ronnie suggested.

"And you haven't seen him since?" Granger asked.

"No of course not. I probably would get another restraining order if I saw him," Ronnie indicated.

"You had a restraining order issued? By whom?" asked Granger.

"I got it issued in New York . In Manhattan," noted Ronnie.

"Was there any violations?" asked Granger.

"Constantly. That's why I had to move away," explained Ronnie.

"Any cyber-stalking, anything on Facebook or any other social media?" asked Granger.

"No I don't think he was into any of that, fortunately," Ronnie stated.

"So this guy I dated briefly, who I call George is really Victorio who is my half-brother, lived with my mother until she committed suicide and then raised by his father. You're looking for him as the person who killed Dr. Solomon and Dr. Zwick?" Ronnie asked.

"That's right, and we're thinking he's looking for Dr. Stern as well," Granger explained.

"But why?" asked Ronnie.

"Well, maybe for the same reason at least initially that you were looking for your mothers' doctors, but Victorio is feeling perhaps something far deeper and is much more enraged over what happened to your mother and is holding her doctors culpable for her life and death. Instead of understanding and learning more about your mother he is out for vengeance," Granger speculated.

As Ronnie was trying to process all of what she just heard, Det. Granger suggested that there was one other thing she wanted to share as part of her investigation but that she wanted Ronnie's assurance that she would be speaking to Dr. Stern about everything during her next appointment.

"Okay... so Det. Granger what else can you possibly inform me about besides my having a psychotic half- brother whose going around stalking and killing my mother's past doctors?" Ronnie expressed in a flippant tone.

Det. Granger, in a delicate fashion, began to probe if Ronnie knew as to who her biological father was. After learning that the private investigator was unable to arrive at that information, Granger decided to assist in that direction. Granger knew all too well that her own past estrangement and now conflictual relationship with her father, most likely influenced how she handled this part of the investigation with Ronnie.

"Ms. Fitz-Morris...following my interview with Mr. Connelly and then with Mr. Armis, I think there is a very strong possibility that your biological father is Giorgio Armis. During my conversation with Mr. Armis it was clear to me he had absolutely no knowledge that your mother gave birth to you and that you were placed for adoption. You see there was a period of just under a year, where your mother had no contact with Armis and that all he knew was that she was pregnant but that she also was planning to terminate the pregnancy. He now knows about you in a general way. Here is his address when you are ready to follow-up," Granger related.

Ronnie was taken aback by this latest information and seemed stunned by Granger's information sharing. "Thank you Det. Granger. None of this was easy to hear and go through but I appreciate what you just gave me," Ronnie related.

"Okay, good. Just one other thing. Be careful. Your brother is out there somewhere and we are not sure yet what his next move might be. Of course, if he turns up and you see him, please let me know immediately, he's very dangerous," Granger advised.

"I certainly will," Ronnie replied.

"Let me arrange for your transportation back home," Granger noted as she called for a patrol car.

***

Det. Granger had one further call to make before her long day and night came to an end. In reaching Ronnie's private investigator, Connelly seemed more forthcoming with information this time around as Granger had speculated that Ronnie already spoke to the private eye. Most everything that Connelly shared simply confirmed information that Granger gathered through her own means. Granger had also asked Connelly if his office in the city was ever broken into. Connelly had confirmed a break-in about four months ago in which the office was ransacked but in the end no records appeared to have been removed. Connelly also reported that some petty cash was taken and an unregistered firearm was missing. Connelly was asked to report the firearm stolen, if he hadn't already, and then notify Det. Munson in Great Neck to check on the type of firearm identified in the Solomon autopsy. Granger subsequently sent an email to Munson as well to follow-up with Connelly should the private eye intentionally forget.

***

# CHAPTER 19

By late September the hurricane season has meteorologists vigilant of any potential activity with tropical depressions and tropical storms developing in the Atlantic, some of which eventually reach the coast of Florida. At first the National Hurricane Center and local meteorologists had downplayed the potential that TD #11 had a sufficient amount of strength to further develop. However, several days later and with the help of two upper atmospheric systems TD #11 quickly developed into Tropical Storm Noah that was taking a beeline right toward the coast. Noah was announced as a hurricane seventy-two hours out with a strengthening profile which was picking up speed. Based on recent metrics from the hurricane hunters, the storm was packing winds upward of 90-95mph and gusts up to 110mph. The counties likely to be impacted were placed in the cone of concern and the communities were advised to take the warning seriously and to begin to prepare. Emergency Management was in the active implementation stage to issue their alert which would open shelters, close schools and request that the State declare a state of emergency in advance should disaster relief funds be requested through FEMA.

Nathan and Joanne went through a few close calls during

hurricane season throughout the years, and had just missed Hurricane Andrew, having relocated from New York a few months after the August 1992 storm, which had left its mark on various communities. With the advisory in place, supermarkets and gas stations began to see a significant bump up in business and the Home Depots and Loews would no doubt run out of hurricane materials within a day. Homeowners, including the Sterns' began to prepare for the worst knowing that statistically the probability of being hit head on by the eye of the storm was still quite negligible. However, as the storm appeared to be quite massive a few hundred miles out at sea, even an indirect hit from the dirty side of the storm could result in significant damage and impact the community for a while. Nathan and Joanne attempted to methodically put their hurricane plan into action although both knew that as prepared as they believed they may be, the intangibles of a storm including the aftermath can never be predicted.

As the University planned to close 48 hours before the storm was anticipated to arrive, Nathan had an extra day to work on getting the house more secure with hurricane shutters as well as to remove any outside furniture or objects that can be launched by the wind and propelled like a torpedo. Nathan and Joanne were also debating as to when to cancel patients who were scheduled for the next day and the day after. Between the two, twenty patient hours would be affected. Nathan and Joanne decided to cancel all clients the day after next but decided to keep their office opened until 5 P.M. during the next day to accommodate those clients that wished to keep their appointments while at the same time not jeopardizing anyone's safety. The meteorologists determined that weather locally would begin to deteriorate around 1 A.M., Saturday morning should the storm maintain its current course and speed.

***

Nathan's first patient to confirm their regular scheduled appointment in spite of the storm warning was Natalie Klingel. Nathan also received a distress call from Ronnie who left a somewhat frantic message insisting on an appointment as well. Both patients, Nathan believed, would be self-involved and probably were not tracking the storm's path, like most everyone else. One additional patient, who was an initial consultation, called as well to confirm the appointment. The patient noted that he had been waiting a while for the appointment and wouldn't want to delay any further. Typically, Nathan would have rescheduled under the circumstances but as his day seemed light to begin with, he went ahead to confirm the session. In the end, Nathan was relieved to know that his day would end much earlier than anticipated, way in advance of the storm.

Joanne, although wanting to be available for her patients, also wanted to be home while making final preparations before the hurricane. Two early morning patients confirmed their sessions which meant Joanne would be out of the office before noon. Joanne also called Myra to give her the next few days off.

***

Within the field of psychotherapy a general principle is to listen very carefully to how certain current events either close by or distant can intrude upon a patient's life and own personal history. Hurricanes and other environmental events would be no different. For Natalie, a sense of being alone coping with the various stressors of Hurricane Noah was certainly appreciated when she initially entered her session with Nathan.

"I don't know how I'm going to get through this. Have you seen this monster out there?" Natalie commented. Nathan was surprised on how well informed Natalie was about the storm.

"I have, it looks pretty bad right now, but let's not try to use words like monster to describe this storm," Nathan noted attempting to bring down the event to the appropriate level and proportion. "You'll get through it as everyone else will. However, what you seem most troubled by is that you are dealing with this all by yourself and once again feeling anxious and overwhelmed, and you are beginning to catastrophize," Nathan added.

"I hear you, Dr. Stern, but you know I just can't stop thinking about how much of my life I had no one to take care of me," expressed Natalie.

"I know, I'm sorry it turned out that way, but you have done a pretty decent job looking after yourself for the most part. Let's find another way for you to emotionally weather this storm," Nathan replied.

Over the next half hour the two worked on an action plan which involved recognizing strengths when faced with adversity, separating the rational and realistic concerns from the irrational ones, and addressing various grounding skills to regain control. Nathan also spent a fair amount of time in addressing Natalie's push to further develop a better level of competence in terms of independence and autonomy even if it meant being on her own.

"Alright Dr. Stern, I think I am better prepared for Noah now and handling whatever comes my way. Make sure you take care of yourself and your family," Natalie noted.

Nathan was pleased to hear that from Natalie as well as to hear Natalie's own concern for him in getting through the storm. Nathan recognized that the work they are doing has clearly helped Natalie in terms of understanding another's perspective and taking into consideration another's feelings.

Ronnie's session on the other hand was expected to begin in an entirely different way. While others would be preoccupied with the storm, Ronnie was emotionally rebounding from the information she was trying to process from last night's meeting with Det. Granger. At least for the next hour, Nathan realized that both he and Ronnie's focus would be detoured away from Noah. Ronnie had reviewed for Nathan every aspect of the interview and her relief that she was able to convince Det. Granger of her innocence when it came to the investigation of the murders of Drs. Solomon and Zwick. However, having learned last night about having a brother, who she actually met last year and briefly went out with, and who was also the primary suspect in the case, was just too crazy and bizarre. And, having further learned the name and the whereabouts of her likely biological father, sent Ronnie into an emotional tailspin.

"This is just too much to take in all at once," Ronnie started to express. "I've always wondered about my father...who he was...why he didn't come looking for me... and now I have all this information to act on."

"It's certainly a lot to think about especially in the context of what's been happening," Nathan replied. "Are you okay?" Nathan asked after sensing that his patient was a little off in session.

"Why... why do you ask?" Ronnie answered back sharply.

"It's just that you seem different today," Nathan noted.

"Yeah, I guess I have a confession to make...after being dropped off at home by the police, I was in a bad way and I went back to an old habit of coping. I hooked up with friend and did a few lines with him and then a few more," Ronnie admitted to Nathan.

"How are you feeling about the slip?" Nathan inquired.

"Not good about myself. I've been clean for seven years," Ronnie replied.

"Okay then. It's a slip under extraordinary stress and we're not going to justify the action but just recognize it as an unhealthy coping style which still needs to be addressed," Nathan noted. "Any plans to work on this to prevent another relapse?" Nathan asked.

"I'm working on it," Ronnie noted.

"Okay, that's good. As long as you feel in control of your recovery program, we can go forward," Nathan replied. "You know, learning about your father and then your brother Victorio would be enough to mess with anyone's coping skills. Your brother Victorio, was a very dangerous man when you first met him last year and still is. I recall that this was the guy "George" you told me about during your first session. The guy who "creeped" you out enough to move away, first out on the Island and then eventually to relocate down here. This is the guy you got a restraining order for… isn't that correct…you did very good trying to protect yourself," Nathan suggested.

"Yes, the same guy. He was fishing around for all that information about me…now I get it…he was trying to figure out if I was his sister without going the next step to tell me that he thought he was my brother," Ronnie described. "We never got that far. He's probably still looking for me. Weird how we were actually looking for the same people though we both had very different personal agendas. I still can't believe I allowed myself to go out with him a few times," Ronnie noted.

"You couldn't know at first but once you picked up the signals, you acted on them correctly and were proactive in making sure the relationship didn't continue," Nathan stated.

"That's for sure. I'm relieved I never let myself get to that next level of a relationship," Ronnie added.

"You never slept with him?" asked Nathan.

"No. Which is surprising. I usually get physical with guys pretty quickly, but George, I mean this guy Victorio, it never seemed about that," Ronnie replied.

"What does it mean to you that you have a brother?" asked Nathan.

"It's all very strange. When I was really young in foster care, I used to pretend that my foster brothers were my real brothers but each time I was sent to another home or they were sent away, the sadness and emptiness in saying good-bye... I know took its toll. I eventually gave up on believing in family and just stopped investing any energy into relationships around me," explained Ronnie.

"So what do you feel about this guy who is going around killing the doctors who were trying to help your mom?" Nathan asked.

"He's a psychopath, who's making me feel confused and angry that he would be doing such a thing," Ronnie noted.

"Any other thoughts?" Nathan asked.

"I'm also thinking about my mother," Ronnie began. "I don't get it. She had me, gave me up after being placed into foster care and then a year or two later, gets knocked up again. But this time, decides to apparently do her best to keep my brother in her home. It's like a whole new level of rejection and abandonment. While I'm out there in foster homes, she's got her son by her side. And then she suicides," Ronnie noted.

"You sound pretty angry in talking about her right now," Nathan observed.

"Totally, she had no excuse to bring another child into this world after what she did to me," Ronnie explained. "And then what she did to my brother, leaving him like that. She fucked us both over," Ronnie added.

"So do you see her desperate act of suicide in a different light now?" Nathan asked.

"What do you mean?" Ronnie asked.

"Well a few weeks ago you commented that you thought your mother took her life a few days after learning about your adoption," Nathan noted. "And now, it seems like there may be an alternative explanation," Nathan added.

"That's right, Det. Granger told me that my mother was being evicted from her home but she also told me that my mother and brother were planning to move to live with Armis in another section of Queens. But for some reason her plans changed and she took her own life before making the move," Ronnie described.

"So maybe her suicide wasn't about you," Nathan suggested.

"That's true, until today I never considered any other possible explanation as to why she did it," Ronnie stated.

"That's good then. Helping you look at things from a different perspective is a big part of the treatment process. As long as you can do some of that work, I'll worry less about you," Nathan noted.

"Okay. But I'm worried about you," added Ronnie. "He's not going to stop, is he?" asked Ronnie.

"I don't know," replied Nathan. "It looks like he is searching for some answers as well and won't stop until he feels his questions have been responded to," Nathan explained.

"What do you plan to do?" asked Ronnie.

"Just go on and be careful in what I do and have confidence in Det. Granger and the police to protect me and my family," Nathan replied.

"What do you plan to do about your father?" asked Nathan

"I think I'm going to wait on it until I can think about it with less emotion and then look him up," Ronnie explained.

"That makes perfect sense. Just don't let your feelings paralyze you from taking action," Nathan recommended.

"I'll try not to. I have his address and phone number and when I'm ready to contact him I will," noted Ronnie.

As Nathan concluded Ronnie's session and accompanied her toward the waiting room, he noticed his next patient already waiting, reading a magazine. Nathan also noticed that the officer securing the premises was not stationed in the waiting room. Upon checking messages, Nathan heard Det. Granger's voice mail message indicating that as a result of an emergency in the city and the pending arrival of the hurricane, all overtime security details, effective immediately, were temporarily suspended due to much needed manpower in other areas. Nathan was able to detect the frustration in Granger's voice over the bureaucratic snafu and reassured Nathan that she would be out by his office, on her own time, within the hour, and then would follow him back to his home.

Nathan's new patient, Frank Mathers, was referred for evaluation and treatment by his attorney following accusations of misconduct and misappropriation of funds while working as the chief financial officer at Conners, Armstrong and Boyd, a large law firm specializing in mergers and acquisitions. Mr. Mathers informed Nathan that prior to the end of the fiscal year, he had arranged for a lavish retreat for his staff which should have been paid through his personal account. However, Mr. Mathers noted that he had "borrowed" from a general fund account which he had access to. And once he dipped into that account, Mathers reported that it made it that much easier to withdraw funds again which subsequently paid for a lease on a new Audi and for a European vacation for he and his family. Mathers anticipated returning the money before it was reported missing, however an unscheduled independent audit by the firms' accountant revealed the irregular funds distribution and eventually the auditors and lawyers caught up with Frank.

"Doc, I haven't been able to sleep or keep anything down since being fired last week," Frank began to report. "I know I messed up real bad but I don't think I can go on this way."

"How do you mean that?" asked Nathan.

"I just don't think I can go through this process...you know initially when I fronted the money to myself, I felt anxious and uneasy, and when I was confronted about it I felt professionally exposed, and then when I was terminated I felt humiliated in front of my friends and coworkers. Now the next part of this is going to be criminal with charges of embezzlement being pursued," Frank explained.

"When you were referred here by your attorney, did he feel that you may harm yourself?" asked Nathan.

"It's crossed my mind a few times, just to end it as an easy way out of the situation, but I love myself too much and wouldn't do that to my wife or kids," replied Frank.

Nathan was relieved to hear the presence of a few protective factors serving as buffers against self- harm as well as his patient's infusion of narcissism to preclude the option of suicide. "So, when you took the money Frank, what did you anticipate the outcome would be?" Nathan inquired.

"I didn't anticipate any other outcome other than returning the money before it was discovered missing," Frank noted.

"So how are you feeling now about your overall conduct?" asked Nathan.

"You know…I've moved funds in and out of this account over the years for the partners and this was the first time I took like a personal bridge loan from the company. No one would have missed it. It didn't impact the operations of the business at any time," replied Frank.

"Sounds like you are using some pretty fancy rationalization to distance yourself from your actions. So tell me why do you think you are having trouble eating and sleeping and having so much anxiety?" Nathan asked.

"Right, that's a good question…that's why I needed to see someone to tell me why," replied Frank.

"Oh, I think you are a pretty intelligent guy that probably could figure that out on your own. I'm not convinced you need to see a psychologist for that," Nathan said. "And, I think it's good in the near term for you to be feeling all these things. I guess I would be much more concerned if you were eating and sleeping as if nothing has changed in your life. Maybe next time we can talk about a persons' moral compass and to see how that developed in your case. But if you aren't interested in examining this area and all you want is some instant relief I can simply refer you to see a psychiatrist for medication," Nathan suggested.

"You know, I'll take that name for the psychiatrist but I want to see you again," Frank noted.

"Okay then. I'll schedule you for next Monday at 6 P.M. The storm should be over by then and everybody should be back to their normal routine," Nathan replied.

As Nathan was completing some paperwork with Frank and arranging fees and payment, he thought he heard the faint chime from the security system indicating the opening of a door. Nathan remembered that Det. Granger's was expected shortly to meet him at the office. However when Nathan escorted his patient to the waiting room, Granger was nowhere to be found.

"Okay, so I will see you next week," Nathan commented to Frank.

"That's right, see you then," replied Frank.

Nathan proceeded to lock the front door , then the waiting room door, and then went to the bathroom. As he was returning to his office, Nathan walked down the hallway and turned the corner entering his office, and as he did he noticed that a picture frame was tilted slightly at an angle. As he approached to restore the picture to the correct position he also saw the reflection of a person standing behind the door. Nathan attempted to quickly reverse course out of the office but the force of the corner of the door closing as it struck the side of his head temporarily knocked him off balance. But it was the second blow to the head that rendered him unconscious.

When Nathan became conscious again he found himself restrained in his office chair with his arms and legs tightly secured by rope and his mouth duck taped shut. He felt a throbbing, pulsating pain on the right side of his forehead as well as on the left posterior side of his head. Nathan's vision was slightly blurry and the ringing in his ear was barely tolerable. He noticed that the outer hallway appeared dark which also meant that the front and rear part of the office also would be dark as all the lights with the exception of the inner offices were controlled by one light switch. Even with his cloudy level of consciousness, Nathan knew quite well as to what had just transpired and knew intuitively that Ronnie's brother was behind it.

Victorio after gaining control of the office, slipped out the rear door, located Nathan's car and with the ignition key he took from Nathan's desk, moved the car a few blocks away. Victorio returned to the office and made himself more comfortable as Nathan sat across from him. "You really should have had that rear door replaced a while ago. So easy to open with the right tool," Victorio announced. "I've been watching your office for a while and I think I lucked out today... no security guard up front and apparently the storm is wreaking havoc in advance of its arrival. Look, I hope you don't mind...I took the liberty to close your office for the day. The office looks closed, so anyone coming to see you would believe you closed up earlier on account of the storm," commented Victorio.

Even if Nathan could have spoken at the time, he probably would have been speechless as his sudden predicament would have overwhelmed him with immobilizing fear and vulnerability. Victorio rambled on to acknowledge his self-declared errors in managing his two previous encounters with Solomon and Zwick and assured Nathan that this time would be different. Nathan heard and stood witness to Victorio's proclamation that he wanted to engage in a discussion about his mother's past, her treatment and therapy, his sister and his own life. "Your friend Zwick, well his departure was premature. I accept my mistake. I miscalculated when I tased him and that second jolt was too much I guess for his heart or something like that. I never got my chance to speak with him." Victorio indicated.

Nathan sat terrified in his chair unable to move but knew no matter what Victorio had in mind, which no doubt was not life affirming, would first begin with some relevant historical information which Victorio couldn't apparently extract from his previous captives. Nathan reflected... *as long as I participate with his inquisition, I would remain valuable to my captor.*

"And your friend Ben, well he thought he was doing my father a personal favor by seeing me...how could Solomon possibly help me after doing such a disastrously poor job with my mother. Solomon had no apologies, no admissions of wrong doings. He just sat there trying to understand my anger and pain. A bunch of bullshit. Anyway, Solomon was halfway gone already. He seemed really depressed to me and didn't seem to care if he lived or died. Well you know what, neither did I on that day, so after I subdued him we played a game of Russian Roulette, somewhat modified. We sat at his desk taking turns with one in the chamber. I even went first and then held the gun to his head for the second round... empty chamber. I thought I was done but I shot another blank and then the fourth chamber...that's all she wrote. He didn't even beg for his life."

Nathan again listened closely to Victorio's words having heard that his captor came up empty handed during the imprisonment of his two friends. No doubt Victorio was on a path to exact revenge but perhaps he would be more restrained in his tactics as he was still not satiated with information he felt his mothers' doctors had at their disposal. Nathan thought that the information he had on Victorio's mother and family could at least buy him some time until a better plan came to the surface. Nathan also knew that time was on his side as Granger would be arriving to the office shortly and that Joanne would be expecting him within the hour or two. Nathan reflected...*keep the guy focused on all the information he may think I have to disclose.*

***

Det. Granger pulled up to the office and as she approached the walkway she had noticed the office was closed. She called both the office number and Nathan's cell number and reached voice mail on both systems. Granger left a brief message on Nathan's cell figuring that he had left early to go home. She then proceeded directly to the Stern home. Victorio who was holding Nathan's cell phone listened along with Nathan to the message Granger left.

"Okay. That's good. I don't think we will be troubled by Det. Granger again," Victorio said.

Up until that point, Nathan's pain level on the side of his head had been subsiding somewhat over the past few minutes. However, when he realized that Granger left the premises, the sensation of pain returned as if he was re-experiencing the initial blows to the head all over again.

Victorio now still sitting across from Nathan seemed to be staring almost right through Nathan. Within a minute or two, Victorio leaned over toward Nathan and checked the tightness of the ropes.

"Dr. Stern, I'm going to remove the duct tape so that we can talk. You can scream if you want but I don't think anyone will hear you. You can ask me anything and I may answer. But most importantly, I'm going to ask you a lot of questions about my mother and her treatment, so please be truthful and honest with me," Victorio indicated. "Your life may just depend upon it... understand?" added Victorio.

By now the duct tape had been removed and Nathan was able to verbalize his understanding. Nathan also was able to ask for the first time of his captor's name. "Can you tell me your name?" asked Nathan, as he noticed the tattoos of Li'l G on both hands.

"My name...right... Victorio or Victor for short," Victorio replied.

"I'm Nathan...Nate for short," Nathan replied as he was attempting his best to infuse a personal element to the situation at hand. Nathan recalled from his readings about hostage and kidnap situations that inserting something personal about yourself in a large way humanizes the circumstances and could be a valuable survivor tool.

"Victor do you think I can get some water and some ice for my head?" Nathan asked in a subservient way. "There's a small fridge in the back," Nathan added.

"Right, don't go anywhere," Victorio chuckled to himself. Victor returned with several bottles of water and a frozen ice pack which he found in the freezer compartment.

"Can you loosen the restraint on one of my arms?" Nathan inquired.

"Nice try, Doc. This will do just fine," Victorio responded as he twisted open the cap and directed Nathan to hold the bottle with his mouth and tilt his head back and take several sips. As Nathan took his third sip, some of the water funneled out of his mouth and ran down his chin and neck. Nathan let go of the bottle which straddled against his thigh before falling to the floor. Most of the remaining contents spilled out onto the carpet.

"That's okay, it will dry in. It's not like it's blood or anything that would stain," Victorio smiled, amusing himself. "Sorry, there's not much I can do about the ice... not your nurse maid, man. Believe me I got a lot of practice taking care of my mom," commented Victorio.

"That's okay. Thanks for the water," Nathan replied. "You took care of your mother? What was that like for a young child?" Nathan inquired trying his best to exert some control over the conversation and over Victorio.

"Hey... I said I will ask the questions," Victorio replied.

"Yes you did, but you also said that I may ask you anything... but that you may not answer, isn't that right?" Nathan noted. At that point, Victorio leaned over toward Nathan and had extended his right arm and hand and grabbed Nathan's throat and squeezed his neck. Nathan felt his airway collapsing under the strength of Victorio's grip. Nathan's face became reddened and his eyes wide open as Victorio showed no signs of release. However, Victorio let go after about fifteen seconds. "No more questions...you got it," shouted Victorio, "or next time I won't let go."

Nathan now further realized that in light of Victorio's actions with regard to Ben and Gerald, he clearly couldn't underestimate his captor's volatility and impulse dyscontrol again if he had any hope of surviving this ordeal. Nathan also realized that his life may very well depend on his skillful interviewing process as well as to become comfortable within himself over this imbalanced powerless equation. With that in mind, Nathan opined that just perhaps he can co-opt Victorio to respond to his non-directive and more importantly non-judgmental comments.

"What do you want from me?" Nathan asked in a rather tired, pathetic fashion.

"What I want... I want to know what happened to my mother. What did you and your people do to her to make her like that. That's what I want to know," Victorio replied with some urgency to his tone.

"You know Victor, I only knew your mother over a short period of her life, just maybe a few months, but I will share what I remember with you. I think I got to learn more about her with those letters you sent to me. Those were your mom's personal writings, weren't they, the ones you sent to me. I read them all and wondered often about the person behind the poems," expressed Nathan. "Your mother...what was her name?" Nathan asked.

"It was Charlene Yarborough," Victorio replied.

"I think people must have called her Charlie, is that right?" Nathan asked.

"I don't know, maybe.. what difference does it make," Victorio noted angrily.

"You know, your mother was already very fragile and broken in so many ways when I first met her in the hospital in New York. All she wanted was to start over but that's never possible, you know. She had a young child and I think she knew she couldn't take care of herself and the baby at the same time, so she had a very tough decision to make. That's your sister I'm talking about. Do you know about her?" Nathan inquired.

"Yeah, I knew about her. I learned about her right before my mother killed herself. Great timing, don't you think. She told me about her being given up to foster care and then placed for adoption. She told me it was her secret and not to tell anyone, but to find her one day. She gave me some old papers from Protective Services and some old Court documents and told me to hide them until I was old enough to look for her. She also left me those poems, a journal and her typewriter and then she was gone. And then, one Friday fucking afternoon... coming home from school she was there all sprawled out... wrists slashed, drugs and booze by her side and a plastic bag tied over her head. I remember her telling me the day before that we were moving to a nice big fancy home and that I will like my new home better," described Victorio.

"What an image. How old were you?" asked Nathan.

"Just turned eight. What a fucking birthday present," Victorio replied.

"That's a lot for anyone to take in, especially an eight year old. Lots of scars from that type of trauma," Nathan suggested. "So did you ever find your sister?" asked Nathan

"I'm pretty sure I did, but she took off again and I haven't found her yet," replied Victorio.

"How did you find her in the first place?" asked Nathan.

"It took some doing. A few years ago, I went back to my caseworker from child welfare services who followed me over much of my eighteen years. See my mother was still messed up even with all that treatment you guys gave her, and for a lot of my childhood I was in and out of her house and placed in foster care. There were many times when she was downright abusive to me but mostly she just couldn't keep things together. So when my caseworker came to visit, without notice, she could see the condition of the apartment, the kitchen and bathroom, and she would see me and knew I couldn't stay with my mom until my mom got better, which she eventually did and we started the whole thing over again," Victorio described.

"And how did you get the information about your sister?" Nathan asked again with a curious tone.

"One day when I came in for a scheduled visit with my caseworker, I created a distraction in the building by starting a small fire and when no one was looking I got my hands on my file which included my mother's first contact with Protective Services and read about my sisters' placement in foster care and there was mention a few times about her name...Veronica... and a final note about being successfully placed for adoption with a New York City family named Fitz-Morris," Victorio noted. "I went around looking for her, stalking some, and it took a while but I finally got to her and met her in an NA meeting. I was never really certain if she was my sister but we hung out a few times and I did my best to probe and get some other information but she freaked and left town before I could be certain. One time in her place, I got my hands on a business card of a private detective she was using. It was only after I broke into the private eye's office and read the stuff he had on her, that I was certain she was my sister. Funny though, she never knew how helpful she was in getting me the information on you and those doctors," Victorio noted.

"Why didn't you tell her who you were?" asked Nathan.

"Enough with your questions, Dr. Stern. I'm here to ask you, not the other way around," Victorio replied with annoyance as he fidgeted in his chair. As Victorio repositioned himself in his seat, Nathan noticed the butt of a handgun holstered in the waistline of Victorio's denim jeans.

"Go ahead, ask me your questions. What is it you wish to know?" Nathan inquired.

"Did you treat her when she was in the hospital?" asked Victorio.

"I did," replied Nathan. "I saw her for a few months when she was an inpatient," Nathan added.

"You remember her?" asked Victorio.

"Yes, I remember Charlene," Nathan responded.

"How is that possible?" added Victorio.

"She was hard to forget, in a good way. I liked her a lot," Nathan commented.

"Don't bullshit me," Victorio warned with an abrasive tone.

"No Victorio. I wouldn't do that. Most psychologists remember almost all their patients in some way. I also had the benefit of recently looking over some of her hospital reports and treatment notes from Dr. Solomon's records," Nathan indicated.

"When did you do that?" Victorio asked.

"After Solomon's death, I was involved in settling some of his office matters. I found one of Charlene's letters on his desk which you apparently sent to him as well. As I was attempting to find specific patients that we both treated... I found your mother's records and her writings. Would you like to see the records Victor?" Nathan asked.

"You have them here?" Victorio asked curiously.

"I do, but you will have to untie me so that I can retrieve them," Nathan replied.

"Maybe in a few minutes," Victorio suggested.

"But first...when my mother first entered the hospital, what was she like...what condition was she in?" Victorio asked.

"She was very depressed with suicidal thoughts. She had post-partum depression and she was withdrawing from some street drugs. She was really troubled over giving up your sister and having her placed in foster care," explained Nathan.

"She told me she was pumped up with meds and given shock treatments, is that correct?" Victorio asked in a demanding tone.

"Yes that's correct. Dr. Solomon apparently attempted to treat her condition very aggressively. Back then, I think psychiatry was still operating more in the dark and probably still experimenting with different procedures. They still didn't know the longer term effects of several treatment procedures like medication and ECT. I think your mother was helped in the short term yet she always seemed to relapse. Therapy probably too helped in the short term but she had a lot of demons to grapple with," Nathan explained. "Tell me, do you know something about your mother's childhood?" asked Nathan.

"No not really," Victorio stated.

Nathan then went on to describe the information about Victorio's mother as related to him from Ronnie. "So now you have a better idea about your mother's emotional condition when she first arrived for treatment at the hospital. Granted, Solomon could have prescribed differently and treatment could have been designed differently, but we were all trying to help her out in the ways our training prepared us for. I know better now after years in the field that our treatments then and still now are imperfect and filled with flaws," Nathan noted as he pleaded his case to Victorio.

"And what about Dr. Zwick?" inquired Victorio.

"Well, I don't know what to say. I have the reports here if you haven't read them yourself. Zwick was called in to evaluate your mother's fitness to parent her infant daughter. In the end, Zwick utilized his interviews with your mother, Solomons' and my opinion about your mother's competence to care for your sister, and some psychological testing to reach his own opinion. And that opinion I think was driven by what was in the best interest of your sister."

"Yeah…so why did they keep using that same god damn evaluation when it came to me?" asked Victorio. "My mother always told me that things will never be right in our home because the Court and Protective Services always went back to Zwicks' report," Victorio noted. "She told me if it wasn't for Zwicks' report I would never have been removed so often and for so long from her home," Victorio added.

"That doesn't sound right. Certainly there would have been additional evaluations about your mother's fitness to parent," Nathan commented.

"Shut the fuck up, that's how it was, that's what she told me," Victorio blurted out. "Those foster homes and those group homes messed me up badly. No one was protecting me or watching out for me. Belts, electrical cords and switches, it didn't matter…look at these scars…" Victorio gestured to Nathan as he removed his T-shirt to reveal the traumatic reality of having spent time in several abusive placements throughout his childhood. "And that's just the half of it," Victorio added. Victorio then went on to recount multiple incidents of sexual molestation where he was forced to perform fellatio on two different foster dads and repeatedly raped in a group home by a male staff member.

"I'm very sorry you went through all that as a child and now still clearly suffering as an adult," Nathan said in a compassionate tone. "There's some assistance you can get with all of this," Nathan suggested.

"Right, I'm sure I can spend years on that couch and get prescribed all those drugs, but I have a much better cure. My mother had the right idea all along," Victorio explained. "Our time is getting short. That cop will be back soon realizing that you aren't home yet and your wife… she'll be calling soon," Victorio commented.

Nathan sensing some urgency in Victorio's tone, knew he needed to elaborate on his earlier suggestion which would give him some additional time. "Look…I don't know what you have planned, but first I want you to read through those records…can you untie me and let me get them in my file drawer?" Nathan asked. "I won't try anything. You are obviously much bigger and stronger and can easily overpower me and you have that gun," Nathan reasoned to Victorio. Nathan's request was honored this time and he was freed at least momentarily to retrieve Solomon's records on Charlene Yarborough. Nathan was directed to sit back down as he handed over the chart to Victorio, who was wielding the gun in the direction of Nathan's torso.

"Sit, don't move," Victorio demanded as he positioned himself across from Nathan. Victorio seemed to scan the records pausing at specific pages, always keeping a threatening gaze toward Nathan. As Victorio was reading, Nathan's office phone and cell phone rang alternatively on multiple occasions. Nathan was certain that this would be calls either from Joanne or from Granger in an effort to learn where he was and when he would be returning home.

Nathan realized he had one other card to play in an effort to barter for more time and proceeded with his next suggestion to Victorio.

"Look Victor…there's something more I think I can do for you, if you allow me to make one call from my office," indicated Nathan.

"And why would I let you do that?" Victorio said.

"Because I can bring your sister, Veronica, to you," Nathan noted.

"How is that possible?" Victorio asked.

"I know you were aware that your sister has been looking for each of the doctors who treated your mother, just like you were, to learn something more about her. And now Victor, I'm about to violate patient-doctor confidentiality so you have the opportunity to meet up with her again."

"How can you arrange that, Stern?" inquired Victorio with disbelief.

"Here's the thing… your sister, Veronica or Ronnie, has been a patient of mine and we've been talking a lot about her life, her mother, I mean your mother too, and I know for certain she would want to have an opportunity to meet with her brother. She just learned about you a couple of days ago having met her father, your father, for the first time," described Nathan. Nathan continued to relate information to Victorio which was in part truthful but also somewhat confabulated to peak Victorio's warped obsession with his sister.

"I think I can get her down here to talk with us. Just let me call her and explain the situation. How does that sound?" Nathan inquired.

"Put it on speaker, and you can call her," Victorio indicated.

"Okay. I can do that, but first get me my appointment book over on the desk," Nathan said.

Victorio passed the book over to Nathan who looked up Ronnie's number and reached over to the phone and began to dial.

"Speaker first," Victorio reminded Nathan.

"Right," Nathan noted and placed the call on speaker. Nathan's first call went right to voicemail. So instead of leaving a message he disconnected the call and attempted again to reach Ronnie. This time, Ronnie picked up on the fourth ring and greeted Nathan as her caller id noted her therapist's incoming call.

"Hi Dr. Stern. I didn't think I would be speaking to you so soon after today's session," Ronnie stated.

At this point, Victorio realized that Stern was telling the truth about treating his sister and realized that he had missed her just by a few hours this afternoon. "Neither did I, but something came up after you left your appointment. Can you come to back to my office?" Nathan firmly suggested.

"You mean like now?" Ronnie replied.

"Yes I mean just like now," repeated Nathan.

At this point, Victorio was holding his gun squarely pressed up against Nathan's forehead and whispered in a low pitch voice "tell her why doc or I squeeze the trigger."

Nathan could see Victorio's finger gripping the trigger in the motion of gently squeezing back on it. "Look Ronnie I need for you come alone...your brother Victorio is here with me in the office, sitting across from me and wants to see you again," described Nathan.

Victorio at this moment, pulled back his revolver, wiped the sweat from his brow with the same hand holding the gun and spoke only a few words to Ronnie. "Hi there sis...you shouldn't have skipped out on me like that a few months ago. I've been looking for you but it seems you found Dr. Stern first. So now I need for you to come to me. Right to the office, tell no one. If you want to have another session with your therapist do as I say, understood," Victorio indicated.

"I can be there in thirty minutes," Ronnie replied.

"Sooner than that or you just may be attending your therapist's funeral in a few days," replied Victorio.

"Hey now…you don't want to do that…you're getting what you want…you're learning about your mom and you are getting your sister back in your life," Nathan commented. "I know you're thinking about ending your life as well, but don't do that…there's much to make sense of, don't you think?" Nathan added.

"I've given up on making sense of things," Victorio replied.

"I could see that, but don't you think there is always a new way to start thinking about things again," Nathan noted.

"Not for me… I don't think so," Victorio replied.

With the information Nathan was hearing from Victorio, he surmised quite accurately that Victorio was not anticipating that his life would continue much longer. Many references suggesting hopelessness and powerlessness combined with Victorio's statement that his mother "had the right idea all along" convinced Nathan that Victorio was planning to suicide or to take part in a murder-suicide. Nathan was hoping that neither plan would be a viable option, but certainly the latter of the two would be an unfortunate outcome for Nathan.

"While we are waiting for your sister, I really got to use the bathroom," Nathan requested.

"Yeah, okay. Move down that way and I will wait by the door. Keep it open. Don't try anything stupid," Victorio indicated.

Given the level of distress that Nathan was under combined with the bathroom door being ajar, Nathan's bladder did not fully comply with his sense of urgency.

"Let's go… finish up in there," Victorio demanded.

"Okay I'll be done in a minute," Nathan replied. Nathan flushed the toilet, washed his hands, and for the first time noted his battered reflection in the mirror. He exited the bathroom having left the light on which dimly illuminated the hallway.

"Back to your office…sit down," Victorio insisted, as he tossed his mother's record on Nathan's lap. "I want you to read aloud your opinion about my mother," Victorio indicated.

"Okay…from what point?" Nathan asked.

"From the beginning. I'll tell you when you can stop," Victorio replied.

Nathan then began to read several condensed paragraphs at length of his opinion incorporated into Zwick's assessment regarding Charlene Yarborough's functional capacity to parent:

> Ms. Yarborough, who is a single parent of an infant daughter, has not shown any substantial clinical improvement in her mental status and emotional functioning which may permit her to be placed in a responsible role of caretaker-parental capacity at this point in time. Her ADL's including grooming, dressing, managing a home and managing funds has been significantly compromised secondary to severe depressive symptoms including anhedonia, anergia, and neuro-vegetative symptoms including appetite and sleep disturbance, cognitive impairment including reduced focus, concentration and attention. Her affect is strikingly blunted and her mood clearly depressed. This patient's judgment on matters of day to day affairs are severely compromised and her direct insight to matters at hand and to her immediate circumstances appears quite limited.

Ms. Yarborough has not to date responded to any extended trial of medication, and ECT trials seem to have impacted her thought process and aspects of memory. Ms. Yarborough is clearly incapable of managing her own life let alone the impressive needs of a young child. I would recommend at the very least an extended period of suspending any and all contact with the child until Ms. Yarborough demonstrates clinical improvement as measured and observed by her mental health providers. It is quite possible that Ms. Yarborough will never recover in a time period suitable to bond with her child and for the child to attach in a meaningful, adaptive and healthy way; and with this in mind, termination of parental rights should be considered by the Court at some near future date.(September 1986/Nathan Stern, Ph.D.)

"Did you write all that?" Victorio asked.

"Yes, I did," answered Nathan.

"Did you believe that?" Victorio inquired.

"Yes. Based on the information I had when I treated your mother that was my opinion," Nathan noted. "Look… what do you want me to say?" Nathan asked.

"It really doesn't matter anymore….what I want you to say… what I want you to say….that you were young, inexperienced and you didn't clearly grasp the gravity of your actions and the impact it may have on someone's life," Victorio indicated in a distinct tone of anger. "But you won't or can't say that," Victorio added.

"Look… mistakes and errors in judgment are made every day in my field, we're not a perfect science and I acknowledge there are things that can be done differently, but in this case, your mom was not prepared to take care of anyone. She tried desperately with you, to keep you in the home but could barely do that. Sadly, she never really got better over time," Nathan noted.

"We're done here," Victorio abruptly informed Nathan.

"What about your sister?" asked Nathan.

"Yes. We will wait for her, and then we'll see," Victorio replied.

*** 

Ronnie, who drove frantically to the office, made the trip in just under twenty minutes. As she approached the street before Nathan's office, the roads were already cordoned off by a police blockade which was initiated by Det. Granger shortly after Ronnie had informed Granger of the call she received from her doctor.

"You did the right thing here," Granger said as she approached Ronnie. "Detective Paulson and I are mapping out a plan to coordinate so neither you or Dr. Stern gets hurt here," Granger added.

"What about my brother?" Ronnie asked.

"Well, that all depends on him, don't you think," Granger replied.

"Ronnie...we need for you to call the office and let them know that you are running late but almost at the office. Tell them there were some delays due to the deteriorating weather and people trying to get around town," Paulson suggested. "You want to make sure you speak to Stern. We want to hear that he is still okay," Paulson added.

Ronnie proceeded to call the office and on the sixth ring Nathan was instructed by Victorio to place the call on speaker. The noticeable silence on both ends of the line for the first several seconds suggested how difficult it was for either party to know what to do next.

"Are you there Dr.Stern?" Ronnie asked.

"He is but you're not," Victorio said to Ronnie. "You got five minutes," Victorio blurted out.

"I'm just a few minutes from the office… there's a lot of traffic out here… I'll be there, but I want to speak to Dr. Stern…I want to speak to him again," Ronnie requested.

Both Paulson and Granger, listening to the conversation, nodded giving their nonverbal approval for Ronnie to continue.

Victorio pointed to Nathan in the direction of the phone advising him to keep it brief.

"Ronnie, it's me, are you close by?" were the only words that Nathan got out before Victorio grabbed the phone and took the call off of speaker.

"You have five minutes, don't mess with me," Victorio indicated as he slammed the phone down.

\*\*\*

"Okay Ronnie…here's what we need you to do. Go ahead and drive your car up to the office, and approach the door but stay a good ten feet away from door and then call again and tell him you're in front but that you want to see Stern before you enter. Stay calm. Whatever happens next do not step into the office. We'll take it from there. We'll have our people in position and have the office surrounded and get Dr. Stern and you out," Granger explained.

Paulson and Granger along with four additional officers went over their strategy one final time in an effort to execute the timing of their plan cleanly so as to neutralize the situation with the least amount of force.

\*\*\*

Joanne after waiting at home for Granger to call back to update her, became overwhelmed with anxiety and fear due to the lack of information and decided to drive herself over to the office. Before leaving she asked her neighbor, Donna Bishop, to keep an eye on the boys. Joanne was met with the same blockade which was diverting traffic away from the office.

"Let me through, I got to get through, I'm Joanne Stern, that's my husband in there…let me speak with Det. Granger," insisted Joanne in a loud, forceful tone which was overheard by Granger.

"Dr. Stern, you shouldn't be here," Granger indicated. "I told you I would call," Granger added.

"Yes you did, but I just couldn't wait any longer without knowing what was going on," Joanne replied.

"Okay then. You got to stand back, calm down, and let us do our job," Granger requested.

At this point, Joanne was clearly unaware that she was momentarily alongside Ronnie who was about ready to depart in an effort to rescue her husband.

\*\*\*

"Come on what's taking her so long," a nervous, twitching Victorio expressed.

"Look …she'll be here. What do you want from her when she comes?" Nathan inquired.

"I don't really know…I want us to be family. I want us to be brother and sister and I want her to hear about our mother from me…the mother who gave her up…the mother she never knew," described Victorio.

"Do you think that could happen given the situation we all find ourselves in?" Nathan asked.

"What are you talking about. We'll talk here for a while, and what the fuck, you can even be like the family counselor," Victorio chided.

At this point, Nathan realized that his captor might have been somewhat detached from reality, given the way Victorio was discussing family and family relationships. Just as Victorio was finishing up on how he anticipated the time with Ronnie to go, the office phone rang again and this time Victorio picked up the receiver and angrily asked Ronnie if she was here.

"I'm right in front of the office. Let me see Dr. Stern," Ronnie demanded.

"Get up now. We have a visitor and we are going to walk slowly to the front door," Victorio ordered Nathan.

Nathan still having Yarboroughs' record in his lap stood up and the two shuffled closely together with Victorio's forearm wrapped tightly around Nathan's neck and his gun angled toward Nathan's temple. The two maneuvered to the front door with Victorio unlocking and opening the door in a swinging rotation. Once opened, both Nathan and Victorio were able to see Ronnie standing several feet away on the walkway. Victorio backed away a few steps into the waiting room and directed Ronnie to enter the office. Victorio was completely unaware that several officers were poised to the left and right of the office awaiting Granger's signal. As Nathan was being instructed to move back toward his office, he was the first to see out of the corner of his visual field that Det. Granger had quietly entered the office through the rear door. Nathan realized that Granger must have entered using Joanne's key and timed the opening of the rear door to the opening of the front door so as to avoid the alarm system chime from going off. Granger must have been made aware by Joanne that both doors were on the same zone. Nathan now knew that this whole event would be over in a matter of seconds with only the outcome still undetermined.

From Nathan's perspective, everything from that moment on appeared to move in slow motion. Nathan , who was now slightly separated from Victorio, heard Victorio command Ronnie to enter the office. As Ronnie was taking baby steps toward the threshold of the door, Nathan almost simultaneously with one hand hurled the record he was holding toward Victorio's head, striking Victorio across his face with the corner of the folder clearly penetrating one of his eyes, and with the other hand struck Victorio on the side of his head with the still distinctly hard ice pack, which Nathan concealed several minutes earlier after returning to his office from his bathroom trip. At this point, with Victorio at least momentarily stunned, Nathan chose to dart pass Victorio's outreaching arms and exited through the front door in the direction of Ronnie. Nathan almost barreled Ronnie over but each kind of caught one another and then both retreated further to safety in the direction of the officers.

Granger who was poised in a kneeling posture with her weapon drawn announced to Victorio to drop his weapon and drop to the ground. "It's over Victorio, you're surrounded, no way out," Granger indicated. "Drop it now," Granger strongly urged.

Victorio sensing his powerlessness over the situation, began to motion his surrender, but then without uttering a word drew his firearm in the general direction of Granger and before he had a chance to fire a round, was shot multiple times and fell slowly to the floor as the hallway in part cushioned his fall. Granger who was still in the same position when she fired her weapon figured that she fired off five or six rounds to bring down Victorio. For Granger, it was the first time she had actually fired her police issued side arm in the line of duty since joining the service.

When Paulson entered the office to confirm that Victorio was neutralized, he secured the weapon, and gave the all clear. Paulson than approached his colleague at which time he still found Granger down on the ground with a tight grip on her weapon. "Hey there Bev, its Paulson, it's all over. It's okay," Paulson noted as he assisted Granger in relaxing her grip and gently guided her to set her firearm down. "Come on let's get out of here," Paulson suggested..

The two stepped over Victorio's body as they exited the office to see both Nathan and Ronnie grouped together with several officers who were beginning to interview and collect information. Granger, who by now was registering all cues around her, approached Nathan and suggested that he go find his wife who was still waiting on the perimeter of the blockade and then get some medical care for his head wound.

"Why did you have to kill him?" Ronnie uttered in the direction of Granger.

"I'm sorry Ronnie, he left me no other choice. It looked like he was giving up but then pulled back and raised his weapon toward me," explained Granger.

"I'm pretty sure his intent was to end his life, one way or another. At some point tonight he told me as much and thought his mother had the right solution when she ended her life," Nathan shared.

Nathan was hopeful that Ronnie would take that information in and perhaps understand that her brothers' intention was not to live through the night. Nathan also thought that the information may also relieve Granger from her thoughts about having any other option. A few minutes later Paulson who had secured Victorio's firearm shared with Granger that the chamber to Victorio's weapon was empty. Given that information, Granger then realized that Victorio was anticipating his own personal resolution via suicide-by-cop.

\*\*\*

Before finding Joanne, who was still posted behind the blockade, Nathan briefly spoke with Ronnie and thanked her for her courage which she displayed throughout the evening. "You know, we both probably should speak to someone about today's events and process some of the emotions," suggested Nathan.

"I thought I could do that with you," replied Ronnie.

"True, that would be the usual way to go, but right now I'm too close to the situation and would be of little assistance to you. The police are giving us a name of a psychologist who specializes in critical incident debriefing. Speak to that individual first and we'll try our best to keep Monday's appointment," Nathan indicated.

"Okay…see you Monday then," Ronnie noted.

Nathan then proceeded to walk briskly across the parking area in the general direction where he hoped to find Joanne. The near gale force headwinds combined with the downpour of rain from the outer bands of the storm reminded Nathan that there was a hurricane out in the Atlantic advancing toward the coast. When he finally met up with Joanne, he was thoroughly soaked but not even the rain was able to wash away the remnants of the physical and emotional wounds that Nathan had just incurred. Both embraced and hugged for quite a while before allowing the paramedic time to evaluate Nathan's status. Nathan was subsequently escorted to an ambulance and taken to a local emergency room for further assessment.

***

Dr. Espinosa, the ER physician attending to Nathan, examined the contusion above his eye socket as well as the contusion on his head which later was noted to have resulted from a blunt force injury with hemorrhage in the adjacent area. Due to Nathan's report of being struck by the butt of a gun and combined with his complaints of headache, dizziness, and ringing in the ear, Dr. Espinosa ordered both an MRI and CAT scan. Both scans however fortunately proved to be negative although Dr. Espinosa noted a diagnosis of concussion with swelling and hematoma. Nathan was advised to take it easy and rest over the next few days and be mindful of any post-concussive symptoms which may persist over the next several weeks. Espinosa also noted his concern for Nathan's emotional well-being and advised

Nathan to seek out support and counseling over the next few days..

"Okay...we are out of here," Nathan commented to Joanne. "Let's go home," Nathan added.

***

With the weather now further deteriorating and the rain coming down in almost a sideways fashion, Joanne drove carefully through the streets of her community until reaching their home.

"It's nice to be home," Nathan mentioned with Joanne echoing the same thought.

Upon entering their home, Erik and Jack, although not being totally cognizant of all the events of the day, were relieved to see that their father escaped any serious physical injury. They were however incapable of seeing or sensing the emotional impact which was likely to weigh upon their father over the next few weeks.

"Thanks Donna for watching the kids. We're good now," expressed Joanne.

"No problem. How's Nate doing?" Donna asked.

"Tired, in some pain, and pretty quiet right now. We'll be okay. Thanks again," Joanne replied.

After Donna left the home, Nathan and Joanne sat down next to the kids and watched with them the latest weather reports from the Hurricane Center. Hurricane Noah which was moving much faster than expected, was noted to be weakening and now posed less of a threat to the Florida peninsula. The report went on to advise of strong tropical force winds and rain accumulations of about two to three inches over the weekend.

"That's pretty good news," Nathan said. "It looks like we'll get back to our normal routine very soon," Nathan added.

***

# CHAPTER 20

Two full weeks had gone by since Nathan was held by his captor. The office, which Nathan and Joanne wondered at one point if they wanted to return to, was in the process of being remodeled. Myra was managing most of the day to day activities of reopening the office which afforded Nathan and Joanne a real opportunity to convalesce and relax together. Any lasting office images of what had happened on that day and early evening would be cleansed by new carpeting, fresh paint and new furnishings. Myra made sure that the rear entry door was replaced and that a secure locking mechanism was installed.

All of Nathan's patients were contacted by Myra on the Monday after the incident to advise of cancellations and rescheduling of appointments three weeks later. Most were very understanding as the news media covered the story quite extensively. Some, who were totally unaware of the circumstances, were initially upset but agreed to come in for their next scheduled appointment. Nathan wanted to directly speak to Ronnie, given their shared experience, but having used better judgment, advised Myra to set an appointment date for the first Monday upon his return and suggested that she could call the psychologist covering for him if she felt comfortable doing so.

\*\*\*

After being cleared by the neurologist to resume normal activity, Nathan began to once again schedule his morning exercise of running a few miles which he essentially had given up due to security concerns. Normal activities with Joanne and the boys became common place again and with the baseball post season just about underway, Nathan's promise to get to the ballpark with Jack was finally fulfilled. An extra bonus included the Miami Marlins having just clinched a playoff berth with a strong possibility of making it back to the World Series this October.

Nathan's respite from the University also provided him with the opportunity to prepare a colloquium to be delivered to faculty and students which would serve in part as the long awaited psychology department memorial for Dean Zwick as well as to deliver a speech on professionalism, clinical integrity and ethical behavior. Given Nathan's recent experiences, he felt he had a special message to offer in terms of advice for the future cohort of psychologists being trained under his tutelage.

\*\*\*

By the third week, Nathan was emotionally prepared to resume his work week. Nathan's colloquium was scheduled to occur on his first day back. Upon his arrival, Nathan entered the medium sized lecture hall which seated approximately one hundred fifty. He was welcomed back by several faculty and greeted warmly by the student contingent present for the colloquium. Several faculty members including the interim dean shared their thoughts about Gerald and paid careful attention to his many accomplishments throughout his career. Nathan spoke next in a moving eulogy referring to Gerald and his own training experiences and subsequent career paths. Nathan welled up with emotion several times as he was recalling special moments with Gerald during residency. As Nathan recounted a few personally meaningful stories, he was mindful of how cathartic the process had become in combating his own grief. As Nathan shifted gears, the lecture began to address his earlier work with reference to his training as a young, beginning psychologist, relationship with supervisors, complex ethical and legal considerations, and financial and billing practices. Nathan began softly and then as his lecture proceeded, he became more forceful in his enunciation in an attempt to engage his audience further.

Many of you know that my internship and residency training was completed in New York alongside two very sharp clinicians, Dr. Zwick and Dr. Solomon, a psychiatrist and also a friend, in an era when inpatient care reached an all- time height in terms of admissions, lengths of stay and financial windfalls for the hospitals. As I reflect on this time period, clearly those we served in the hospital required our significant help which unfortunately paved the way for treatment plans which in retrospect probably were excessive as well as aggressive in nature. What we thought were clinically indicated treatments turned out to be ambitious efforts to treat and yes even cure some psychological conditions, which we now much better understand how to work with. There certainly has been an evolution in our field and I think we are much better equipped as a profession to effectively treat and manage a wide array of psychological conditions. As we go on, we should all keep in mind that we are imperfect professionals who often do not comprehend or are blinded to our own limitations. Some of us also lather in our own narcissism and feel we are brilliant and beyond reproach and often impose unusually harsh and abusive methods to train our students, making it almost impossible for them to challenge authority, power and control. Yet as young, developing psychologists you may be faced with such challenges and will need to confront your supervisors' failed logic or wisdom and thus rise to the occasion to right their wrong. Failure to do so can ultimately lead down the road to an unfortunate therapeutic rupture or failure or even an unanticipated consequence. We need to remind ourselves that we are not only treating our patient, who we have a fiduciary responsibility to do no harm, but also we have a responsibility to all stakeholders who are in relationship to our patient. I knew this all along, but the events I recently faced, convinced me more than ever to critically assess the impact that we have on how treating one individual can impact in a positive way or sadly in an adverse way on connected or disconnected family members. We are naïve and myopic to think that our precious work, which most of us perform hour by hour with one patient, would not have a cascading effect on our patients' family system and result in a kind of living legacy of our work in either a favorable or unfavorable way. Please always consider this as you go forward in your professional life, as to ignore this advice may result in unforeseen and unwarranted events.

Nathan's lecture was well received by most as they congratulated him on making several pointed comments which in the end Nathan hoped would change the way his colleagues and students look at their work.

\*\*\*

Nathan's first day back to the practice was met with some degree of apprehension as he had not been back to his office since running out of the front door escaping from Victorio's forced detention. Nathan admired how fresh and clean everything seemed to be. His office once again appeared to be a safe and secure place for patients' to bring their worries and issues to.

One of Nathan's first order of business was to go through the mail which Myra had stacked in separate piles categorized by level of importance. On one stack was an envelope which caught his immediate attention as the return address was from Ronnie postmarked New York from one week earlier. Handwritten in a sophisticated cursive style, Ronnie first apologized as she informed Nathan that she was cancelling her next session and all additional visits. The letter continued:

> Dr. Stern, thanks for all your help and assistance. What I started is now finished. I'm back in New York getting to know my father and new family. You helped in so many ways. I don't think you can even begin to imagine how you have resolved things for me. I've tried to capture some of this but my writing is a bit rusty...see what you think.

Nathan then turned the first page over which was stapled to the second. He began to read the typewritten prose:

As the end drew to a close and the final act was before us

I can see the evil within would be destroyed forever

From a distance with both rain and wind striking harshly at my face,

I could see your frail, wounded self, at once

vulnerable and afraid yet strong and resilient.

Who would be taken?

Why was it he who would be taken?

But the choice was never in doubt.

You now stand tall and we both are finally at peace.


And as Nathan read the last phrase he wondered in earnest.

***

# Author's Note

About the letters...several letters containing various lyrics, prose, and quotes were actual letters sent over a decade ago, anonymously but directly to the author as described in narrative. The original letters, which in part inspired this novel, did include fragmented phrases of prior work under copyright. To preclude any copyright infringement, the letters were set aside and substituted with fictional narrative to avoid any resemblance. The author never was able to establish who might have sent the letters and to this date remains an unsolved mystery.

# Acknowledgments

I would like to acknowledge and immensely thank my wife and lifetime partner, Cathy, who read and assisted in editing the early version and several additional drafts of this book, as well as offering both constructive criticism and continued positive encouragement toward the completion of this project. She is an avid reader herself of suspense and mystery, and her objective sense of a good story and plot greatly assisted in the process of writing this book. Without her literary mind this work would not have been possible.

I would also like to acknowledge Ingrid and Jane who read a later draft of the work and offered their feedback as well.

All parties were instrumental in their encouragement and support for this book to find a home in the personal libraries of so many other eager readers.

A special thank you to Alex Ross, the illustrator, who designed the book cover. Through his creative efforts and energy, Alex intuitively interpreted the correct mood and tone for the written work.

# About The Author

The author, a practicing psychologist in Florida writing under the pseudonym, D.S. Leonard, has thirty-five years of clinical experience working in various treatment and university settings as well as in private practice. Married with two adult children, the author has resided in the metropolitan New York vicinity and has made South Florida home for some time now.

With Inexact Vengeance, Leonard brings a provocative debut work of fiction which engages the reader to gradually unfold and appreciate the suspense surrounding the main character, Nathan Stern. Leonard presents an engrossing psychological suspense novel which captures both the mundane as well as the complexities of the treatment process. For a new author to this genre, D.S. Leonard sculpts a wonderfully, riveting first novel.

Follow the author on Twitter @dsleonard1
Contact the author via email: d.s.leonard@aol.com

Made in the USA
Columbia, SC
31 March 2020